A Wink and a Smile

A SMALL TOWN MADISON ROMANCE
-BOOK 1-

S.J. CUNNINGHAM

A Wink and a Smile: A Small Town Madison Romance
by S.J. Cunningham

© Copyright 2024 S.J. Cunningham

ISBN 978-1-964369-06-8
Paperback Edition

This is a work of fiction. All the characters in this book are fictitious, and any resemblance to actual persons, living or dead, is purely coincidental. The names, incidents, dialogue, and opinions expressed are products of the author's imagination and are not to be construed as real.

This edition published by S.J. Cunningham: www.sjcunningham.net.

To Robert: Endless Happy Birthdays!

Chapter 1

Your experiences this week will all make sense within the year.

Rose Glasser stared down at the words on the slip of paper she had just pulled out of the folded wafer cookie.

She avoided the eyes of the man across from her, who was watching her, eyebrows raised, waiting. He was nice enough, she supposed, if a bit overeager. And his looks were…fine. Dull brown hair, thinning on top. Hazel eyes, full cheeks, thin lips.

He was wholly unremarkable.

But Rose wasn't looking for remarkable. Was she?

Actually, she wasn't looking for anything. She hadn't even been looking for this date, which she'd only agreed to because her coworker Alyssa wouldn't stop pushing for the connection with her brother's friend. Rose presumed the best way to get her employees off her back was to agree to at least one of their suggested excursions—if only so she could say, "I told you it wouldn't work out."

Rose had also done some convincing on herself—

acknowledging it wasn't healthy for a moderately attractive woman of thirty-three to remain at home or hang out with her sixty-three-year-old boss every single Friday night. Even if her boss happened to be Mid Higgins, who'd been like a mother to her in every way for nearly half of Rose's life.

But now she deeply regretted accepting this date in the first place. She didn't need a man at all, and the only good thing to come out of this encounter so far had been to cement this certainty.

Rose placed the slip of paper on the table, smoothing it with her thumb.

"Well? What does it say?"

Rose gave him a small smile. "That doesn't really matter much, does it? It's just a silly fortune."

"Oh, come on. It's a bit of fun to read the predictions. Who knows—maybe you've gotten a glimpse into the future."

She was trying to be a good sport about the date, truly she was. And because withholding the words from a fortune cookie would have been petty, as well as a bit silly, she read the prediction aloud, but she didn't put much heart into the recital.

He didn't notice the tone and gave her a sly, smug grin. "Very interesting," he said, drawing out the syllables as though the words held some deeper meaning or significance. He cleared his throat. "Mine says, 'You will soon meet the love of your life.'" He wiggled his eyebrows.

Rose managed a kind of grimace. The love he might eventually meet was certainly not with her.

She didn't know what else to say to this man, whose name she was having trouble remembering, so she popped half of the stale fortune cookie into her mouth and chewed, planning her escape. Thankfully, she'd driven to the restaurant. She reached into her purse and placed a twenty-dollar bill on the table between them.

The man looked at it, crestfallen. "You don't want any dessert?"

She glanced around. "We're at an Asian buffet. The dessert is on the island." She pointed to the stainless-steel pans on the buffet table to their left. "And no, I don't particularly want any Jell-O. Or tapioca pudding."

"We could go somewhere else. Maybe order a glass of wine, or a cup of coffee? Whatever you would prefer."

Rose wavered between being polite and being honest. In the end, she decided it was kinder to be honest. "Thank you, but I'm afraid I will have to pass. I appreciate the offer, though," she added.

She simultaneously had two thoughts.

Number one—she was being awful. This was a perfectly nice, if boring and somewhat unattractive, man. Why should she think she was too good for him?

It wasn't like she was some prize specimen who had men knocking down her door.

And number two—is this what her life had come to? Was she meant to settle for something that didn't make her heart sing? Didn't make her feel completely alive? She'd rather be completely alone.

Both thoughts led her to the same conclusion.

"It's not you. It's me."

He didn't seem to get it. "Well, maybe we could have dinner sometime this week? Or even next weekend," he said in a rush of words. "I'd like to see you again."

"Look," she said in the kindest voice she could muster. "You seem like a really nice person…"

The man's face fell again.

"…I'm just not sure I want a long-term relationship. I know Alyssa thought we'd be perfect for each other, but the truth is, I'm not looking for anything right now—"

"I thought we were just having a good time," the man interrupted. But his words held a note of desperation. "It's not as if I'm making life plans because we had one date." He offered a small laugh.

His argument was reasonable, but Rose did not believe it. Still, it was tempting to acquiesce. Instead, she resisted and said, "It's just I have a lot going on right now."

A shadow of anger passed over the man's face. "I

think I get it."

He looked as if he wanted to say more, but he kept his lips resolutely closed.

She'd given him an out. A reason not to feel too badly about himself. She hoped he could take that, make her out to be the bad guy, and never call her again.

The server appeared, deposited the check on the table between them, then disappeared quickly. The man pocketed the cash Rose had left on the table and placed his card in the slim black folio with old food crusted atop the faux leather.

Before the server returned to collect the bill and the card, a female voice rang out from across the dining room.

"Rose Glasser! Is that really you?"

Rose looked up sharply, alarmed. The woman approaching the table looked familiar, but it took Rose a second to place her. She summoned the name from the bowels of her memory. *Samantha McClintock*. To say this woman had been an acquaintance would have been a stretch. Rose had graduated from high school with her nearly fifteen years earlier. They had played together on the volleyball team once upon a time.

"It's been ages," said Samantha.

The man across from Rose eyed them both. He appeared as if he wanted to be anywhere else but at the table.

Samantha looked at him and then at Rose expectantly. Rose said nothing.

Finally Samantha said to the man, "Have we met?" She held out a slim, manicured hand.

The man declined to take the proffered hand.

Rose exhaled. She wanted this encounter to be over. All of it. "We were just about to leave."

Samantha, her face rounder and her hair three shades blonder than it was the last time Rose had seen her, said, "I didn't realize you were seeing anyone."

Rose stared at her. "Why would you?" In fact, why would this woman have realized *anything* about her?

"It's just that my aunt—" Samantha interrupted her thought as she dropped her abandoned hand. "Do you know her? Tilly Barker?"

Rose did know Tilly. Tilly came into My Pink Wink—the salon that Rose managed—every other week to have her hair blown out and styled. Tilly and Mid, who owned My Pink Wink, were friends. Rose thought Tilly seemed like an elderly version of a mean teenaged girl. She gossiped in a way that verged on nastiness but held the unmistakable passive aggression of plausible deniability.

"Anyway," Samantha continued, "Tilly mentions you from time to time. She said it was a shame such a pretty and smart young woman like yourself remained unattached. Mid worries about you, you know. Something she probably shouldn't have to do in her condition."

Samantha made a face—a show of knowing concern for both Rose and Mid. "And even though you and I haven't talked for quite some time," Samantha said, "I still want to know my old teammates are thriving. According to Tilly, it just doesn't seem like you are." Samantha arranged her face in an expression of carefully constructed worry.

Rose's cheeks burned. She was both appalled and fascinated by the sheer gall of this woman. What business of it was Samantha McClintock or her busybody Aunt Tilly what was happening in Rose's personal life? She was shocked into silence.

The man across from her lifted his lip in a sneer. "Too busy for another date, huh?" He let out a snort. "Just like the rest of them. Too good for any man." He held up the portfolio and waved it around, looking for their server. "I don't know why I even agreed to this date," he said, unaware of Rose's embarrassment or Samantha's surprise and barely concealed glee.

Rose imagined Samantha would return to her table and immediately begin texting every mutual acquaintance they had.

"You wonder why you can't find a man?" her date continued. "It's because you're looking for something that doesn't exist. You're looking for the perfect person. Well, guess what—you're not going to find him."

His voice had risen, and the server, sensing an impending scene, hurried over with the card reader to take care of the check.

"I guess I should be happy," the man went on. "I dodged a bullet with the likes of you."

Samantha opened her mouth, her eyes wide, then shut her mouth again. She gave Rose a smile that smacked of pity, amusement, and superiority. "I guess I'll leave you to it," she said. "It was good to see you," she called over her shoulder.

When Samantha had rejoined her party, she leaned forward and began talking in low and excited tones to the women across from her.

Rose reluctantly turned back to the man on the other side of the table. Her initial instinct was to try to smooth things over, make things right, tell him she'd been wrong. Apologize. But his face was a mask of barely concealed rage, and his hand shook as he signed his name on the electronic card reader.

She thought it was a bit extreme that this man had become so angry with her for trying to let him down gently. They'd known each other for less than two hours. Furthermore, she was upset with Alyssa for thinking that she and this person would have anything in common at all. Rose supposed that also said something about how Alyssa—and the rest of her staff for that matter—thought of her. *Poor, sad Rose, sitting at home every night of the week with nothing to do.*

And that also made her angry, but she didn't want to make a scene. Not with Samantha watching. And not when her date seemed to be unpredictable. Best to stay where she was and wait it out. In public.

After the man had scrawled his signature and the server had hurried away without making eye contact, he placed the card back into his wallet and stood without a word then walked out of the restaurant without a backward glance at Rose.

Rose sat quietly for a minute, gathering her wits. Her cheeks were hot, and she was aware every eye in the place was focused directly on her. Was it her imagination, or had a hush had fallen over the patrons?

Not only is she embarrassed, she is also mortified at the way she'd been treated. She hadn't deserved that.

Did she?

Well. At least the date was over.

She knew Samantha and her family were also watching, and she avoided looking in their direction. She waited until she was sure the man had gotten into his car and driven out of the parking lot before she stood.

Looking down at the table, she picked up the slip of paper holding her fortune and shoved it into the pocket of her heavy jacket. As she walked out into the chilled night air, she rubbed the small piece of paper between her thumb and her forefinger, removing any creases that remained there.

Then she climbed into her sedan, started the car, and pulled out onto the main street of the blink-and-you-miss-it town of Madison, Pennsylvania.

When she arrived back at her cozy home—her haven—Rose hung up her coat next to the front door and unwound the scarf from around her neck. She sighed, glad that the entire experience was over. It was the last time she would go out on a blind date. Her friends had her best interests at heart, she knew, but honestly, she was all set. She was more than happy at home. Alone.

She noticed a red light blinking on the house phone.

She knew it was unusual to still have a wired phone, but her friend Mid only barely acknowledged the arrival of mobile phones into the world.

Instead, eccentric and quirky Mid used the landline exclusively and insisted on calling Rose on her house phone, a vestige from a bygone era. Mid thought reliance on cell phones and other electronic technology would eventually lead to the downfall of society. She believed in human connection, which was why she'd opened the salon in the first place.

Still young in her early sixties, the woman was normally feisty, active, and vibrant. But a few years earlier, she'd been diagnosed with late-onset lupus, which had wreaked havoc on her health. Then she had struggled to fight a lingering cold she'd picked up after

Christmas when a nasty virus had torn through the town, the church, and the employees of My Pink Wink. Earlier that day, she'd been running a low-grade fever. Rose should have insisted she visit the doctor. Instead, she had prepared for her date.

Rose headed to the phone on the small table in the corner of the living room and pressed the button. Mid's voice was raspy and punctuated with a cough.

"Rose?" the disembodied voice said. "You there?" A pause. "I'm not feeling so well. It's probably fine. I'll be fine." Rose detected an unexpected tinge of fear in Mid's voice. Rose's alarm grew.

"Well," the older woman said, and drew out the syllable, as if she were hoping Rose might pick up any second. "I guess you're not home yet. Don't worry about me. I'm going to head to bed. I'll just see you tomorrow and hear all about how it went. Maybe a trip to Dr. Cole's is on the cards in the morning. Good night, dear. I hope you made a love connection."

The message ended, and Rose picked up the earpiece. She dialed Mid's number. It rang five times before her greeting-less answering machine beeped in expectation of a message.

"Mid, are you awake?" Rose asked. She waited, but the silence of the recording stretched out for seconds. She replaced the receiver and glanced at the time. It was nearly eight o'clock. Mid had sounded tired. She'd probably fallen asleep watching her crime shows with the volume turned up too high.

For a moment, Rose contemplated climbing back into her car and driving the mile up to Mid's house on Mill Road. But she talked herself out of it. It probably wasn't necessary. Mid would be annoyed at the disturbance, and Rose would be annoyed she'd wasted both of their time.

Still, she lingered on the sofa in the living room, scrolling through the news on her phone without processing any of it, waiting for Mid to call back.

The phone remained silent.

Finally, Rose sighed and switched on her television set to stream an episode of a limited-series British crime drama. Every so often, she glanced at the phone. She was mildly worried, but before long, her thoughts returned to the mortifying interaction at the restaurant. Not only the encounter with Samantha, but the entire failed date.

Had the man been right? Was Rose really looking for something that didn't exist?

Even though she hadn't expected—nor had she been looking for—a love connection, some of what the man had said struck a nerve. And so, there must have been at least a kernel of truth to his remarks.

Did she really want to spend the rest of her life alone?

As the crime drama droned on in front of her, Rose considered her own existence.

She'd been working happily at My Pink Wink for over eighteen years, from even before she'd graduated high school. She loved her clients, she loved what she did, and she loved her coworkers.

She even loved the administrative aspects of running the business, which she'd almost completed assumed from Mid five years earlier. My Pink Wink may as well have been Rose's salon now.

When Rose's parents had passed away unexpectedly, Mid had taken the rebellious sixteen-year-old girl under her wing. She'd given her a job, security, structure. She'd steered Rose off the dangerous path she'd been about to head down. She'd saved Rose's life.

When Rose considered her future, ten years from now, she saw herself in exactly the same spot—working at My Pink Wink, living in Madison, attending Sunday church service, and perhaps spending time with her surly and jaded brother, who owned the Sweetwood Saloon at the far end of town.

At no point did a man make an appearance in this vision of hers.

Rose began to relax as the killer on television was revealed.

She was not being picky or looking for something that didn't exist. In fact, she had everything she needed already. Despite what her coworkers thought, Rose was exactly where she needed to be, and she was just fine at home, alone, watching her crime dramas. In fact, after watching many of her former friends getting married and then divorced, and listening to the drama that was revealed every day in the salon, Rose wanted nothing to do with it. She was fine just as she was.

Rose woke the next morning at her usual time of five thirty. She checked the weather app on her phone. It was a relatively warm morning for mid-April at forty-nine degrees. She dressed for the cool weather in spandex leggings, a long-sleeved compression shirt, and quilted vest. Then she tucked her chestnut brown waves into a high ponytail and covered her ears with a black headband.

She went out, pulling the front door shut and locking it behind her. Though she was convinced the town of Madison was the safest place in the country, she didn't want to tempt fate. Tucked away in the rolling hills of Western Pennsylvania, Madison wasn't on its way from or to anywhere. If you were in Madison, that is where you intended to be—your final destination.

My Pink Wink tended to bring in a few outsiders to the salon, but those customers typically drove in for the day, and perhaps walked next door to the Tin Roof Café for one of Olivia's delicious brie grilled-cheese with fig jam and apples and a mug of her signature mocha coffee.

But for the most part, everyone in Madison knew everyone else, which was both a blessing and a curse. The residents shopped at Alsops' convenience store, worshiped at the town's one non-denominational church led by Pastor Phillip Ballentine. Sometimes they had a burger and a beer or three at Teddy's Sweetwood Saloon. They whispered at the post office run by postmaster Fanny Albright and golfed at the Rolling Meadows golf club just outside town.

But no one except Rose was out at 5:45 in the morning.

She jogged down the deserted sidewalk, her breath coming in light puffs as she ran. She crested the gradual hill of Main Street toward Mill Road, and ran the half mile north until she reached Mid's small ranch-style home atop the sloping hill. The light in the living room window shone brightly; Rose breathed a sigh of relief. Mid was already up and moving.

With that lingering fear quelled, instead of turning into Mid's driveway, Rose ran in the opposite direction, toward the overgrown ballfield across the street from Mid's house.

The ballfield had been built on land owned by the church. A year earlier, Pastor Ballentine had used church funds to refinish the walking and running trail around the old ballfield which was rarely used anymore. The track was a half mile in length, and Rose ran around the path six times, gradually increasing her speed until her quads burned and her heart pounded.

The run took her approximately half an hour. Rose was perspiring by the time she stopped, stretched, and slow-walked the distance to Mid's front door. It was too early for flowers—the threat of frost had not passed—but in a few months, Mid's front stoop would be filled with petunias, geraniums, and begonias of red, pink, yellow, and purple.

Rose had a key to the door, but she didn't need to use it. The front door was not locked. She pushed her way inside. "Mid?" she called lightly, not wanting to surprise the older woman.

She could hear the hum of the television as she walked into the small, neat living room, where the morning news droned on. Mid, however, was not in the room.

Rose moved to the television set and turned down the volume. "Mid?" she called again. She rounded a corner into the kitchen, half expecting to find the woman sitting at the kitchen table or standing in front of the sink.

Upon first glance, the kitchen appeared empty.

Rose was about to go check the back bedroom, when something on the floor on the other side of the kitchen table caught her eye.

Rose took a step forward.

It was a hand.

She blinked, trying to comprehend the sight. Then

she recognized Mid's plump pale hand with its fuchsia-tipped fingernails.

"Mid!"

Rose rushed forward. She knelt down and took the soft, pale face of the woman in her hands.

Mid didn't move. Her eyes were shut, and her mouth was slack, as if she were sleeping.

Rose lightly tapped the woman's cheek. "Mid," she breathed, and sang out in a sing-song voice, "Wake up, Mid. You're scaring me."

No response.

Rose lifted Mid's shoulders and cradled the woman's head on her knees. Mid's frosted curls spilled over Rose's lap. "Come on, Mid," she said, with a little laugh that caught and bubbled into a sob. "This isn't funny anymore."

The sorrow pooled at the back of Rose's throat, and she began to rock back and forth with the woman still cradled on her knees. "Mid," she sang. "Mid, Mid, Mid…"

Mid was gone. The tears slid from Rose's eyes, wetting the woman's lifeless forehead and cheeks.

She wondered if she should start CPR anyway, but she knew there was no point. The violence of chest compressions, the rush of Rose's breath into Mid's empty vessel—it would all be too much.

Rose could not say how long she knelt on the kitchen floor rocking her dear friend. It might have been minutes or hours. But after a time, she laid Mid gently back down on the floor and went to the phone in the corner of the kitchen.

A small red light on the handset blinked steadily with a message. Rose's message from the evening before.

Rose shut her eyes. That pulsing red light meant Mid had likely been lying on the kitchen floor all night. If Rose had just listened to her first instinct and driven up here after her stupid, ill-fated date, Mid might still be alive. If Rose hadn't gone on the date at all, she may have brought Mid some dinner and would have been able to get her to the hospital. If Rose hadn't sat mindlessly in front of a forgettable television show, pondering her existence and her future, she could have gotten Mid the help she needed.

Rose sucked in a breath. She wanted to scream at herself in frustration. It was too late. It was all too late.

She dug her fingernails into the palm of her hand and did her best to push away her guilt. For now. She pulled herself together and dialed 911.

Chapter 2

Rose quickly discovered Mid had prepared nothing for her death. A call to Howard Lincoln, Mid's attorney, revealed Howard was near certain Mid had not named an executor of her estate, nor did he believe she had prepared a will. But since it was early, Howard planned to call Rose back when he had access to all of his files at his small office in the neighboring city and county seat.

A call to the funeral director, Jack Cummings, owner of the only funeral home in town, also confirmed Mid had made no funeral arrangements, nor had she thought about a cemetery plot.

Jack had been extremely helpful in walking Rose through the entire process, and was willing to allow Rose more flexibility than the law might have allowed in starting the arrangements.

Then Rose had called Pastor Ballentine, whose kindliness and sympathy had made her cry all over again. She didn't deserve his kindness. Not after she'd abandoned Mid in her hour of need.

Rose dreaded telling the employees at the salon,

who would be devastated by the unexpected news. Even though Mid had gradually given up involvement in the day-to-day operations of the salon, she was a daily fixture inside the business. Her blunt pronouncements and tough advice had made them laugh and made them think.

Mid had walked them all through breakups, marriages, divorces, births, and deaths. She was their entertainment and their mascot. She was their leader and their cheerleader. And while most of the employees considered Rose the manager, the business would change drastically now that Mid was gone.

Just how drastically remained to be seen.

After the initial phone calls had been made and the first round of chaos had subsided, Rose went home and stood under a spray of scalding water and sobbed until she felt empty. Then, exhausted, she dressed and walked the two blocks down Main Street to My Pink Wink where she opened the shop like any other day.

She knew Mid would not have wanted the salon to close. The woman had been nothing if not practical. *Your tears aren't going to do anything to bring me back,* she could almost hear Mid saying. *May as well make a bit of money before you put my body in the ground.*

When Rose unlocked the door, she could swear she felt Mid next to her. She was with Rose as Rose turned on the lights. She was beside Rose as Rose made the coffee. She was next to Rose when she turned on the old CD player and sound system Mid had installed nearly twenty years earlier.

Rose picked up a disc titled *Soothing Sounds of the Spa*. Then she put it down.

She asked the empty air, "Do you want some Harry Connick Jr. today?"

For Mid, the answer was always and undoubtedly 'Yes'.

Rose switched out the CDs and the tinkling, upbeat piano filled the shop, followed by the crooner's distinct voice. 'A Wink and a Smile'. Mid's favorite song. The music made Rose simultaneously smile and sob.

The distinct scrape of the front door sounded, and Rose dashed the tears away with the back of her hand.

It was Della Davidson, the middle-aged receptionist. The last of Della's three children had graduated from college two years earlier, upon which Della's husband, a career politician and state senator, immediately left Della for a staffer half Della's age.

Della, who had dedicated her life to her husband, his career, and her children—in that order—found herself alone and jobless. She was fond of saying that Mid and her family at My Pink Wink had saved her life.

"How was the date?" Della said excitedly when Rose emerged from the back of the shop. Then she saw Rose's face. "Oh, honey, are you okay?"

Rose knew her eyes were red and swollen from the

tears. "I'm fine," she said after a pause. She thought it would be best to tell the entire staff at once what had happened, but she didn't have a plan for delivering the news.

"Was it that bad?"

It took Rose a minute to figure out what Della was talking about. "Oh, the date," she said, thinking back. She sighed. "It wasn't a love connection. He was a nice enough guy. He just wasn't *my* guy."

"Bummer," her coworker said mildly. "But you'll find someone. You're young, smart, kind, and beautiful."

"You know, Della, I'm not really all that interested in finding a man, to tell you the truth. I appreciate that you all are concerned for my long-term well-being..." Her words trailed off as she thought about Mid. A sob bubbled up into her throat.

Della rushed forward and put her arms around Rose. "Oh, honey. It's going to be okay. You're going to be okay. You'll find someone soon..."

Rose wanted nothing more than to cry on Della's shoulder. But she pulled herself together, straightened, and held up a hand. "I'm fine," she said, speaking as much to herself as to Della. "But there's something I need to tell you—"

Before she could finish her thought, Alyssa, the youngest of the stylists, burst into the shop. "You'll never guess what happened to me on my way here," she said, her arms flailing around her. Alyssa was also the most dramatic of the group, and her pronouncement could have been something amazing, something devastating, something horrific, or something completely trite.

Rose didn't have it in her to entertain the girl, so she was glad when Della turned her attention from Rose and gave it to Alyssa. "What happened?"

"Some jackass ran a stop sign and hit the car right in front of me. Can you believe it?"

Alyssa lived with her boyfriend in the nearby town of West Newton, along the Youghiogheny River. "Luckily, no one was hurt," she continued. "But if I would've left just thirty seconds earlier, it could've been me." The girl placed a hand over her heart and shook her head.

"Well, I'm glad you're okay," said Della, her arms now around Alyssa's shoulders instead of Rose's.

"Am I a bad person for being glad it didn't happen to me but to the guy in front of me?"

"Of course not," Della assured her, and the conversation turned almost, but not quite, philosophical.

Rose was glad for the excuse to stop listening.

Hallie Bosch, the lead stylist, arrived next. Hallie ignored the profound conversation happening between Della and Alyssa at the front desk, mumbled a hello to Rose, and walked to the back room, which held a washer and dryer as well as a small kitchenette and table. This was also where the coffee was brewing.

Hallie was about Rose's age and lived with her two young children on the west edge of town. She'd been born and raised in New York City, but had relocated to Western Pennsylvania a few years earlier after her younger sister attended college close by, then moved here permanently and had a baby. Hallie's parents had relocated first, and Hallie had grudgingly followed after the unexpected death of her mechanic husband in New York.

Rose wasn't sure Hallie would ever love Madison, or the entire area for that matter, but she seemed to have made peace with her home, and her children were settled in the local school district.

Her lone male stylist, Jay Gaffney, was not on the schedule until later in the day.

Rose went to the back of the shop to pour herself a coffee. She hadn't eaten breakfast, and a headache was forming behind her eyes. She knew she had to tell Della, Hallie, and Alyssa about Mid, and she had to do it soon, but wasn't sure if it was quite the right time. Or if she even had the right words. How do you break that kind of news?

Hallie stirred some cream into her coffee, and Rose poured herself a cup. Hallie eyed Rose closely. "You okay?"

Rose blinked. The image of Mid on her kitchen floor kept appearing in her mind. "I'm—Yeah, I'm fine." She took a scalding swallow of coffee from her pink mug with its signature winking-eye logo, and attempted to push the memories of that morning out of her mind. She squeezed her own eyes shut.

Then Alyssa walked into the room.

Hallie must have decided she couldn't deal with Alyssa's drama because she abandoned the conversation with Rose and ducked out of the room.

Alyssa didn't seem to notice Hallie's exit. She looked at Rose, a pouty expression on her pretty face. "Is there something you want to tell me?"

Rose regarded Alyssa's accusatory expression, and her heart leapt into her throat. "I-I…" she stammered. "I was trying to figure out the right way to tell you. How did you find out already?" she asked, wondering not only how Alyssa had heard the news, but who else knew already.

"Jamison told me."

Rose cocked her head. *Who the heck was Jamison?*

"My brother?" Alyssa prompted. The word was a question followed by a scoff. "Andrew told him you were rude, but I said that couldn't be, because you're one of the nicest people I know. At least *most* of the time," she added.

Rose tried to keep up. "Oh," she said suddenly. "The date." She'd completely forgotten the guy's name. She wasn't sure she'd ever even known it. She hadn't been rude, she thought, a tad defensively. At least not outright. She'd been *honest*. Men hated honest women.

But now she had other things to worry about. She didn't give a damn about Anthony. Or whatever his name was.

"I didn't want to say anything out there," Alyssa continued. "But it's just disappointing because Andrew is, like, really nice. And you're nice. I know he isn't as good looking as, like, Austin Butler, but you could do worse."

"Who's Austin Butler?" Rose asked, mystified.

In her back pocket, Rose's cell phone buzzed. She pulled it out. Howard Lincoln's name lit up the screen. "Excuse me, Alyssa. I really need to take this."

Alyssa made another face. "Rude," she confirmed. Then she flounced out of the room in a huff.

Before Rose accepted the call, she heard the front door of the salon scrape open. The first customer of the day. Rose's head pounded harder, and she answered the phone.

"Howard," she said.

"Rose? Is that you?"

"Yes, this is Rose, Howard."

"This is Howard Lincoln," Howard said loudly into the phone.

Rose exhaled. "Hi, Howard."

He cleared his throat. "I'm at the office now, and I have all my files…"

Rose swallowed and pressed her lips together. At

least things could move forward now.

"I can confirm with certainty Mid did not file a will."

She hadn't realized how strongly she'd hoped Howard would come back to her with a different answer.

She shut her eyes and then opened them again. "Can you explain to me exactly what that means?"

She needed to know what it meant for the whole ordeal—the funeral planning and costs, the medical examination, the burial, Mid's house, and most importantly, My Pink Wink. Rose had assumed, based on Mid's comments over the years, that Mid was going to leave the business to Rose. And while Rose had in no way been wishing for it to happen, she couldn't ensure the staff would have jobs if she had no control over the ownership of the salon.

"Well," Howard began slowly, "since there is no beneficiary or executor named for the estate, I have the authority to appoint someone so long as I can get signoff from the Register of Wills."

"Is that a difficult process?" Rose asked.

"Not particularly, though depending on their back-log, it might take a bit longer than it needs to."

"But will it delay anything? With funeral planning or operation of the salon?"

"No," Howard said, but there was something be-hind his words. "My advice is to move forward with

Jack Cummings on the planning and keep the salon humming along as normal."

"I haven't told the team yet. I'm still trying to figure out the right way to break the news. They'll be devastated, but relieved to know they still have jobs."

Howard hesitated. "Rose, before I go down the path of preparing all the paperwork, I do need to perform some due diligence on potential beneficiaries."

"Beneficiaries?" she asked.

"Blood relatives."

Rose shook her head. "I don't believe Mid has any relatives. She'd mentioned a sister a few times…" Her words trailed off.

"Madeline," Howard interjected. "Mid's twin."

Rose had heard scant stories about Mid and Mad, and a few infrequent mentions of some of their antics as young women and teenagers. From what Rose could gather, Mad had married and moved away, and that had been that.

It had never occurred to Rose that Mad might have had children, though the possibility certainly existed. Surely, Mid would have said something.

She took a breath. "Are you telling me if Mid has nieces and nephews somewhere, even though she's never met the children, they would be entitled to her estate?"

"I'm afraid so," said Howard. "Now, we still have to perform an inventory of Mid's assets. You know better than anyone what she has in the bank and the value of My Pink Wink and her home. Even if there are relations, they may decide they're not interested in the hassle of becoming the executor of the estate. They'd likely need to travel here, or hire someone to take care of business in Madison. And as you also know, while the salon is profitable, it also takes work to manage it, to keep it operational. In other words, it would not be profitable without the staff in place. And without you in particular. I will certainly explain all of this to any relatives, should they even exist."

Rose felt the flutter of anxiety in her chest. She tapped a short unpolished fingernail against the edge of the counter. How was she going to handle all of this on her own? "What about the funeral arrangements?" she asked aloud. "I've already begun the process with Jack."

"Mid certainly has enough in her personal savings to cover that cost. But you won't have access to those funds until the question of inheritance is answered."

Rose wasn't concerned about the money. "If relatives exist and they don't like the arrangements I've made, can they change them?" She was much more worried about some stranger trying to save money by having Mid cremated and kept in a box in a basement. Mid should be buried in the town cemetery right along with everyone else. She would have wanted that.

"It's a possibility, but it's not likely."

In response to her silence, he continued. "You were like a daughter to her. I will do my duty and search for a blood relative, but the search will not take long, if you catch my drift."

Rose let out a shallow breath. She wasn't Mid's daughter. Not really. Howard's remark didn't completely alleviate her anxiety, but all the same, she said, "Thanks, Howard."

"I'll give you a call later. Take care of yourself, my dear. Even though you weren't Mid's daughter by blood, she certainly thought of you that way. You have every right in the world to grieve like a daughter."

Rose felt the tears rise again. If she'd been a good daughter—a *real* daughter—she wouldn't have been on that stupid and completely disappointing date last night. She would have been home with Mid.

She managed to thank Howard without breaking down completely, and after she hung up, she took a few moments to steady herself.

Harry Connick Jr. was still crooning. The beat of 'There Once Was a Man' rang out through the speakers.

She dashed her tears away, and when she was certain she wasn't going to start bawling, she stood up straighter and walked into the belly of the salon. It was time to tell the team.

What met her were stony stares and heavy silence.

Rose took this all in, and quickly discerned what

had happened. She hadn't looked at the appointment log when she'd come in, which was a mistake. Because the first appointment of the day was Julie Newlin, the church's administrative assistant and operations manager, who was sitting in Hallie's chair, looking ever so smug.

Rose had spoken to Pastor Ballentine earlier, which meant Julie likely already knew about Mid's passing. And Julie, in turn, had shared her knowledge with the staff, who were in various states of tears, shock, and anger—all directed at Rose.

Julie said, "I'm sorry, Rose. I would've thought you'd have told the staff straightaway." Her perfect face was the picture of perfectly arranged innocence.

Rose gritted her teeth. She didn't want to think ill of anyone, but right now, her thoughts about Julie were anything but warm.

Della spoke first. "Rose. How could you not have told us immediately?"

Alyssa cried softly, didn't look at Rose.

Hallie said, "I thought we were a family here. I guess I was wrong."

Julie said nothing else, but just the hint of a smile played at the corner of her lips. Maybe that was Rose's imagination. She knew it was not.

How had she not anticipated this happening?

She shut her eyes for just a moment, and then announced to her staff, plus Julie: "I wanted to tell you, but I needed to get some information first. It was a shock to me, too, and I'm still processing the information myself."

"You let me go on and on about a car accident that didn't even affect me. But I can't think of more important information than the fact that Mid is dead," Alyssa wailed.

The Harry Connick Jr. song continued its trotting beat. Rose wished the song would end soon; its energy was completely misplaced.

"A lot is up in the air right now," said Rose. "I needed to call Jack Cummings about the funeral, and figure how to get all that accomplished. And Mid didn't leave a will, so Howard Lincoln is trying to help me figure that out."

"Who cares?" Alyssa wailed, her voice accusatory.

Della broke in, "But, honey, we could've helped you with all that."

Rose looked at Della gratefully.

But it was Hallie who understood the deeper implications of Rose's words. "Are we going to lose our jobs?"

Rose held out her hands. "Not if I can help it," she said. She could only pray Howard would be able to appoint her as executor and that she had the opportunity to, if not inherit the business outright, take a loan to purchase it from Mid's estate. She'd remortgage her small house if she had to. She'd borrow money from Teddy. Hell, she'd even date what's-his-name, if it meant financial stability. Then she pulled back on the thought. That was going a little far.

They were still watching her. Hallie said, "Should we be working today? Maybe we should all go home."

The rest of the women murmured.

Julie's face lost some of its superiority. "But I need my highlights," she said, her voice close to a whine.

Everyone ignored Julie, and Rose said, "Right now, I think what would be best for all of us is to move forward as if nothing has changed."

"But everything has changed," said Alyssa.

"Yes," Rose agreed. "Everything has changed." A tear slid down her cheek. She wanted nothing more than for Mid to walk through the front door in one of her colorful flowing kaftans, a smile on her face and a laugh in her voice.

She forced some steel into her voice. "But we're going to serve our customers." *Even Julie*, she thought bitterly. "You all know that's what Mid would've wanted."

Dubious looks were exchanged, but no one argued with her, and no one walked out.

A few minutes later, Helene Graff entered the salon for a trim at Alyssa's station, and Hallie set to work stoically on Julie's highlights.

Rose walked to the desk at the front of the shop where Della said quietly, "How are you, really?"

Rose blindly picked up a stack of appointment cards. She sucked in a breath and held it.

"It's okay not to be okay," Della whispered.

Rose let the breath go on a rush of air. "I'm the only one holding this place together right now."

Della laid a hand on Rose's arm. "As long as it's not *you* who falls apart."

Grace Blackburn was Rose's client, and she wasn't due in until noon, so Rose went to the back room to call Jay only to find out Alyssa had somehow already made the notification. At least he hadn't seemed as angry as the others had been.

The day moved on almost normally, apart from Mid's glaring absence and the myriad offers of sympathy and tears shed by clients. But it was comforting, Rose realized, to be around these people who had become family.

And when her phone buzzed at five in the afternoon, and Howard's name flashed again on her screen, she left Becky Greenawalt in her seat to answer it in a marginally better frame of mind than she had been that morning.

"Rose, I have some news."

She didn't like the grim timbre of his voice.

"I'm afraid Mid has a nephew," he continued.

"A nephew," Rose repeated. "This is Madeline's son?"

"Yes," Howard said. "His name is…" There was a

pause, as if he was searching for the appellation. "Griffin Stangel."

The name sounded vaguely familiar, but she couldn't remember Mid ever having uttered the moniker. Perhaps someone else in the salon who had known Madeline had mentioned it.

"Okay," Rose said, trying to process this news. "Is he coming here?"

"I haven't been able to get hold of him yet," said Howard, "but I'll keep trying, and I'll let you know. I just wanted to give you this information as soon as possible."

"I appreciate that." She was about to end the call, but before she did, Howard said, "Remember, Rose. All is not lost."

Rose nodded and hung up. She looked around her at this place that had become her home. Somehow it seemed that, in less than twenty-four hours, *everything* had been lost, including Rose herself.

Chapter 3

Griffin Stangel slumped forward on the high wooden bar stool at South Boston's Red Bull Tavern. It was three in the afternoon on a Tuesday, and even though the bar was warm, he kept his heavy wool coat folded around his broad shoulders.

For now, he had the place to himself, but he knew in a few hours, the place would be filled with the blue-collar crowd—constructor workers, laborers, plumbers, maybe some cops and firemen. But right now, it was just Griffin, served by a middle-aged Boston native named Hank.

"You want another?" Hank asked in his thick accent, nodded to Griffin's empty glass in front of him.

Griffin wasn't drunk yet, but he was well on his way.

He didn't answer, just nudged the glass forward.

He caught the almost imperceptible shake of Hank's head. Griffin felt like punching Hank right in the face, but he didn't have the fight in him right now. He was tired. It was less than a year since his life had started its downward slide into the pile of shit where he currently found himself.

On the television set fixed high on the wall opposite the bar, the early season Red Sox game played.

One year ago today, Griffin himself had been on that field at Fenway Park. Then, plagued with a bum shoulder, advanced age, and a bad temper, he was quickly dismissed without so much as a 'thanks for the memories'. He went into free agency, but no other team wanted a guy with as many forewarnings on and off the field.

His agent had gotten him a few offers, but they'd been lowball propositions for crap farm teams in shit locations. At thirty-eight, Griffin Stangel was a has-been.

There had been a bright spot for a white-hot minute, until Griffin had ruined that too.

His bad-boy reputation and roguish looks had made him a minor celebrity off the field, and the Sports News Network, or SNN, in Boston had offered him a sweet gig as a game-day commentator. With no education, no prospects, and no experience, it was perhaps the best outcome Griffin could've hoped for. He'd been grateful. But then he'd set the whole thing ablaze. In spectacular fashion.

On the bar's hazy screen, a new rookie, twenty-one-year-old Colton Crews, hit a double. The commentators fell all over themselves praising the kid while the crowd cheered.

"Hey," Griffin called to Hank at the other end of the bar. "Would you turn that shit off?"

Hank peered at Griffin levelly under his heavy brow, looking like he was going to argue. Just to push Griffin's buttons. Griffin decided he had enough fight in him to punch Hank in the face before the afternoon was over.

But Hank shrugged, picked up a remote, and switched off the set.

The quiet was unsettling.

Griffin took a swig of the strong whiskey and felt sour all around. When he'd been a player, his nickname had been 'the Stinger', a play on his last name. But he'd earned it. In his position at left field, he could throw the ball so hard and fast that often the opposing team didn't even see it coming. And once upon a time, he'd been an excellent hitter too.

Then they'd started calling him 'the Grifter', a play on his first name. These days, that was the one used and remembered. Just the idea of it made Griffin pull the collar of his coat higher around his neck, even though no one was there to recognize him.

He'd been out of work for months. He still had money, but it wasn't going to last forever. He needed to figure his shit out, and he needed to do it soon.

But not today. Today he was going to drink this whiskey and feel sorry for himself. It didn't matter he wasn't as lean as he'd once been or that fleshy pouches sat under his dark, dark eyes. Today, none of it mattered. Because today, he could do nothing to change it.

The door opened, and a blast of chilled Boston air rushed into the space. A pair of female voices broke the silence in the Red Bull. Griffin scowled into what was left of his whiskey.

They took the two seats directly to his right. He looked around pointedly. Every other seat in the bar was vacant.

They didn't seem to notice his irritation and continued to chatter.

Griffin studied them in his periphery.

He estimated they were older than his thirty-eight years by roughly a decade. Both wore fashionable leggings and puffy vests over designer long-sleeved tops; they were fit and toned, and their makeup was perfect and not a hair of their sculped and highlighted hairstyles was out of place. They had unnaturally full lips and extraordinarily smooth faces.

The one closest, a pretty brunette, glanced at him, offered a soft smile, then looked away.

For a second, he wondered if she recognized him. She didn't look like a typical baseball fan, but then again, you didn't have to be a baseball fan to know Griffin's face.

Hank approached. "What are you ladies drinking?"

"Do you have a menu?" the other woman—the

blonde—asked stridently. She looked harder and more severe than the smiling brunette.

The Red Bull Tavern wasn't exactly the kind of bar where you needed a menu. Most customers ordered draft beer, or whiskey from the long dusty row of bottles behind the bar.

Hank made a noise at the back of his throat, rummaged around for some sticky menus, and slid them down the length of the bar top unceremoniously. They stopped in front of Griffin.

"Thank you," the blonde said loudly. Then just loud enough so Hank could hear, she added, "Customer service is dead."

The brunette leaned over to slide the menus closer, and as she did, she brushed Griffin's forearm with her toned shoulder. A tiny electric shock ran through him at the contact. It was a few months since he'd been with a woman. It wasn't that he couldn't have found companionship—women still found him plenty attractive. He supposed a part of him may have been punishing himself for his past humiliation.

He glanced over at her again and found she was watching him with a sly smile.

"Hello there," she said as she handed a laminated menu to her companion.

He smiled back but didn't speak.

The pair stopped chattering and studied the menus in silence.

Griffin wished Hank would turn on some music or something. But the bartender had moved down to the other end of the bar, his back to his trio of customers.

"What's a gal need to do to get a drink around here?" the blonde asked loudly.

The brunette called out, "Excuse me!"

Hank continued to ignore them.

The brunette looked up at Griffin, and Griffin sighed. So, this was the game. He'd been cast as the hero.

"What are you drinking?" he asked. His voice was low and slow. Not because he was trying to be seductive, but because he hadn't spoken more than a handful of words that entire day and his voice was rusty.

"I'll take a Manhattan," the brunette said.

Griffin snorted. "A Manhattan in Boston. Original." She didn't seem to take offense, and giggled.

Her friend said, "Cosmopolitan."

He walked to the end of the bar, repeated their orders to Hank, and told the bartender to add them to his tab.

Hank raised an eyebrow but didn't comment further. He set about mixing the concoctions.

When Griffin got back to his seat, the brunette said, "Do you live in Boson then?"

Griffin studied her to gauge whether she was trying to game him. Her expression was innocent.

"Yeah."

"Born and raised?"

He thought about that. He'd been here long enough, and he had no plans to leave.

"Yeah."

There was a silence. The blonde had a coy look on her face, and the brunette studied her ringless, manicured left hand stretched out on the bar in front of her. An invitation, he recognized.

"What about you?" Griffin asked.

"Columbus, Ohio."

Griffin winced. The Clippers had been one of the triple-A teams to make him a lousy offer.

Hank set the drinks down in front of the pair and raised his eyebrows at Griffin's glass. Griffin shook his head. The quick look Hank gave in the direction of the brunette was so subtle Griffin thought he may have imagined it. But Hank recognized the pre-hookup dance.

"What brings you to Boston?" asked Griffin.

"My friend Beth is here visiting her daughter." She glanced at her companion.

"And you?"

"I'm Michelle. I'm just tagging along for a bit of fun." There was a lilt in her voice when she said the word 'fun'.

Beth laughed and sipped her drink.

Griffin spun his glass around between thumb and forefinger. "What kind of fun you looking for?"

There was a slow, anticipatory pause. Michelle took a long drink of her Manhattan. Then she plucked the maraschino cherry from atop the ice, and held it between her lips before she bit down.

Griffin's heart started to thrum in his chest.

The women hadn't even finished one drink before Griffin closed out his tab. Beth took an Uber west to Newton, the home of her daughter, and Michelle and Griffin climbed into their own Uber and headed north to the Seaport and Michelle's hotel.

Griffin didn't overthink this decision. He was just living in the moment, and an opportunity had presented itself.

In the backseat of the black sedan, driven by a silent man who paid them absolutely no attention, Michelle let her hand linger on Griffin's knee.

"Tell me about yourself." Her fingers made small circles over the fabric of his jeans.

"What do you want to know?"

She lifted a shoulder. "What do you do in Boston?"

That was a loaded question, and there were many ways to answer it. He was glad this woman didn't want a real answer. He said, "I like to do a lot of things."

Her fingers inched higher up his leg, and her mouth came closer. "Like what?"

He leaned into her. "I like to play games, for starters."

Her hand shifted to the inside of his thigh. He let

out a slow breath.

"I like games too," she said, and pressed her breasts against his arm as her lips found the sensitive skin of his neck.

He moaned as her tongue flicked hot against his throat.

Her fingers traveled higher; the anticipation was painful. Just as she reached his erection, he grabbed her wrist and held it at bay.

She laughed, low and throaty. "Ah, you like the long game." Her voice was a purr.

He dipped his head and kissed her, pressing her into the back seat of the car. *May as well give the driver a good story for later…*

He let go of her wrist and slid his fingers under her shirt. Her hand immediately went back to his pulsing erection; she squeezed his shaft, her fierce grip belying her hunger. Griffin's manhood strained as the desire overcame him. He sucked in a breath and growled softly.

Her hands felt so good touching him, teasing him, tempting him…

Mercifully, they pulled up in front of the Seaport Hotel just as Griffin began to question how much longer he'd be able to control himself.

The driver didn't acknowledge their departure as they tumbled out the passenger side door. Michelle held on to Griffin's arm, still pressing her body hard against his.

Griffin's mind had cleared from the two drinks he'd had earlier, but he was still buzzed enough to feel the hazy, giddy high. He smiled down at his new friend.

Griffin quite liked that this was an anonymous encounter. The fact that Michelle was interested in him for no other reason than she liked his looks pleased him beyond measure. He didn't have to perform. He could simply be himself.

He wondered if he remembered who that was.

The doors to the hotel's lobby slid open, and Michelle let go of Griffin's arm to rummage through the contents of her small purse for her key card.

As they walked toward the elevator bank at the back of the lobby, Griffin noticed some sort of gathering to the right side near the bar. It appeared to be an event, or a press conference, with a media avail.

A gaggle of reporters milled around as a young woman who looked vaguely familiar readied herself at a microphone.

Griffin turned to hide his face. Too late. A man with a handheld microphone and a cameraman glanced in Griffin's direction and caught his eye.

Shit, Griffin thought, and must have muttered the word out loud because Michelle glanced up sharply.

"What?"

Griffin didn't answer. The man had broken away

from the scrum and was headed their way, his cameraman, camera hoisted on his shoulder, looking confused. But he followed behind the reporter obediently.

"Well well well, if it isn't Griffin Stangel…" The man's brown Oxford shoes moved soundlessly across the floor. "The *Grifter*," he added. "Long time no see."

Griffin gritted his teeth. He wanted to keep walking, but he knew the camera was filming. Better to play it cool and defuse the situation. He attempted to hide his annoyance.

"Hi Mike," he said mildly.

Michelle's key card was visible in her hand. "What's going on?" she whispered. Her voice was quiet, but Mike McCaffrey, one of the more aggressive field reporters for the local NBC affiliate, heard her.

"And who do we have here?" Mike asked.

Some of the other reporters from the avail had noticed the interaction and were glancing in their direction. The woman at the microphone looked furious. Griffin didn't know who she was, but it just went to show how the whiff of a scandal could leave an odor in its wake for months.

Griffin kept his voice low. "There's no story here, Mike."

Mike was a typical reporter—always looking to break the next story with the most shocking, shameful, and unflattering angle. Griffin couldn't blame the guy.

He was just doing his job. But it was sleazy and gross, and Griffin hated that he was still in the nasty cross-hairs of the press.

Mike smiled, and his face lit up. "When someone tells me there's no story, there's usually a story."

Michelle had assumed the expression of a fawn in headlights. She was staring straight into the camera. Its big lens was staring right back at her. Griffin knew they weren't live. The news crews were most likely gathering footage for the five-o'clock early news, which would be replayed at seven, and then again at eleven. But the edited footage would be streamed online endlessly.

If he could just play it cool for a few minutes, they wouldn't end up on any of those broadcasts or the internet.

"So…what have you been up to since we last spoke?" Mike asked, looking pointedly at Michelle.

"Not a thing," said Griffin, and that part was excruciatingly true.

Michelle asked in a high-pitched voice, "Are we on camera?"

Mike made a tsking sound with his tongue. "It sounds like you don't want to be on camera…ma'am," he added after a pause. He turned to Griffin. "Looks like you've gotten yourself a taste for…experience."

It was an insulting comment, to both Griffin and Michelle, and Griffin's blood started to run hot. He reminded himself to breathe, but he couldn't stop his fists from clenching at his sides. He attempted to herd Michelle behind him.

But Mike smelled blood. He shifted his body to get a better look at the woman. He made a feline and animalistic noise Griffin could only assume was supposed to sound like a cougar.

Griffin's face flushed. He clenched his teeth, trying to keep his temper at bay.

You've been here before, he reminded himself. His reputation could not survive a repeat of that terrible incident a few months earlier.

Sharp heels clicked on the floor as a female reporter from WCBV headed their way with her own cameraman and a microphone bearing the call sign of the station. Two print reporters trotted behind with notebooks, phones, and handheld mini voice recorders thrust forward.

Griffin took another breath. "I'm just headed to the bar with my friend to have a drink, that's all. No story."

Mike looked at the key card in Michelle's hand. "Didn't know the bar here required a room key. Looks like you're after more than just a drink."

The woman reporter who Griffin had never seen before, but who clearly knew him, started speaking into the camera. "We're here with former Major League baseball player and Red Sox MVP Griffin Stangel, who has just walked into the lobby of the Seaport Hotel."

Griffin tried to keep his face passive. He knew this

woman also wasn't live, but was just gathering potential footage for later.

Michelle, however, did not know any of this. Coming out of her frozen state, Michelle put her hands over her face, the key card and room number visible to the cameras.

"I'm married!" she cried.

Mike let out a whoop of laughter. "Well of course you are, sweetheart." His tone was filled with glee. He turned to his cameraman and said into his microphone, "Some things just never change. We've just run into Griffin 'the Grifter' Stangel and his married lover who are heading to their room at the Seaport Hotel. Let's see what Griffin has to say for himself." Mike, the woman, and the two print reporters, shoved their microphones and recorders into his face.

Griffin turned around quickly and started walking toward the hotel's exit, hauling Michelle behind him. She was sobbing now. They would definitely make it onto the local news affiliates. But with any luck, they'd stay out of the national spotlight.

Behind him, Mike said, "Looks like a change in plans is in store for the Grifter, as he's been confronted by multiple interveners and his afternoon delight has been interrupted."

The woman reporter teetered on her high heels as she attempted to run in front of Griffin and Michelle. She thrust her microphone into Michelle's face. "What do you think your husband will have to say about your affair with scandal-plagued Griffin Stangel?" she asked Michelle, who stumbled and tried to tuck her face into Griffin's arm.

Jesus Christ, these people were vultures, Griffin thought as he pushed is way outside and hurried down the street. And Mike McCaffery was the worst of the bunch. If there weren't so many witnesses, he'd be tempted to lay him out on the sidewalk.

Hell, he hadn't known she was married. She wasn't wearing a ring, probably on purpose, now that he remembered the way she flaunted her bare hands on the bar in front of him. She hadn't offered that piece of information while she'd been caressing his leg on the car ride over here. But even if she had, it probably wouldn't have changed anything.

He kept his mouth shut, because nobody cared about his excuses. They wouldn't believe him anyway.

He and Michelle pushed past the female reporter, but just as quickly, Mike was in front of them again.

The man's breath came in puffs as he struggled to keep up and talk into the camera. "Griffin Stangel has had a track record of scandal over the years. And here he is again, caught with a married woman on a Tuesday afternoon. It looks like you can take the baseball out of the Stangel, but not the grifter out of the Griffin."

Griffin rolled his eyes at the silly soundbite as he

juked and quickly turned down an alleyway between buildings. But the still crying Michelle, left hand covering her face, slowed him down.

Mike easily followed and moved back in front of them. He shoved the microphone into Griffin's face. "I imagine you're hoping this older lady might teach you a few things in the bedroom?"

Griffin tried—he really did—to stay calm. But the attention was ludicrous. Why in the world was this city so fixated on his movements and his love life?

He let a "Fuck you" slip past his lips, and Mike laughed again cheerfully.

"It looks like we're getting under the skin of Griffin Stangel, the former MVP and left-fielder for the Red Sox, who was unceremoniously dismissed after injury and mayhem on the field, and a number of scandals off the field. As you might recall, during Stangel's brief stint as a sports commentator, his affair with former newscaster Victoria Bryant, the wife of SNN Boston's CEO Charlie Bryant, was broken by yours truly. Both Stangel and Mrs. Bryant were dismissed from their positions."

Griffin saw red as he listened to Mike's summary of his past year—the worst of his life.

He also heard Michelle gasp as she attempted to pull her hands from his.

They reached the end of the alleyway and a dead end. There was no place to go.

Griffin turned around to the crowd of reporters who'd followed them.

"Can you comment on your spectacular fall from grace? We've rarely seen someone fall from such a height, so far so fast."

Griffin tried to move forward, but Mike and his cameraman blocked his path.

"Get out of my way, Mike," Griffin warned.

Mike continued into the camera. "We've been calling him Stinger, we've been calling him the Grifter, but what we really need to call him is the Homewrecker."

At that, Griffin snapped. He pushed Michelle roughly behind him, reared his arm back, and punched Mike McCaffrey in the jaw with his powerful arm.

There was a collective gasp from not only the reporters and the cameraman, but from a crowd of spectators who'd followed into the street to watch the spectacle.

Mike went down hard and out cold. None of the camera people missed a beat. They continued to film while concerned bystanders rushed to Mike's aid.

"Fuck," Griffin spat as he looked at Michelle. "Go back to your hotel!" he yelled.

She stared up at him, shocked. "Who the hell are you?" she demanded, disgust coloring her voice.

"I'm someone you don't want to fucking know."

Chapter 4

Griffin was booked at the Nashua Street Jail and released at 8:00 a.m. the following morning when his lawyer, Irvin Abbott, Esquire, finally showed up to bail him out. Griffin was tired and hungry. His anger had bubbled and boiled all night. At around 2:00 a.m., he'd been resigned enough in his jail cell that his rage had reduced to a low simmer that caused an irregular heartbeat.

"Thanks for coming so quickly," Griffin said sarcastically as he walked across the booking room toward Irv. A cop smirked as he handed Griffin back his wallet, cell phone, and coat, all of which had been confiscated after his arrest.

"I suppose I couldn't leave you in here to rot," Irv responded, missing the sarcasm. Or perhaps the grizzled man who was just on the other side of sixty caught it and decided to ignore it.

Griffin kept his mouth shut because he hadn't been sure if Irv had planned to show up at all.

"You're all over the news, by the way. Even made the national press again. Congrats."

Irv was a high-powered defense attorney in town, and held a grudging respect among the cops. He'd defended famous dirtbags, but Irv himself was no dirtbag. He'd started his career as Boston P.D., and he was tough and sharp as a tack. The cops still saw him as one of their own.

A tall, uniformed man motioned Irv toward the back of the room. "You can go out this way, Mr. Abbott."

"Thanks, Sargent Sullivan," Irv said.

"Just Sully is fine."

Irv nodded once, a sign of mutual respect. "Tell Captain Rodriguez 'Hey' for me."

"Will do, sir." He gave a tight-lipped smile at Irv and scowled at Griffin. "See you soon, pretty boy," Sully said.

Irv glanced back at Griffin, probably to make sure he was behaving. But Griffin had no desire to get into a fight with a cop. In a police station. Even *he* wasn't that stupid. Clearly his attorney disagreed.

They emerged from the station into the brisk April morning. Griffin shivered, pulling on his coat as they walked.

Before he'd climbed into the passenger side of Irv's car, Irv peered at him over the roof of the black luxury SUV. "Not looking so pretty these days," he quipped.

Griffin wondered if the comment was supposed to hurt his feelings. It didn't. He'd never cared about his looks, even when the world had wanted him to. His black hair—a tad too long—and his scruffy unkempt beard were a product of his lack of concern. Even if the press wanted to believe it was a carefully cultivated branding decision.

Irv started the car and turned right on Nashua Street; Griffin couldn't see if there were any paparazzi waiting outside jail for him. Maybe he flattered himself, but he thought there was probably a camera or two awaiting his release. Punching a reporter while the cameras were rolling was a good way to build up some staying power in the press.

When Irv turned left onto Cambridge Street, Griffin looked around. "I thought you were taking me home." He wanted a hot cup of coffee and a hot shower, and then he wanted to fall into bed. His own bed.

"No, no, my friend. We're going to talk about this thing."

"What *thing*?" Griffin asked.

"Your situation."

"That's what I pay *you* for."

Stopped in morning rush-hour traffic, Irv leveled a glance at Griffin. "If you want me to continue defending you, we're going to have to talk about your behavior. I don't think I need to remind you, this isn't the first time you've punched a high-profile target in the past year. I've only got so much goodwill. And you, my boy, have none."

Griffin let out a noisy sigh and leaned his head back against the posh headrest.

"Your arraignment will be scheduled for later today, so I'll have you out of here in time to go home, shower, and *maybe* take a nap."

"Arraignment?" Griffin asked. "That didn't happen last time."

"No, it didn't. But as I said, this isn't last time. Last time, you were charged with a misdemeanor. We're well beyond that."

There was no sense in arguing his case. Not with Irv. Griffin set his jaw and looked down at his cell phone and tried to power it on. It was dead. Not that it mattered. There was no one left to try to get in touch with him.

"You expecting a call?"

Griffin shook his head.

"You can charge it at the office." Irv's voice softened slightly.

Griffin just shrugged.

The building housing the office of Abbott and Associates just off Broad Street had secured underground parking, so they didn't have to worry about anyone popping out with a camera. No one in the office even looked in their direction, other than Irv's receptionist, Katy, who gave Griffin a wave from behind her big glass desk. She didn't seem offended when Griffin scowled in return.

"Can you bring us two coffees, Kate?" Irv asked. "And order some breakfast for Mr. Stangel."

"My pleasure," she said and smiled in Griffin's direction. "What would you like to eat?"

Honestly, he would've eaten just about anything, and he was taken off guard by the question. She seemed to understand. "I'll take care of it," she said.

They sat down in Irv's posh modern office, with its sleek minimalist furniture and abstract art. Griffin always felt uncomfortable in the room. The décor seemed so juxtaposed to the rough-around-the-edges lawyer.

But the chair, though streamlined, was comfortable, and Griffin knew he would struggle to stay awake. A minute later, Katy sashayed back into the room, two cups of coffee in her manicured hands. She leaned closer to Griffin than he thought necessary when handing over his mug. Her hand brushed his. He nearly spilled the coffee, trying to get away from her.

He hadn't consciously decided it, but he would be swearing off women. Maybe for the rest of his life.

Katy walked out and shut the door behind her.

Irv had powered up his laptop and was pawing through some files on his desk while Griffin gulped down the coffee. It scalded his throat.

"Feel free to use that," Irv said, pointing to a charging block on the corner of his desk.

Griffin took another gulp before pulling his phone out of his pocket and laying it on the charger.

Irv leaned forward, his dark reading glasses perched on the end of his nose.

"Okay…" He drew out the word as he read over the file in front of him. "They're charging you with aggravated assault and battery, which is a felony."

"Aggravated?" Griffin exclaimed. "They guy goaded me. There are witnesses."

"The witnesses all say you punched him in the face and knocked him out. Doesn't matter if he deserved it or not."

"Shouldn't it be a misdemeanor?" Griffin knew it should, because he'd been here before.

"If it was your first time, maybe. It's not, and you're a known offender."

"Okay, but what if it was self-defense?"

"Was the guy threatening you?"

"He was threatening my name."

"Your safety?"

Griffin didn't say anything; he didn't need to. Irv knew the answer to the question.

"You don't have self-defense, you don't have defense of property, and you don't have defense of another."

"What if I was defending my friend, who was terrified?" Griffin tried to remember her name. "Melanie," he said, then frowned. That wasn't it. "Melissa."

"Michelle," Irv said flatly.

Griffin snapped his fingers. "Right. Michelle."

Irv stared at him, then looked down at the sheaf of papers in front of him. He thumbed through them. "She actually gave a statement."

"Great," Griffin said triumphantly. "That has to count for something."

"Oh, it does. It's a witness statement on behalf of the victim."

Griffin deflated. He felt unexpectedly betrayed.

At the corner of the desk on the charger, Griffin's phone began to vibrate. Irv glanced at it. "Expecting a call?"

Griffin shook his head and peered at the unfamiliar area code. Probably spam or a wrong number. The vibration stopped.

"We might be able to work this another way," Irv said when the phone was quiet. "I know a few of the attorneys over at Mike's affiliate station. We might be able to make some kind of a deal with them to get Mr. McCaffery to drop the charges."

"Ha," Griffin said, without mirth. "Fat chance. Mike will push this as far as it can go. Hell, it'll be like a real-time documentary starring himself." Griffin shut his eyes. It was going to be a nightmare.

Griffin's phone started vibrating again. Irv looked annoyed. "You want to get that?"

Griffin glanced over again. It was the same unfamiliar number. Had some enterprising reporter found his private cell number? He silenced the call.

Irv laid his hands out on the desk in front of him. "What if we were to offer something in return? Something he wants?" Irv paused while Griffin stared at him. "A public apology, on-air, from you. An exclusive."

Griffin sighed and pushed his hand through his hair. "Absolutely not."

"Short-term pain to make the problem go away."

"I'll be humiliated," he said.

"I got news for you..." Irv didn't finish his statement. He didn't have to.

"What's the punishment for felony aggravated assault and battery?" Griffin took another long swallow of coffee.

"Depends on whether a judge wants to throw the book at you. Could be up to twenty years in prison."

Griffin choked and sputtered. "Twenty years?"

"Obviously that's the maximum. And I wouldn't be any kind of lawyer at all if I allowed that to happen—"

Griffin's phone began to vibrate for a third time.

"Jesus Christ," Irv exploded. "Would you answer the goddamn thing?"

Griffin snatched it up. "Who is this?" he growled into the receiver.

There was a pause so long Griffin nearly ended the call. Then a tentative male voice said, "Is this Griffin

Stangel?"

"Who's asking?"

"Uh…my name is Howard Lincoln. I'm an attorney for Mid Higgins."

Griffin frowned. *Mid Higgins.* He wasn't great with names, but this one rang a bell. "Mid Higgins," he said, this time aloud and into the phone.

"Your aunt."

Griffin's frown deepened. *Holy hell*, he thought. Mildred Higgins was his mother's twin sister. His mother had been dead nearly five years, and he'd never once met, spoken to, or heard from his mother's sister. The woman may as well have been dead herself, and he said as much to the man on the phone.

There was a shocked pause, then the man said, "Actually, Mr. Stangel, that's why I'm calling. Ms. Higgins passed away yesterday morning. I've been trying to get in touch with you for the past twenty-four hours."

Griffin glanced up. Irv's expression had changed from annoyance to curiosity. "For what?" Griffin asked, then mouthed to Irv, 'My aunt died'.

"…My Pink Wink."

Griffin started listening to the man again. "Excuse me?"

The man repeated the strange and obscene-sounding phrase. "My Pink Wink."

"I'm sorry—what are you saying?"

The man on the other end of the phone sounded confused. "Mid Higgins, your aunt, passed away suddenly—"

"No, I got that part…"

"Put it on speaker," Irv said in a loud whisper.

Griffin did as he was told, and Irv announced himself to the man on the other end as Griffin's attorney.

"Oh," Howard Lincoln said. "Well, isn't that convenient." He sounded both surprised and relieved. "As I was telling Mr. Stangel, his maternal aunt Mildred Higgins has unfortunately passed away suddenly." His voice became low and somber. "She was a great woman, business owner, and community leader, and she will be missed."

Irv raised an eyebrow at Griffin, who shrugged. He'd never met the woman.

Howard continued. "She didn't name an executor or leave a will, and I've been tasked with identifying her next of kin. Her assets aren't vast, but she owns outright a small house, a not insignificant savings account, and her profitable business—My Pink Wink."

"My Pink *what*?" Irv said, frowning.

"*Wink*," Howard said.

The two men looked at each other. Irv said, "What the hell kind of business is that?"

"A beauty salon."

Griffin rubbed at his eyes. He was exhausted, and this conversation was dreamlike. Surreal. A dull pressure pulsed behind his eyes—the beginning of a monster headache.

The door to Irv's office opened, and Katy walked in with a tray holding a huge breakfast sandwich of sausage, bacon, egg, cheese, and hashbrowns held between two full-sized, golden flapjacks. Despite the headache, Griffin's stomach grumbled loudly at the sight.

Irv said, "And what is it you're asking of Mr. Stangel?"

Griffin smiled gratefully at Katy, who beamed back. Then he reached for the sandwich and took a huge bite.

"Well," Howard said slowly, "I'm informing Mr. Stangel he is Ms. Higgins's next of kin, and as such, he's entitled to her property if he's interested in it. I'm also hoping he'd be willing to act as executor of her estate. If not, I can petition the Register of Wills to appoint someone. I have someone in mind, if Mr. Stangel will agree to it."

His sandwich in his right hand, Griffin made a slicing motion across his throat with his left. He wanted no part of being an executor, his strange aunt's meager estate, or My Pink *anything*.

"And where is this property?" Irv asked.

"Madison."

"Wisconsin?"

Howard laughed as if it were a silly mistake to make. "Pennsylvania."

Griffin could see something going on in Irv's mind. The wheels were turning. He swallowed down his bite of sandwich and mouthed 'No' to Irv.

Irv held up a hand and nodded, indicating Griffin should trust him.

"Mr…What did you say your name was?"

"Lincoln. Howard Lincoln."

"Mr. Lincoln, I'm not sure Mr. Stangel has the capacity to serve as executor right now. He's got his hands full at the moment. But he would like to visit and take a look at the assets if that is agreeable to you."

Griffin's mouth dropped open. And in the subsequent pause, Griffin interjected, "I'm sorry, Mr. Lincoln, Mr. Abbott and I are going to need to discuss this—"

Irv snatched the phone from the charger before Griffin realized what was happening. He took it off speaker and held it to his ear. Griffin put the sandwich down directly on Irv's shiny desktop, egg yolk and bacon grease running out of the sandwich and onto the surface.

In his haste to reach Irv, Griffin lost the thread of his attorney's conversation. As he tried to reach around the side of the desk to grab back his property, Irv said, "I completely understand, Mr. Lincoln. No, that's understandable too." He stood and easily sidestepped Griffin, then held his hand out, keeping Griffin at bay.

Son of a bitch! Griffin thought, fuming. He tried

again to reach for the phone, but Irv gave him the stiff-arm. "Just send me the details." He recited his email address. "I will arrange everything with Mr. Stangel." A pause. "Okay, Mr. Lincoln. Yes, I look forward to hearing from you." Another pause. "Sounds great. Talk soon."

The lawyer ended the call and handed Griffin back his phone.

"What the *fuck*, Irv?"

Irv was unbothered. "Look, your career is nonexistent, and your life is going down the tubes fast…" He sat back down behind his desk, leaving Griffin to stand alone, impotent and filled with rage. "…and you're facing felony charges, Griffin. I don't think you appreciate the gravity of the situation."

"If that's the case, how the hell am I supposed to go to Pennsylvania?" Before Irv could answer, he exploded, "I don't *want* to go to Pennsylvania. I don't want whatever is being left to me. An obscene-sounding hair salon? Tell Mr. Lincon to sell it and donate the proceeds to charity. It can't be worth much anyway."

"I couldn't give a shit about the inheritance. But I'm going to go into the arraignment today with a story. A story of a grieving nephew who needs to go home to take care of the death of a beloved aunt who passed away yesterday, right before he attacked a reporter. And then I'm going to work like hell to get the district attorney to let me plead this thing down to a misdemeanor. And *you're* going to get your ass to Pennsylvania and do your part."

"What am I supposed to do once I'm there?"

"Meet with this guy Lincoln and find out what's up. Poke around your aunt's house and business. Make a show of interest. Then when I tell you, you can come home."

Griffin stared at his attorney, then sat back down in his seat. The breakfast sandwich was flaccid and soggy, and his coffee was cold.

A chime on Irv's laptop sounded, and the man peered at his screen. "You're scheduled for a two-o'clock arraignment with Judge Raymond Postlethwait. He's tough, but more importantly, he's a man. I can work with that."

Griffin scowled.

Irv peered at him over his glasses. "Get an Uber, go home, and grab a shower and some sleep. I'll see you at City Hall outside courtroom 25, seventh floor at half past one. Wear a suit. And get a haircut if you have time."

Griffin would not be getting a haircut. He didn't respond.

Irv shook his head then blew out a breath. "Look, Griffin, I like you. I really do. But this is your last shot. You screw this up, and I can't help you anymore." He opened his mouth then shut it again. "Let me amend my comment. I *won't* help you anymore. I'll do my best to get out of this bind, but this is it. Your last chance. Our time together is coming to a close. Because if you don't do exactly as I say and keep yourself out of trouble, you're on your own. And that, my friend, is a place you don't want to be."

Chapter 5

Rose had barely slept. When she *had* managed to drift off, she dreamed of Mid's smiling face, of the woman dancing around My Pink Wink to the tune of 'Let's Call the Whole Thing Off'.

She'd woken with Harry Connick Jr. in her head and Mid's laugh ringing in her ears.

It was disquieting how lost Rose felt without Mid as her anchor. She hadn't realized how much she'd come to rely on those morning visits to Mid's for breakfast, and even though Mid's frequent calls to Rose's landline had annoyed her, Rose found herself waiting expectantly for the line to ring, a sound that would never come again. A voice she would never again hear.

She thought of Mid's body lying at the funeral home. She worried about what would happen next. One thing was sure—Mid wouldn't want to be there for long. Rose had chosen an outfit—a dress in a pale pink, Mid's favorite color. But she suspected Mid's body would be naked now until final arrangements were made. And final arrangements couldn't be made until Howard either located, or didn't—here she crossed her fingers—Mid's next of kin. A person who would be a complete stranger to her, and maybe to Mid as well. The thought made her queasy.

Rose skipped her morning run. In her small kitchen, she was just about to pop a piece of bread into the toaster when her cell phone buzzed with a call from the attorney.

She answered the call on a breath, her heart thrumming in her chest. "Hello?" *Please, be good news*, she prayed, and realized she was praying to Mid.

"Rose? This is Howard."

"Yes, Howard. It's Rose."

He didn't bother with pleasantries, which she appreciated. "I have some news," he said in a neutral voice.

Rose waited. He didn't say if it was good news or bad. Maybe to him it was all the same.

"I've made contact with Mid's nephew, Griffin."

Rose's heart sank. The fact that Howard had actually spoken to him was a step in the wrong direction.

"Do you want the good news or the bad news?"

Rose stood corrected. "The good, I guess." She didn't believe in saving the best for last. May as well have the best first, before life ruined it for you.

"Mr. Stangel isn't interested in being named the executor of Mid's estate."

"Okay," she said slowly. "What exactly does that mean?"

"I can petition to have you named as administrator if you're willing. It means you'll have control over Mid's arrangements, at least. And you'll have access to funds for the service and the cemetery plot. You'll have the task of performing the inventory of her assets and ensuring their value."

Well, that was something, though she didn't know if she'd classify the news as good. She was marginally relieved, she supposed.

"What's the bad news?"

"Mr. Stangel *is* interested in Mid's assets, including the house and the business."

Rose's heart fell further. That meant while Rose would be doing all the work ensuring Mid's bills were paid, taxes were filed, and affairs were in order, her nephew could just waltz into town and take all her assets, without so much as a 'thanks for your service'. She would do all the work, and he'd take all the reward.

Rose hated the direction of her thoughts. This wasn't about money, she reminded herself. It was about memorializing Mid. It was about ensuring her wishes were carried out, whatever those wishes happened to be. It was about ensuring My Pink Wink didn't shut its doors.

"So, how does that work?" Rose asked.

"I spoke to Mr. Stangel's attorney. Mr. Stangel has some prior commitments, but he'd like to spend some time there in the next week or so."

The next week or so. The man wasn't even planning on coming to Mid's service. She scowled and tried to remember if Mid had ever mentioned this person. She'd rarely even mentioned her sister. Any memories Mid had shared of Mad were from long, long ago.

Rose couldn't remember Mid uttering the name Griffin at all, even once. Though something about the name had been vaguely familiar to Rose when she'd heard it. Even now, there was a recognition there, but she couldn't for the life of her place it.

She already disliked this man. She wasn't looking forward to meeting him.

"Can I start clearing out Mid's house?"

Howard hesitated. "I have to officially petition the court to have you named the administrator, and that could take a few weeks. Let me discuss the contents of the house with Mr. Stangel first. As the beneficiary, he technically will own the house and all its contents. We may want to have a conversation with him about his preferences for the process."

And by 'we', Rose knew Howard meant 'me'.

Rose got it. Her frown deepened. "And what about My Pink Wink?"

Howard cleared his throat. "As part of Mid's estate, he'd ultimately be entitled to that, too, though as administrator, you'd be the one to have it appraised and evaluated. I suspect this man might not want to be saddled with the ownership of the salon. He might decide to sell it to you," Howard said hopefully. "Mr. Stangel is not from the area, and I got the distinct feeling he is not interested in moving here." Howard paused again. "I don't want to get your hopes up, but I have some questions as to whether he's interested in Mid's property at all. He's coming to look first, that's all."

None of this raised Rose's hopes. At all. The fact that this man didn't even know Mid. Had never made any attempt to contact her. And now, he wasn't even coming to her funeral, but would waltz in like some picker at a flea market, rifling through her stuff to see what was most valuable. It made Rose sick.

Her voice had taken on a strident, demanding tone. "And you don't know when he's arriving?"

If Howard noticed her dismay, he gave no indication. "No, unfortunately. His attorney mentioned some pressing commitments he had to address."

Pressing commitments and an attorney. That sounded high-maintenance to Rose. "Can I call him?"

Another pause. "Why don't you let me meet with him first? I can talk to him, get a sense of the direction of his thoughts."

"Should I not at least let him know what arrangements have been planned?"

Howard made a long humming noise, as if he were considering. "I'll tell you what. After you finalize everything with Jack, just send me a written summary of the plans and the costs."

Rose let out a noisy breath. She reminded herself Howard was just trying to help. Then she remembered Howard would get paid for this too, out of Mid's assets, she assumed. That raised her blood pressure all over again. "If I'm not technically the administrator and it can take days or weeks for it to be approved by…whomever," she waved her hand in front of her, "can I even move forward with plans for the funeral?"

"Yes, yes," Howard said. "I'll talk to Jack. I'll let him know the situation. This happens more often than one might think."

Rose had never thought about any of this before. She tried to remember back to when her parents had died, but she'd been sixteen. Teddy had returned home from college to deal with all the details. At twenty, he'd somehow navigated the process alone while Rose had been off taking her anger out on the world. It was a wonder her brother didn't hate her.

She quickly pushed the thoughts away. There was no sense in punishing herself by recalling those memories.

She ended the call, and after she'd eaten a piece of dry toast without tasting it, Rose put on her light spring jacket and stepped out into the cool April morning to walk the half mile to the Sweetwood Saloon. The temperature was supposed to rise to a balmy seventy-five degrees today, but the morning air was still damp and chilly. She wrapped her arms around herself.

The rustic tavern sat on a partially wooded half acre of land near the end of town, and adjacent to the town's cemetery. Teddy lived in a converted apartment on the second floor of the saloon, but Rose fancied her brother would already be in the bar, readying for the after-work crowd. Even though weekends were the bread and butter of the business, plenty of people from both in town and out came by in the evening for a bite to eat or a drink to take the edge off their day.

Teddy employed a cook, a bartender, and a part-time server, but he was seldom anywhere else but the Sweetwood. Rose wasn't sure if his constant presence was because he loved the place, or because this was the place he felt most comfortable. Her brother was a creature of habit; he hated change.

Rose certainly understood. Like hers, Teddy's young adult years had been punctuated by traumatic change.

But the problem with lack of change was also lack of growth. Rose worried Teddy might just die alone, an old man, behind this bar. He was only thirty-seven years old, but he was crotchety and set enough in his ways that he seemed much, much older.

The main parking lot of the salon was empty. Rose walked up the gravel drive to the front entrance. The sign on the door read 'Closed', and the heavy wooden entrance was locked.

She didn't bother knocking, instead walking around to the back of the old two-story wooden building.

The residence had once belonged to a woman named Sabina Beer, a spinster who owned her own land and property. It was rumored she housed male fugitives in the early nineteenth century. It was also rumored she had stolen a large sum of money—coins and gold—from some of these men, then hidden her pilfered treasure in the walls of the house. Sabina's body was buried in the cemetery where Mid would also soon reside.

No one had ever discovered Sabina's hidden for-tune.

Rose was curious as to whether Teddy had searched the building he owned. He'd grown up with the same stories she had. But she never asked. Teddy would have thought the question frivolous.

About one hundred feet behind the main building was a small outbuilding which at one time had probably been some sort of stable or shed. A few years after Teddy purchased the building and converted it into the saloon, he had installed a bed and washroom in the outbuilding. The space was not infrequently used by patrons who'd had a bit too much to drink.

The interior was decorated in a surprisingly femi-nine style—light-blue blanket on the bed, yellow curtains, and decent scented soap and towels in the washroom. Rose often wondered if Teddy may have been dating someone who had supervised the decorating of the place. But if there had been a woman, he hadn't shared that information with Rose. Teddy was notoriously private, and Rose respected that about her brother.

Rose spotted Teddy's Jeep parked near the rear entrance. The door was unlocked, and she pushed it open. Music was playing inside—an old Moody Blues song.

"Teddy?" she called, walking into the commercial kitchen area which smelled vaguely of fried food. The Sweetwood Saloon did not have an extensive menu, but Teddy employed a man named Buster Harrison, a former chef down on his luck, who prepared food in the evenings. Buster made the best burgers, fish and chips, chicken wings, and chicken sandwiches Rose had ever tasted.

She continued into the main bar which smelled lemony and fresh. Teddy leaned over the bar intently, concentrating as he polished the gleaming mahogany with a soft cloth.

The bar itself, with its leaded stained-glass inlays, tongue-and-groove joinery, and dental molding and millwork, had been rescued from abandonment and ruin in the northern part of the state. The wooden marvel had been built by the original bar's owner, a woodworker who had immigrated from Scotland. During the prohibition, the tavern had been shut down and the bar moved to an old barn, where it had been forgotten until a new family bought the property and discovered the piece.

Rose didn't know how Teddy had come upon the find. But he had, and the idea for the Sweetwood Saloon had been born. After a knock-down, drag-out fight with the town council, none of whom had wanted a bar within the town limits, Teddy had managed to gain approval for the business, largely due to Mid's influence. Now, Teddy himself was president of the town council and a voice of reason on the still unpredictable council, with its egos and odd little power trips.

Over the bar's speaker system, the singer lamented about needing a miracle. Rose felt like she could relate.

"Teddy…"

Her brother, engrossed in the task of cleaning the intricate etchings carved into the wood, startled.

He stood from his position in a crouch at the front of the bar and scowled deeply, before noticing it was Rose. His face softened and became handsome. "Hey, bud," he said, a shortened version of her old nickname, Rosebud. "I should've texted. How ya holding up?"

She knew he was talking about Mid's sudden passing, though he wouldn't mention it directly. By nature, Teddy didn't recognize anything he didn't want to exist. But the fact he even acknowledged that he should have texted was more sentiment than anyone could expect from him, and she gave him a wan smile.

She shrugged. "I'm okay. Sad."

He gave her an awkward half smile. "And everyone else?"

He meant the salon staff. "Sad, too. And worried about their jobs."

He rubbed at a milky spot on the top of the bar's counter with his oiled rag. "Why would they be worried about that? I assume you'll just keep right on going."

"Mid didn't leave a will," Rose said, then added, "Apparently, Howard Lincoln has found a nephew."

Teddy's eyebrows shot up, taking in this new information. Finally, he said, "Rosie. That stinks."

Rose shrugged. She hadn't come here for sympathy, and frankly, sympathy at this point would just make her angry. "It's fine," she said briskly. "It'll be fine," she amended. "I have some questions for you."

Teddy stiffened, and she saw the glazed look in his eye. She gave him a minute and shifted her gaze to the bottles of liquor and spirits laid out in neat rows behind the bar. Teddy didn't shirk on the good stuff. The top shelf was lined with the very best alcohol you could buy.

To her surprise, he indicated a bottle of good scotch on the top shelf with his gaze and a tip of his head.

Rose wasn't much of a drinker, but she considered it for a moment. Then she shook her head. She took a deep breath. "When Mom and Dad died, you were the administrator of the estate, right?"

A muscle ticked in Teddy's jaw. "Why?"

"This guy—the nephew—isn't interested in being named executor of her estate. So, Howard offered that position to me."

"But he's the beneficiary?"

Rose nodded.

"Sounds like a bum deal."

Rose sighed. "At least I'll be able to make sure she's given a proper goodbye and all her property is properly assessed."

Teddy didn't say anything for a minute. "So, what's your question?"

She thought about that. "Did you—?" She stopped abruptly, trying to decide what she wanted to ask. "You were only twenty. How did you handle all that?"

A shadow passed over Teddy's face. "I am not sure how to answer that, bud. Like you said, I was twenty. I had no idea what I was doing."

Rose felt the familiar twinge of guilt and shame. Even though she'd been just a teenager, she could have helped. *Should* have helped.

"Did you have someone helping you through the process?"

He exhaled all the breath in his lungs then breathed in just as deeply. "There was a lawyer, I think. I can't even remember his name. Rosie, to tell you the truth, I don't remember much. I think I may have blocked it out."

He lifted his cloth again, and Rose knew that was the most she would get out of him on the subject.

But he said, "This isn't the same situation anyway. You know what Mid's assets are, for the most part. And you have Howard. You'll get through it. If that's what you want."

"What do you mean, 'if that's what I want'?"

"I mean, you don't have to accept. You can let Howard and this nephew figure it out. I didn't even know Mid any siblings, let alone a nephew. Did she ever talk about these people?" Teddy had gone back to lovingly massaging the mahogany.

"No." She stood there until another song came on. It was something she didn't recognize that had a beat reminiscent of something from the 1970s.

She loved her brother a lot, but she wished he was more self-aware. She should have known better than to ask for more from him.

Unsatisfied, she sighed and turned to leave the way she'd come in. She supposed what she'd been looking for was some sense of comfort. Or at the very least, someone to make her feel less alone. Teddy had never been the best person for that job.

In the past, that job had belonged to Mid.

She felt a sob bubble up in her throat, and she tried to swallow it down.

"Hey," Teddy said just as Rose had reached the doorway to the kitchen.

She stopped and looked up at the ceiling covered in its decorative tin ceiling tiles. When she felt like she could speak clearly, she said, "Yeah?" just a bit too brightly.

"It's all going to be okay."

She took three deep breaths and nodded.

"Rosebud?"

Rose hazarded a glance behind her and found her brother's face looking kinder than she ever remembered.

"I promise," he said softly.

Rose turned away so he didn't see her tears.

Chapter 6

The next few days were filled with arrangements, details, flowers, and food, with Rose shepherding nearly all of it. She barely had time to breathe let alone grieve, and when she fell into bed at night, sleep crept over her with a black heaviness she welcomed like a blanket.

All the while, My Pink Wink was even busier than normal. Nearly every woman in town visited the salon in honor of Mid and to prepare for the final sendoff of their friend. When Rose wasn't at the funeral home or the church, or making phone calls to the florist or on the phone with the salon's accountant, she was setting curls, applying toner, folding foils, or snipping split ends.

Everyone she met asked her how she was holding up, but they barely listened before sharing their own sorrows. Rose had learned a long time ago to smile, listen, and make the appropriate noises. And she had learned sharing was futile. Not many people wanted to listen nearly as much as they wanted to talk.

It was Rose who happened to be standing at the

front desk when Julie Newlin walked in at three o'clock in the afternoon the day before Mid's service. Rose had no idea how old Julie was, but she estimated the woman to be in her early forties, though Julie took meticulous care of herself. She wasn't native to the town, but had been married to a man named Thomas Newlin whose family had once owned the property on which the golf course was now situated. When they'd divorced, Thomas had disappeared, but Julie became a permanent fixture, securing a job with the church and inserting herself neatly into everyone's business.

Rose sighed inwardly at the overly sympathetic smile on Julie's face.

"Hi Julie," she said as brightly as she could. "What can I help you with today?" The woman had had her hair styled only a few days earlier, and her artfully colored and shaped waves hung beautifully around her perfectly made-up face.

Julie held up a platter filled with what looked like homemade cookies. "Someone dropped these off at the church, and I figured you girls could use them more than I ever could."

Rose inadvertently glanced at the small table to the right of the front desk filled with nearly every type of baked good you could imagine: cookies, brownies, turnovers, scones, muffins, tarts.

"That's kind of you," she said to Julie, trying to convince herself Julie had not intended the veiled insinuation that the workers at My Pink Wink were unhealthy, overweight, or otherwise inferior to the toned and fit woman holding out her plate like a prize.

Rose took the plate and made room for it on the table with the other pastries.

After she'd found a spot between a plate of brownies and a tin of fudge, she looked back to find Julie with her head cocked and her lips pursed.

"I've heard about Mid passing on without leaving a will," Julie said. She waited for a response.

Rose took a calming breath. She had no idea how the information had made its way to Julie, but the flow of gossip in the town had always been beyond Rose's realm of understanding.

"It was an unexpected passing."

"Well, I certainly hope nothing happens to the shop." Her eyes were wide.

Rose managed a small smile. "We hope that as well."

"Are you talking to someone? You know, a lawyer?"

"I'm handling it."

"Because I might be able to help you." She leaned so close Rose could see the foundation caked into the fine lines around her blue eyes. "I know some people." Her breath smelled like cinnamon over stale garlic.

Rose shut her eyes briefly. "I'm handling it," she said again. Slowly. Deliberately. This time, there was a bite in her voice, and she didn't try to breathe over it, smile through it, or soften her tone.

Julie straightened. Her mouth was tight. "I was just trying to help."

Rose wanted to assume positive intent. She really did. But it was hard with Julie. Even when Julie did something good or kind for the church or for someone in need, she immediately gave in to her instinct to tell the entire community about it. And since she'd come to town, she'd out-gossiped even the most well-established of the town matriarchs. There was no way Rose would accept help from the woman, knowing details of the assistance would become common knowledge.

But before Rose could respond, Hallie said hotly, "Did you ever consider Rose might not need your help?"

Julie reared back. She placed a hand on her chest. "Well. Excuse me."

Rose moved quickly. As much as she did not want or need Julie's help, she also didn't want it spread all around town that the team at My Pink Wink were insulting to customers.

Rose shot Hallie a look, and said to Julie, "I appreciate the offer, I really do. But I've been in constant contact with Howard Lincoln, Mid's attorney, and I'm all set." Rose smiled. "Thank you, Julie. Truly."

Julie's shoulders lowered a few inches, and while

she didn't look pleased, the horrified expression had faded from her face. Still, she remained silent.

"We're all a little emotional after the shock we've had. Sometimes those emotions get the better of us." It was as close as Rose would get to offering an apology on Hallie's behalf. Rose knew there would be no apology from Hallie herself.

But this seemed to satisfy Julie, who said, "You know, when my dear grandmother died what helped was a nice spa day—a massage, a mani-pedi, a sit in a steam room, a facial."

Hallie made a noise, and Rose said, "Thanks, Julie, we'll take that under."

It seemed to be lost on the woman that while the staff of My Pink Wink were the ones grieving, it was they who were pampering everyone else in the town.

Julie nodded. "Oh, I also wanted to let you know Pastor Ballentine will be calling you. He's going to need some sense about Mid's eulogy. Of course he's known her for quite some time, but in absence of any real family, you're going to have to do."

All Rose's goodwill toward the woman faded.

It didn't matter. Whatever Julie's intent for the visit was had obviously been accomplished. She turned toward the door. "I suppose the next time I see you will be at the service. Such a loss for the town."

Then she pushed her way out of the door, slipping on her oversized sunglasses even though the day was gray and dreary.

After the woman had gone, there was a pregnant silence from both staff and customers. Rose met Hallie's eye and gave a small shake of her head. There was no need to fuel gossip, speculation, or idle chatter.

Della came walking out of the back room from her break and sensed the shift in energy. "What did I miss?"

"Julie Newlin," said Hallie.

Della just smiled, and when she sidled next to Rose at the front desk, she said under her breath, "Thank god."

"Be nice."

"Always."

"Don't you get tired of that, though?" Alyssa asked from her station on the other side of the shop.

"What?" Rose asked.

"Being nice. You're always so nice."

Rose didn't know why, but the comment made her defensive. "I'm not always nice," she said indignantly.

Jay, their male stylist spoke up from his chair at the far end of the shop. "You're one of the nicest people I've ever met."

While the words sounded like a compliment, his tone did not.

Teresa Taylor, a middle-aged woman from a neighboring town, caught Rose's eye in the mirror of Alyssa's station. "You're very nice, honey."

Alyssa said, "It's like the whole thing with Andrew…"

"Who?" Rose asked, frowning.

"My brother's friend. You went on a date with him?" Alyssa shook her head. "Anyway, if you hadn't been so *nice* in trying to tell him you didn't want to date him, he mightn't have been so completely humiliated."

Rose was shocked. "I didn't mean to humiliate him. And I try to be nice to everyone."

"And where has that gotten you?" Hallie asked, with censure in her voice.

Rose's mouth fell open. "I think I'm doing okay."

No one said anything, and Rose went from feeling defensive to feeling hurt. Did they really think her life was that bad?

Della seemed to sense Rose's change in mood. "Hey, don't let Julie get you down."

"I'm not sure it was Julie who brought me down," she responded.

Della glanced toward the employees, who were now morose and quiet. One of the stylists started a hair dryer, giving their conversation some cover. Della's voice was still low when she said, "They're just scared."

"Of what?"

"That you'll lose the salon, and they'll lose their jobs. Not only their jobs," she added. "But their family."

"I don't want that either," Rose said, just as quietly. "I'm doing what I can."

Della pursed her lips and raised her eyebrows.

"What?" Rose asked.

Della lifted a shoulder. "I didn't say anything."

"You didn't have to. Your face says it all. What does that expression mean?"

Della exhaled. "It's just…" She paused. "Mid was having health problems for a while before she passed. Some of the staff think, as the office manager, you should have addressed this earlier."

Again, Rose felt defensive. Partly because she'd been feeling the same way. But she snapped. "It's not exactly the easiest thing to have a conversation about. Especially when the person was fine just a few days earlier."

"Mid wasn't fine. And I agree—it's *not* easy," Della agreed. "And it's not *nice*. But sometimes it's necessary."

Rose blinked and stared out the shop window at the busy Main Street traffic. It wasn't fair they were ganging up on her for this. Not with everything else going on.

"No one is blaming you," Della said. "They want to blame Mid, but Mid's not here. You're the next best thing."

"Interesting choice of words."

"Because it's true," Della said. "You are the best.

You're the leader, and everyone here is looking for you to protect them."

"I'm not even sure I can protect myself," Rose remarked.

"Then stop being so nice, and start kicking some ass," Della whispered.

Rose laughed as a walk-in customer entered the store. Della checked her in, and Rose ushered the young woman to her chair. But as she washed the woman's hair, she couldn't get Della's words out of her mind.

After her all of her sorrows, her frustrations with Julie Newlin, and the uncertainty surrounding this mystery nephew, she'd love nothing more than to kick some ass. If only she had someone's ass to kick. Other than her own.

Chapter 7

Griffin had half expected Judge Raymond Postlethwait to deny Irv's petition for him to leave town. But, as usual, the situation worked out just as Irv had predicted, which was why, Griffin supposed, he paid Irv the big bucks to represent him.

Judge Postlethwait was old and crabby, and he'd looked at Griffin with a crooked eyebrow and a scowl. But Judge Postlethwait was also a fan of baseball and a critic of the media, and it had worked in Griffin's favor. Despite getting a lecture on public conduct, the judge had granted Irv's request for reduced bond. And despite the prosecution's heated argument, the Honorable Postlethwait had agreed Griffin could travel to Pennsylvania to settle his aunt's affairs, so long as he checked in with Irv on a daily basis and was in reach at all times.

After the arraignment hearing, as they'd stood in the hallway of the city courthouse, Irv had gripped the back of Griffin's neck harder than Griffin felt was necessary. "Go," he'd said. "Lay low for a few days. Pretend to be interested, and let me figure this out."

Griffin ducked out of his grasp and rubbed the back of his neck with the flat of his hand. "I can lay low right here," he grumbled.

"No, Stangel, apparently you can't."

Griffin exhaled loudly and tried to ignore the other people who stared at him as they walked by. He wasn't sure if they recognized him from his days as a player, his days as a broadcaster, or his days as a news story. Maybe it had been all three. Somehow, he'd become notorious. A scoundrel. A cad. A reprobate.

Someone snapped a photo, and Griffin caught Irv's smug 'I told you so' glance.

"I'll check in with you every day," Irv said. "To make sure you're staying out of trouble."

"What kind of trouble could I possibly get in, in a Podunk little town in the middle of Nowhere, Pennsylvania?"

"I shudder to think," Irv quipped, then turned on his shiny red Santoni leather Oxfords.

It took Griffin a full day of procrastination to finally work up the motivation to leave, but Irv was on his case nearly constantly.

And so at eleven o'clock on Thursday morning, he packed a carry-on suitcase and dumped it in the trunk of his late mother's white 2019 Mercedes-Benz C300.

Patrick Sullivan, the retired owner of a large construction company and Griffin's neighbor, strolled up the sidewalk with a grocery bag just as Griffin was about to climb in the driver's seat.

"Whoa, Stangel," he said. "You borrow your mom's car?"

"Something like that," Griffin said.

"I haven't seen you around in a couple of days. Not since your most recent situation."

Griffin clenched his jaw but said nothing.

"What's going on with you, anyway? You're getting a little long in the tooth to be fighting in the streets, huh?"

"I guess, Pat."

Griffin liked Patrick. He was an outgoing, boisterous guy who knew plenty of characters and had plenty of stories. He was a blast when he'd had a few beers, and he was easy to talk to. Griffin had cried into his own beer more than once with Patrick as a friendly ear on the barstool beside him.

But without a beer in his hand, Griffin didn't really feel much like talking. Besides, since he'd made up his mind to leave, he just wanted to get on the road.

Patrick didn't take the hint. The older man glanced in the backseat at Griffin's suitcase. "You skipping town?"

"Something like that," Griffin repeated.

It was clear Patrick thought that's exactly what he was doing. Griffin didn't feel like correcting him or explaining himself.

"Well, you know me. I won't say a word. But, Griff,

you sure you know what you're doing?"

Griffin let out a huff of a laugh. A humorless noise smacking of resignation and desperation, even to himself.

"Can I give you some friendly advice?"

"Can I stop you?" While Griffin had meant it as a joke, the words didn't come out that way.

"You need to find yourself a purpose," Patrick said. "When I left the military all those years ago, I imagine I felt a lot like you're feeling—rudderless, adrift, unnecessary. It wasn't a great feeling. It wasn't until I started my construction business and channeled my energy and focus that I turned things around."

"I'll keep that in mind," said Griffin. He was done waiting for Patrick to walk away, so he lowered himself into the driver's seat and twisted the key in the ignition. It had been years since he'd driven this car, which had been sitting at the garage of a mechanic buddy. The guy had religiously maintained it for him.

Griffin didn't know why he'd kept the thing. God knew it wasn't out of any sense of sentimentality. At the time his mother passed away, Griffin hadn't spoken to the woman for well over a decade.

"I'm not trying to get into your business," Patrick said, leaning on the frame of the car so he was nearly inside the car itself.

Griffin looked up, his hand on the wheel.

"It's just that I know how it feels to be a..." The

man's words trailed off, and Griffin's defenses came up.

"A what?" he asked, a challenge in his voice.

"You know." Patrick straightened and shifted his shopping from one hand to the other.

"No, I don't think I do. Why don't you tell me?"

Patrick shook his head and started to walk away.

"Say it, Patrick…"

When Patrick didn't speak, Griffin yelled "Pussy!" after him. It was a low blow, but one designed to ensure Patrick, a macho man, would talk.

Patrick's congenial countenance darkened into a harsh and intimidating expression. "A *has-been*, Stangel. You're washed up. You've outlived your usefulness. It's why you're chasing the thrill instead of the substance. The cheap women, the low blows. You're trying to shock people into thinking you're still relevant."

Griffin barked out a laugh. If the guy was going to insult him, he'd have to do better than that.

"It's sad," Patrick continued, and those words got under Griffin's skin, but not enough to cause more than a twitch of his jaw. It was Patrick's next words which caused him to see red. "Actually, it's more than sad. It's boring and tedious. It's a joke. By sleeping around and throwing punches, you've become a punchline."

Patrick barked out his own laugh, and Griffin realized he was nothing more than one of Patrick's characters. The man would go down the street to his favorite Irish pub, and he'd tell the story of Griffin Stangel, his washed-up ballplayer neighbor, who was facing charges after fighting over yet another anonymous woman. He'd probably add in a detail about the old woman's car to add a pop of humor to the desperation of the story.

People loved a fall from grace with a hint of black comedy.

Griffin couldn't think of a witty comeback, so he returned a lame "Fuck you, Patrick."

Patrick chucked. "See you later, Griff. Or not. Safe travels to you."

Griffin started the car and punched the gas, pulling out into Charles Street in front of a large SUV that screeched to a halt, the driver laying on the horn.

"Watch where you're going, you idiot!" the man yelled.

Griffin took a sharp right onto Stuart Street. He didn't calm down until he was nearly twenty miles out on Interstate 90.

By the time he'd driven under gray cloud and rain through Connecticut and into New Jersey and finally Pennsylvania, Griffin actually felt relaxed, which was the opposite of what he'd expected to feel during the trip.

After years of spending long, boring hours on first

buses, and then planes, traveling around the country with his teammates, the last thing he expected to feel during a solitary car ride on the infamously awful highways of New Jersey and Pennsylvania was a sense of peace.

Late in the afternoon, Griffin stopped for an early dinner and quick break near Pennsylvania's state capital and made small talk with the father of a mini-van full of kids at a gas station near Carlisle. The man may or may not have recognized Griffin, but if he had, he'd not said a word about either Griffin's career or his recent headlines. Griffin found himself both relieved and disappointed. Patrick's words came back to haunt him. He was a *has-been*—boring and uninteresting.

He finished the last leg of his journey on the Pennsylvania Turnpike, on winding, mountainous roads. When he finally sped through the last of the highway's tunnels, he emerged into clear skies colored, in the last vestiges of daylight, with soft pink and purple clouds. But it wasn't until he'd exited the highway onto a winding two-lane roadway that he realized it hadn't occurred to him to call his aunt's attorney to alert the man he was coming to town. Nor had he thought to book a hotel room for himself.

He fumbled with his phone in the dark, and scrolled through his missed calls until he found what he thought was the lawyer's number.

"What was his name?" Griffin mumbled aloud.

Hank? Harry? Henry?

He pressed the number, and the tone trilled three times before a message came on. An old man's voice.

"You've reached the law office of Howard Lincoln, Attorney at Law. Our office hours are from 9:00 a.m. to 5:00 p.m., Monday through Friday."

Griffin hung up. It was well past five o'clock. He didn't wait to see if there was an after-hours number listed in the message.

For a minute, he considered checking in with Irv, but then decided against it. *Screw Irv*, he thought with some vehemence. Irv was the reason he was on this two-lane road in bumfuck, nowhere in the first place, squinting past open farmland between sporadic, unimpressive houses.

He had next to no hope he'd find a hotel in this small town, but he'd passed a busy interchange along the highway about five miles back. He was sure he could find a vacant room. But since he'd come this far, he figured he may as well check out what Madison, Pennsylvania, had to offer in the way of nightlife.

A few miles past the last expanse of farmland, his GPS directed him down the final stretch of road and triumphantly announced that he'd reached his destination. Griffin slowed the Mercedes and peered around in the dark.

He crawled past a concentrated cluster of tiny brick houses, a church, and what looked like a post office. He came to an intersection, looked both ways, then continued straight. More tiny houses, a shop of some sort, and perhaps a restaurant. A large building with a lighted sign announced the volunteer fire department, and next to that, a marquee in front of a white stone building heralded a funeral home. The parking lot was filled with cars.

Griffin kept going until the houses became more sporadic, then he looked for a place to turn around. He ended up in the parking lot of an ancient-looking building, and to his surprise and delight the sign read 'The Sweetwood Saloon, est. 2014'. In Griffin's experience, there was no better way to get a feel for a place than to visit the place where the locals let their guard down. And that place inevitably served alcohol.

There were only a few cars in the parking lot, but the lights were on. When Griffin cut the engine, he could hear the faint pulsing bass of music coming from inside.

After the long drive, a drink and a barstool sounded great; so much so, he physically craved the experience: The feeling of the stool on the backs of his thighs. The smooth glass tumbler against the tops of his fingers. The yeasty, hoppy smell of alcohol in the air.

He would worry about the hotel room later.

He climbed from the low sedan and stretched out the tight kinks in his body before he walked through the misty April night. The air was brisk, and the wooded lot around them perfumed the night air with springtime and new growth. Griffin breathed deeply as he crossed the empty parking lot toward the entrance.

He pushed open the heavy wooden door, a century old perhaps, maybe more. The structure had clearly been converted from an old house.

Inside, the interior had been transformed into a spacious gathering room with rustic-looking wooden tables scattered about, atop roughhewn hardwood floors. But the centerpiece of the room—where Griffin's gaze was immediately drawn—was the impressive bar itself. The dark wood—Griffin thought mahogany—gleamed in the dim lights. Brilliantly etched stained glass decorated the back bar next to two polished mirrors.

The back bar also appeared to house an impressive array of spirits. He squinted. Macallan 26, Woodford, Glenfiddich, Guillotine Vodka. Griffin was shocked to find an establishment of this caliber at the end of a nowhere town, in Nowhere, Pennsylvania.

A young couple sat at a small corner table, their heads bent close together. Two older men and one woman occupied stools at one end of the bar. They were laughing loudly over the music—a raucous, bluesy composition that made Griffin feel like he'd wandered into a different era.

At the sound of the door opening, the lone bartender glanced up at Griffin, raised his chin in a silent acknowledgment, and then turned around to whatever task he was performing, his back to the patrons.

Griffin took a seat at the opposite end of the bar from the other clientele. He looked around, wondering how a place this impressive, yet this empty on a Thursday evening, managed to stay in business so far away from the rest of civilization.

After a minute, the bartender, who appeared to be around Griffin's own age, walked over. "Need a menu?"

Griffin glanced at the rows of bourbon against the back of the bar, and his eyes went to the top shelf.

He ordered a variety called The Saint, neat. The eyebrows of the bartender shot up before he peered at Griffin closely. Griffin glanced away.

"Don't get too many people ordering that."

Griffin didn't think the comment required an answer, and the bartender continued, "Anything to eat?"

Griffin shook his head. He probably should eat something, but the fast food he'd had on the turnpike was still sitting like a ball of lead in his stomach.

A few seconds later, the man placed a heavy leaded-glass tumbler on a cocktail napkin in front of Griffin and poured a generous slug of the amber-colored liquid into the glass. Griffin's mouth watered at the sight.

"Cheers," the bartender mumbled, then wandered

away.

The drink was smooth and strong. It tasted of cherry, chocolate, and tobacco. Griffin took two small sips, savoring the taste, then knocked it back, allowing the warmth of the alcohol to flow through his limbs. He shut his eyes for just a minute, and listened to the sounds of the bar.

A big-band version of 'Rhapsody in Blue' was playing over the speakers. Another group of customers had come in and taken a table. The laughing, voices, music, smells, and sounds mingled in a way that made Griffin feel both unsettled and completely at peace. He was half tempted to keep his eyes shut—as if he could shut out the modern world completely and just exist in this strange shadow place in his imagination, away from all his modern problems.

He wasn't sure how long he sat on that stool as lone resident of his own reality. But presently, he felt an energy in front of him. He opened his eyes to find the bartender frowning.

Griffin blinked, then smiled, letting the guy know he was fine. He tipped his glass forward, indicating another round without a word.

The bartender refilled it without comment, and as he poured, Griffin said, "Slow night?"

"Most of the town is over at Cummings," the bartender said, as if Griffin had any idea what, or who, Cummings might be.

"I suppose you're not there because there's no one else to man the bar?"

The bartender shrugged. "Along with the fact that I'm allergic to the place." He turned away again and went to check on the table with the young couple in the corner.

Griffin sipped the bourbon more slowly, observing the bartender out of the corner of his eye. The guy was a one-man show, tending to all the customers in a nimble and unhurried manner.

The trio at the other end of the bar ordered another round of drinks, and Griffin watched as the bartender practiced his craft—expertly mixing a concoction of absinthe, whiskey, bitters, sugar, and cold water. He garnished the drinks with lemon peel, as the customers oohed and awed over the beverages. He made a bit of small talk, but not much. This was not a bartender who'd get in your business. Griffin liked that about him, and that realization along with the numbing effect of the alcohol caused him to warm considerably to both the man, the bar, and the town.

Griffin was staring into his half-empty glass when one of the men at the end of the bar called over to Griffin, "You new in town?"

Griffin was surprised it had taken this long for someone to notice him. "Just passing through," he said.

"Passing through to where?"

"The next place," Griffin said easily. And it was the

truth. All his life, from his chaotic childhood being passed between his mother and father, to his career as a baseball player, he'd been moving from here to there, never quite settling in one location. The closest he'd gotten to a permanent home had been Boston, where he'd last played, and where he thought he'd settle down when his career had abruptly ended.

Now, he'd been exiled to this remote place. But one thing was certain—he would not be here for long. He'd perform his assignment, and he would get the hell out.

The woman next to him, nearly old enough to be his mother, winked at him. "A guy that looks like you is welcome here anytime."

Griffin looked terrible. His hair was too long, his beard was too ragged, his skin was sallow, and it had been far too long since he'd last gone to the gym or even gone for a run. He was as unhealthy and out of shape as he'd ever been.

The third man said, "You a baseball fan?"

This caused Griffin to stiffen, but he cautioned himself to act casually. He shrugged and said, "I've been known to catch a game or two."

"Anybody ever tell you you look like Griffin Stangel?"

Griffin considered the best way to respond in this situation. It wasn't the first time he'd gotten the question, but he wasn't sure how many people in town would have known his name, or even cared. He highly doubted his aunt had mentioned his name to anyone in town, considering she'd never once attempted to reach out to him.

To the bar patron, Griffin said, "I've heard it a time or two."

The man laughed. "It's not exactly a compliment, I guess." He snickered. "That guy's had nothing but trouble. Much of it of his own making."

"I wouldn't know." He turned back to his drink, shutting down the conversation. He lifted his glass toward the bartender, who looked as if he might say something. Mercifully, he just poured him another glass of The Saint.

Griffin sipped, allowing the heavy-limbed comfort to leach through his bones. The bourbon was going down as smooth as silk. He hadn't realized how tense his body had become until the alcohol loosened his muscles and all the tension melted from his body.

His senses felt both dulled and heightened. The Big Band swing seemed to get louder, and the tables around him began to fill up with more and more people dressed remarkably well for a Thursday evening. By comparison, he felt scraggly and disheveled. He sank down further into the bar and huddled around his glass.

As he sipped, he lost himself in the jazz and the buzzing of the crowd around him. For just another moment, he closed his eyes.

Again, he felt a presence close by. He opened his eyes again when he sensed someone sitting next to him. He glanced over and found a very attractive young woman, her green eyes misty, and her nose slightly red. She was well dressed in a simple black dress, and her chestnut-colored hair was pulled back into an elaborate twisted style. She wore lipstick, but no other makeup. She didn't look at Griffin at all.

The bartender approached and said softly, "How you holding up, Rosebud?"

The woman—*her name couldn't possibly be Rosebud, could it?*—lifted a shoulder and let out a breath.

"Oh, Teddy," she said. "At least that part is over." There was a hint of a wobble in her voice.

"Looks like just about the whole town showed up."

"Are you surprised?" she asked cynically. "There's nothing like a funeral, followed by a stiff drink, to get the social juices flowing."

"Come on. They're grieving too."

She dipped her head.

"Can I get you something to drink?" the bartender asked. Teddy, she'd called him. For some reason, Griffin was gratified to finally learn the man's name.

The pretty woman paused, then shook her head. The movement caused the soft musky scent of her perfume to waft toward Griffin. It mingled with the woody smell of his bourbon, and he breathed in deeply.

For the first time, she glanced over at him then looked away just as quickly. She shifted away from him. It was nearly imperceptible, but Griffin noticed the movement.

She turned back to the bartender. "It will be an early morning. But I could use something to eat. Do you think Buster would make me a club sandwich?"

"For you, yes."

Teddy walked away. Griffin noticed another bartender was also now behind the bar, and a server taking care of the suddenly crowded dining room.

He felt a physical awareness of the woman next to him. It wasn't sexual in nature; rather, like the scent of her perfume, it was simply a mingling of senses. He wondered if she felt it too. Maybe he was imagining things. Perhaps he'd had too little to eat and too much to drink.

Still, he sipped his whiskey, knowing the three glasses of bourbon would run him well over a hundred dollars. He didn't care.

A few minutes later, Teddy returned, checking on customers as he made his way back down the bar.

Teddy stopped at the woman next to him. "Buster's making your sandwich now."

She nodded.

There was a lull, and then Teddy asked, "So…did he show up?"

She shook her head. "Howard hasn't heard from

either him or his attorney in a few days." She let out a long, noisy breath. It was a sigh, but one filled with frustration or anger.

Griffin's ears perked up and the hair on the back of his neck prickled. *Howard.*

"Is he going to communicate with you when he does decide to show up?" Teddy asked.

The woman shrugged. "I assume he'll communicate with Howard. He probably wants nothing to do with me. I'm standing between him and his money." She let out a brittle laugh.

Teddy shook his head. "Considering you're doing all the heavy lifting for him, I would think he'd at least want to meet you." There was a pause. "Honestly, Rose, I can't believe you even agreed to administer the will. Had Mid wanted you to be this involved, she would have arranged it ahead of time."

"It's not like she knew she was going to die."

"The whole town knew she'd been having health problems, Rose. Including you. No one wanted to have the hard conversation."

Griffin swallowed. He couldn't believe the providence. He thought about how he should introduce himself. *If* he should introduce himself.

Then he remembered the man at the end of the bar. *Anyone ever tell you you look like Griffin Stangel?*

He certainly didn't want to get into *that* conversation here, in this crowded bar, in front of people who may have recognized him. Maybe it'd be better to communicate through Irv and Howard anyway.

He didn't want any of his aunt's property, but something told him it may not be wise to let this woman know that piece of information. Not here. Not yet.

"A responsible person would've taken care of things," Teddy said. "You felt indebted enough to take care of every single business and life complication for her, for the past five years, at least. The very least she could've done was to ensure you could take care of her assets after she was gone. And the very least *you* could've done was to take care of yourself."

Griffin took another long swallow at his drink and hazarded a glance at the woman. *Rose.*

She looked angry, but she also looked as if she might cry. His earlier warm feelings toward the bartender faded. Was he this woman's husband? Boyfriend? Whatever their relationship, he was acting like an asshole.

He felt compelled to say something, and opened his mouth, but then then man spoke again, this time more softly.

"I don't mean to be harsh," said Teddy, "but we've seen this before. The difference is, they were much younger and didn't expect to get in a fatal car accident. You'd think with everything Mid knew you'd gone through, she'd have been a little more cognizant of circumstances. I'm just upset on your behalf. That's all."

Griffin tried to remember his conversations with Howard and Irv. Had they mentioned a woman? He didn't think so. As far as he knew, he was the only next of kin. So, who was this person, and how was she involved in this situation?

One thing was sure—he needed to talk to Howard before he tipped his hand.

He realized instead of feeling the pleasant warmth in his head, now his mind felt fuzzy and cottony, and his tongue fat. He didn't think he was in any shape to have a coherent conversation about a serious subject, even if he'd wanted to.

Teddy the bartender walked away, and the woman beside him checked her phone. She seemed to have forgotten he existed, and in his inebriated state, he snuck another glance at her. She was definitely younger than him. Her skin was smooth and unblemished. And while she was very pretty, she also had a small permanent looking line between her eyebrows, and fine lines etched at the sides of her mouth—from frowning rather than smiling.

Griffin liked a woman with some life in her. A woman who'd seen some things and knew how to have some fun and share a laugh.

He did not think this woman laughed much at all.

He wanted to stay and catch more of the conversation between Teddy and Rose. He wanted to discover if they had anything more to say about him. But he really needed to use the restroom.

He stood up and turned to walk away from the bar, but his foot hooked over the foot of the stool. He tripped, dragging Rose's seat back with him.

"Hey," she said loudly, grabbing onto the bronze railing. She steadied herself and her stool before it tipped over. She shot him a hostile look. "Watch yourself," she scolded.

Griffin felt chastened and embarrassed when he realized most of the conversation around the room had stopped, replaced by stares, uncomfortable silence, and a few snickers.

"I'm not drunk," he said loudly, mostly to the woman, but loud enough, even over the music, for the closest diners to hear him. At least he didn't think he was drunk. Maybe a little buzzed. But his clumsiness was much more a product of the exhaustion, long drive, and lack of sleep and proper nutrition than the alcohol. He tried to say "Excuse me" and "I'm sorry" at the same time, and it came out "Ex-scory."

The woman peered at him with her fine dark eyebrows knitted together. He stared at her. With her black dress, elegant chignon, pale face, and serious expression, he had the oddest sense he was staring at a woman from another time; another era.

"Are you okay?" she asked. Gone was the annoyed

tone. She sounded legitimately worried about him. Her concern annoyed *him*. He didn't need this serious young woman's concern, pity, or attention.

"I'm perfect." Even to his own ears, the response sounded forced and unnatural, as if someone else were speaking, and he was listening with judgment.

Disgusted with himself, he scowled, and started walking toward the back of the dining room, where he assumed the bathrooms might be located.

Someone yelled, "Hey…"

Griffin turned. It was the bartender, Teddy, with his hands out, palms up in questioning. "You skipping out on your check?"

"Just looking for the restroom."

If the tavern customers hadn't been paying attention before, they sure were now. The only sound in the place was the music piped through the hidden speakers. The lyrics floated through the air, uninterrupted.

You stepped out of a dream…

Teddy pointed in the opposite direction to the right side of the bar.

For some reason, Griffin saluted. Then headed to the tavern's washroom.

The washroom was mercifully empty, and Griffin used the facilities before splashing some cold water on his face. He dried his hands then took a few breaths, and walked back to the bar, determined to let both the woman and the bartender know he wasn't an idiot, and he wasn't a drunk. But by the time he returned, Rose was no longer on the stool. Someone else had taken her seat—a man who glanced in Griffin's direction and looked as though he might say something.

Griffin scowled, and the man looked away then joined the conversation on the other side of him.

Griffin sat back down at his end stool where his glass sat, a reminder he still needed to settle his tab. Teddy was at the other end of the bar, but Griffin noticed him watching carefully.

He pulled his phone out of his back pocket and checked the time. It was after 10:00 p.m. He sighed. He needed to find a place to stay.

When Teddy came back, Griffin pulled cash from his wallet. "I'm hoping to find a hotel close by."

Teddy sucked his front teeth his lips. "Closest hotel is right off the interstate, about eight miles away. You drive here?"

Griffin thought it was a stupid question. How else would he have gotten there? But he nodded anyway.

"Then I can't let you leave."

It took a moment for Griffin to process the man's implication. "What do you mean?"

"You've had three generous portions of pretty strong bourbon, and I watched you nearly knock someone over, before stumbling to the restroom. We have a safety policy here. I will not let any customer drive drunk."

Griffin opened his mouth then shut it again. His brain wasn't completely clear, and it took him longer than normal to come up with a response. He decided to appeal to the guy's sensible side. "Look, I don't want any trouble. I just need a place to stay. That's it. I'm fine to drive."

"You're not even fine to walk."

The smarmy comment stuck in Griffin's craw. It was comments like those which made him want to throw his weight around. If he hadn't had so much horrible press coverage over the past few months, he might've shot his mouth off. But he didn't want these people to know any more about him than absolutely necessary.

"I think it might be best if I just spoke to the owner," he said. He tapped his cell phone. "I'm happy to make a phone call. You won't get into any trouble."

Teddy drew himself up straighter and crossed his arms across his chest. "I *am* the owner."

Shit.

Griffin let out a silent breath through his nostrils. He changed tack. "I know you don't know me, but I can assure you—I'm not a drunk, and I have nowhere else to go."

Teddy wasn't moved. "I can try to get you a ride-share, though those are few and far between in these parts." He hitched his chin over his shoulder. "We have a place out back."

"Huh?"

"It's not fancy, but it'll do for the evening. Save you from waiting for a ride and then needing to come back for your car. You can at least sleep it off."

Griffin felt the color climbing into his face. "I'm not staying in the back of a bar." He must have raised his voice again, because a number of diners glanced in their direction. As much as he was attempting to stay under the radar, he sure was attracting his fair share of attention. He'd be the talk of the town by the next day if he weren't careful.

"It's a room," said Teddy, sounding offended. "There's a bedroom and a bathroom. It's private."

The guy next to him leaned over. "It's actually pretty nice. Stayed there a time or two myself."

Griffin ignored the man. "Absolutely not. Just let me pay my bill, and you'll never see me again."

"Might see you, or god forbid, someone else over at Cummings. No can do, sir. We'll settle up in the morning before you leave."

"We'll settle up now, and then I am getting out of here."

Teddy's unsmiling face hardened further. "If you try to leave, not only will you be driving above the legal limit, you'll be skipping out on your bill. If you drive out of this parking lot, I will call the police."

Griffin blinked at him. "You can't be serious…"

Teddy didn't look like he was ever anything *but* serious. He didn't bother to answer.

Griffin couldn't believe it. How his opinion of this laid-back, easygoing tavern had fallen. But his hands were tied. He knew he couldn't get arrested in this small town. One look at his name and the police would make the connection between him, his failed career, and his recent legal troubles. He'd have to call Irv. Again. And Irv's words haunted him. Irv was done representing him. Oh, he was sure he could pay someone else to take him on as a client—the notoriety he brought would absolutely be enough to entice a new legal team. But he'd never find anyone as good as Irv.

He had a nearly overpowering urge to punch this bartender right in the face. His fists clenched at his sides.

As if Teddy could read his mind, he squared his shoulders and set his feet. Griffin knew this guy would give him a run for his money. He wouldn't go down easy. Not like Mike McCaffery.

Griffin deflated. He'd been defeated, at least for the evening. "Fine," he said through clenched teeth. "Let me just get my bag from the car."

Teddy held out his hand. "Go ahead and unlock it, and hand over the keys."

Griffin blinked at the guy again. They stared at each other, but in the end, there was no doubt who'd won this round.

With the bar patrons looking on, Griffin hit the unlock button on the key fob and handed over the set of keys to his mother's Mercedes. As he moved toward the door, again his foot caught on the foot of the barstool and he stumbled. Then he swore loudly.

Teddy followed him out and watched him grab his suitcase, then ushered him through the back of the bar, a smattering of whispers, plenty of stares, and a few giggles. Griffin knew this feeling well—the combination of anger and shame that accompanied some stupid decision he'd made without thinking about the consequences of his actions.

He thought about his mother. She'd always said he was a screw-up. Someone who wouldn't amount to anything. He'd spent a lot of time trying to prove her wrong, and every time he got close, every time he did something that might come near to greatness or be worthy of praise, he immediately did something ill-conceived enough that he knew she'd always be right.

He could almost feel her sneering at him from beyond the grave. His face burned hotter.

The night air was cool, and after crossing the back parking lot, the bartender opened the door to a small outbuilding with a set of keys. He switched on a dim overhead light, walked to the other side of the room and adjusted the knob of an electric heater. A blast of heat shot through the chilled air.

Griffin looked around. The room looked comfortable enough, and as much as Griffin didn't want to stay in a dry tank at the back of some backwoods tavern, he had to admit he was glad he didn't have to search for a hotel room. Plus, he was exhausted, and the bed looked inviting.

Teddy handed him a bottle of water.

Griffin wasn't ready to thank the guy. He'd still like to fight him.

But Teddy just walked away, back into the bar, while Griffin watched him go.

He closed the door to the small room and silently cursed himself. As much as he wanted to blame the bartender for his situation, he knew it wasn't Teddy's fault. Griffin had done this to himself. As Madeline Higgins would've said, and seemed to whisper right into her son's ear, "Griffin, you are nothing but a fuck-up, and I wish you'd never been born."

Chapter 8

S itting at home in her kitchen, Rose chewed the club sandwich Buster had made for her and thought about the handsome stranger in the bar. For a second, Rose thought the stranger might have been *him*. But it was impossible. Howard had told her the man was dealing with his own legal issues and would let Howard know when he'd be arriving in town. Howard hadn't heard a word from the elusive Griffin Stangel. Rose had asked.

At the thought of the man's name, Rose's mouth puckered. She thought it was an evil-sounding name. There was something too mythological about it. He sounded like the villain in a grainy film noir. She tested the name by saying it out loud. *Griffin Stangel.* It was sharp on her tongue. Dangerous.

The man at the bar hadn't been sharp. He'd reminded Rose of those high-school athletes who couldn't get out of their own way. The ones who still harbored some ornery little boy inside them.

Oh, he'd been handsome, with his intense amber eyes and rakishly unkempt, unshaven face. He hadn't looked homeless or destitute, but he appeared down on his luck. Or at least his mood. And it had triggered something in Rose. The need to take care of him.

She had looked at Teddy with a questioning glance, but Teddy was the world's most antisocial bartender. He believed in giving people privacy to cry into their beers, or in this man's case, their bourbons. So Teddy had simply shrugged and said not a word.

Rose had, however, caught Teddy's concerned glance when the man had stumbled over the barstool attempting to make it to the restroom. Teddy took his responsibilities when it came to the administration of alcohol—a controlled substance—very seriously. She doubted Teddy would allow him to leave. He might just be the first guest the charming little outbuilding had seen in quite some time.

She imagined him there right now, the frilly bed-spread covering a lean body. She thought of his dark beard, long straight nose, and pronounced brow. When she felt her face flush, she quickly altered the direction of her own thoughts. He probably snored, she decided.

Sitting alone at her small kitchen table, she glanced down, surprised to see she'd finished her sandwich. She didn't remember tasting much of it.

Annoyed with herself, she pushed the handsome stranger out of her mind and thought of Mid.

Mid would have gotten a kick out of the stranger,

Rose knew. Though Mid was in her early sixties and suffered from sciatica, gout, and high blood pressure, the woman retained her ability to flirt shamelessly. She could not understand why a girl as pretty as Rose couldn't bring herself to let go and have some fun with a handsome man.

But Rose didn't see the point. If an interaction wasn't heading somewhere, she just wasn't interested.

But Mid wasn't here, and Rose's shoulders slumped.

She rose from the table and threw the remnants of the sandwich and its container in the trash.

The viewing had gone as well as could be expected. There had been plenty of laughs, plenty of tears, plenty of memories, and plenty of sympathy for Rose.

There had also been plenty of questions as to what she would do next. Most people assumed she wouldn't be able to purchase My Pink Wink on her own. And a number of people had heard about the nephew; how, she had no idea.

The amount of people who had simply assumed Rose would not be able to either purchase the business or would just roll over and let this strange nephew walk away with all of Mid's property irked her. She knew she was relatively young, but at thirty-three, she felt plenty old enough to take on this challenge. Plenty of women her age were business owners. And Rose had been running My Pink Wink for over half a decade. There was no reason why she couldn't continue the business on her own. As discouraged as those conversations had made her feel, they had also made her determined.

If only she knew what she was facing with the evil Griffin Stangel.

She changed out of her black dress, washed her face, unpinned her hair, and went to bed early so she could get an early-morning run in before Mid's final viewing and service. She needed a burst of exercise to clear her head and work out some of her anxiety.

Then she'd go to the funeral home earlier than the other guests to ensure Jack Cummings had everything in order. After a brief gathering of family and friends, Pastor Ballentine would perform a short eulogy before everyone would pile in their cars to drive the quarter mile to the town cemetery where Mid's plot had been prepared and she would finally be lowered into the ground.

After Teddy had dealt with all of these details at the age of twenty for their parents, Rose understood why he'd opted to stay at the Sweetwood instead of taking part in the morbid festivities. It was exhausting, and he'd likely been traumatized.

The salon would be closed tomorrow for one day only. That made Rose feel guilty. But the staff wanted to pay their respects, and everyone in town would be at the service, along with their out-of-town regular customers. She had rescheduled all of the appointments, and she knew closing for one Friday wouldn't hurt them. She wondered what Griffin Stangel would think of that.

Rose went for a brisk run in the misty April morning. She found herself running to the edge of town where the Sweetwood sat on its wooded plot of land. A lone white Mercedes was parked in the front lot. It had a Massachusetts plate.

Rose peered at the vehicle as she ran past. The car did not look like something the handsome stranger would have been driving. She felt unexpectedly let down, which was embarrassing.

Then she wondered if maybe his car was in the back lot. She briefly considered jogging around the building, then immediately decided against it. Teddy would likely see her and wonder what she was doing, skulking around the saloon at this early hour.

Worse, maybe the handsome stranger really was in the outbuilding. What if he were to see her and suspect she was there for him? She would be mortified.

Before someone noticed her on the roadway, she turned around and ran the distance back to her own house.

Once there, she showered and dressed in her best black suit, which she'd had for years. Had she known

Mid was going to up and die, she may have gone shopping for some new clothes. But since she hadn't known, and she'd been busy with other, more pressing matters, the jacket, which was out of style, and the pants starting to show wear on the backside, would have to do.

Today, she decided to apply some light makeup to her face, if only to mask her exhaustion. At least that's what she told herself. There was the smallest, most miniscule part of her, still thinking about the stranger.

And there was a niggling in the back of her mind. *What if he really were Griffin Stangel?*

But, no. Howard would know. Besides, the man the evening before had heard her conversation with Teddy. Based on his straightened posture and alert energy, Rose could tell he'd been listening to at least part of the conversation. If he'd been the subject of their conversation, surely he would have spoken up.

She could almost feel Mid's glee at Rose's imagination running wild, as if in death, Mid could read her mind.

Rose didn't like that sensation one bit.

With a scowl, she finished getting ready and drove to the funeral home. She met with Jack, and made sure the hundreds of pink flowers—as would have been Mid's preference—were arranged correctly.

And then she said her own personal and private goodbyes to Mid.

There was a strange finality in the air around her. Almost as if Mid were silently communicating to her this is exactly how things were supposed to have worked out. And Rose couldn't shake the feeling Mid was standing beside her, telling her to get over herself and make this day a party.

Rose rolled her eyes.

Suddenly, Rose thought about the piece of paper she'd pulled from the cookie at the Asian restaurant with the forgotten man a few days earlier. *Your experiences this week will all make sense within the year.* It was such a jolting and unexpected memory that the hair on the back of Rose's neck stood up, and her skin prickled with goosebumps.

She rubbed her arms and shook the feeling away.

Mercifully, Jack Cummings chose that moment to walk into the room. He was a tall pale man, with glassy kind eyes. He was unobtrusive yet attentive. Rose couldn't think what else he would have done with his life besides being a funeral director.

She managed a smile for him, still feeling somewhat like an imposter, grieving like a daughter for this woman who was not her mother.

Jack smiled back. "Are you ready for me to open the doors?"

"I am." And the final hours of Mid's existence above ground began.

After it was all done—the words, the tears, the

memories, laughter, the service, the final lowering of Mid into the ground, and the brief buffet-style luncheon in the gathering room of the church—Rose went home to her silent little house. She glanced at the landline phone and fought back another wave of tears.

She changed out of her suit into a pair of leggings and a plain white T-shirt. Then she glanced in the mirror at the remnants of her makeup and washed her face clean. The brief attraction to the stranger in the bar had faded; during the course of the morning she'd nearly forgotten about him.

She was glad she hadn't made a fool of herself.

She had seen Howard and spoken with him briefly at the luncheon. He hadn't yet heard from either Mid's nephew or the man's attorney. When Rose had mentioned the stranger, he'd shaken his head. "His attorney assured me Griffin would not show up announced." Then Howard had leaned in close. "I got the feeling the nephew is kind of a…Well, let's just say he's had his fair share of problems." Rose had no idea what that meant, and she didn't ask. Frankly, she didn't want to know.

He told Rose he'd try contacting the nephew later in the afternoon, but she should go home, relax, and try not to worry. "Everything will be fine," he'd said.

But Rose didn't feel fine.

She made herself a peanut butter and jelly sand-wich and considered heading to the Sweetwood to sit at the bar, not to drink, but just to feel the presence of other people. It was a Friday afternoon, so there would be a few early patrons, maybe even some of the people from the funeral. But Rose couldn't bring herself to face everyone again.

She wished Teddy might sense her loneliness and call her up, but that wasn't Teddy. Even if she sat at the bar and spelled out for Teddy exactly what she needed, she had a feeling her brother wouldn't quite understand.

She supposed she could go on another run, but she was cognizant of overdoing it. She'd known too many runners with injuries—torn menisci, popped Achilles tendons, sciatica, inflamed hamstrings, strained calf muscles. Although she was still young, she wasn't as nimble and flexible as she had been in her late teens and early twenties.

So she moped around the house, scrolled through mindless videos on her phone, and periodically glance at her unused landline which would never ring again.

She had an imaginary conversation in her head. "Mid, what have you gone and done?"

I did what I was supposed to do.

"But what am *I* supposed to do now?"

You're a smart cookie. You'll figure it out.

"You could have made this so much easier on everyone involved."

Well, where would the fun have been in that?

"This isn't fun at all."

Then you're doing it wrong, my dear. You need to change the way you look at things.

Rose could almost hear her full, hooting laughter. It was a bittersweet sound. Rose had to stop believing she could actually still be communicating with her old friend and mentor.

After an hour of this self-punishment, Rose grabbed her keys and walked the short distance to the salon. It felt almost surreal to see an empty parking lot on a Friday afternoon. Except for major holidays, the shop was open seven days a week, though they kept shorter hours on Sundays so the staff could attend church or spend time with family. Rarely, the shop might close a bit early if there were no customers and they didn't expect any walk-ins. But for the most part, there was always *someone* here.

Rose unlocked the door and looked around the empty salon. Mid would never be here again, in this place she had built. And Rose didn't know how much longer she herself had in the shop. It was all dependent on the decisions of a man named Griffin Stangel.

She went to the back to play some music so the space didn't feel so still and hollowed out.

She chose a CD of funk and blues, one of Mid's favorites, and took a deep breath, trying to lose herself in the music instead of the grief. She was glad this music lent itself to joy rather than sorrow. And of course it did. The owner of the CD was not one for wallowing.

Because Rose didn't want to wallow either, of all the tasks on her list, she chose to clean and mop the salon floors. Something mindless and physical, where she could get lost in the movement.

She set about sweeping, first with a broom, swaying to Bobby Short's version of 'You've Got that Thing' and humming along to the music. She dimly wondered, as the singer crooned, what it was like to 'have that thing' that would make a man run off to Cartier's for a wedding ring. Whatever *that thing* was, Rose didn't have it.

After finishing, she glided over the floor with the high-powered, heavy-duty vacuum she had purchased a year before. And when she was convinced not a single stray hair remained on the white floors of the shop, she filled an industrial-sized bucket with scalding water and a disinfecting floor cleaner that burned her nose.

Then she grabbed her squeegee mop and went to town, scrubbing, rinsing, wringing, and repeating.

Another of Mid's favorite songs began playing. The liquid tones of 'It Had To Be You' flowed through the speakers. Rose belted this one out, and swayed her hips as she scrubbed at the floor, pausing to use the mop handle as a dance partner.

Again, Rose had the strangest sensation Mid was

there with her, her full face shining, her eyes laughing. And Rose, giving into the sense, sang a little louder and twirled around, as if Mid might have been dancing along with her.

But when she turned, her heart leapt in her throat. Rose let out a yelp.

A man stood just inside the front door, watching her.

She dropped the mop handle as her hand went to her throat; the mop clattered to the floor, flinging water all over the back of Rose and sloshing water from the bucket onto the clean floor.

Rose stepped back and nearly fell over the bucket, causing even more dirty water to splatter.

The man put his hands in front of him, palms forward, as if to indicate he was not a threat.

All of this took place in less than five seconds. Rose quickly recognized the man as the handsome stranger from the Sweetwood Saloon. The one who'd nearly knocked her off her stool the night before. The one she'd thought might be Griffin Stangel.

The one she'd nearly stalked that morning.

The one she couldn't get out of her mind.

And while she wasn't exactly afraid, she was definitely wary.

"What are you doing in here?" she exclaimed. "We're closed."

He seemed both alarmed and amused. But he

hitched a thumb behind him toward the entrance. "I saw movement inside, and the door was unlocked."

Rose glanced at the door. She may have forgotten to lock it behind her, but the 'Closed' sign was clearly affixed to the window.

She didn't bother to argue with him. Instead, she bent to pick up the mop and began to clean up the mess.

The man started forward as if he was going to help. Then he stopped and rocked back on his heels, his hands shoved into his pockets.

She snuck a glance in his direction. He looked just as disheveled, but maybe more handsome in the light of day. He was tall—well over six feet, she estimated. Even though he was wearing a jacket, his body appeared to be toned and lean. To her chagrin, she found herself remembering the random daydream about his body on the frilly bedspread in Teddy's outbuilding.

She knew she was blushing, and to cover up her body's betrayal, she asked, "So, what can I do for you?"

"I was just hoping, since I was still in town, I might be able to get a haircut. It's been a while."

Rose put the mop aside and allowed herself to study him openly. His thick dark hair was curling over his ears inside the collar of his black jacket. She eyed his ragged dark beard that was too long. She wondered what he might look like without the beard. She imagined the skin would be smooth…

He raised his eyebrows. Rose realized she was staring, rather than assessing, and she looked away quickly.

"But if you're closed, I guess I can come back…"

He made a move as if to leave, and Rose found herself blurting out, "I can cut it."

What was she doing? It wasn't as if she *couldn't* cut this guy's hair. Though her primary role these days was manager, she had her own regular clients and often took walk-ins. In fact, Rose's cuts were the reason My Pink Wink was as popular as it had become.

Seven years earlier, her layered inverted bob with chunky pastel highlights had been so popular that clients were driving from out of state for the trend. Rose may have single-handedly changed the look of that year's collection of senior photographs. The trend was quickly copied, and a year after, Rose had popularized the edgy fade-undercut for women, a look that parents didn't always love but that the younger generation had adored.

She had been recruited by some of the nation's most well-known master stylists and wooed to relocate to New York City, but Rose was a hometown girl. And so, as it turned out, was Mid. Offers to buy the salon, at least at the time, had been firmly rejected.

My Pink Wink, with its quirky name and stellar reputation, had retained its local popularity, but its national appeal had eventually faded. Still, Rose kept her skills as sharp as her scissors. And she was glad she'd done so. She might need the expertise after all.

But none of it meant she should be cutting *this* particular man's hair. Especially alone in the shop. They didn't have a policy against it, but they probably should have had.

Rose ignored the instinct and indicated he should sit at the porcelain shampoo bowl near the back of the store. She preferred to work on clean, damp hair, but also, there was a small part of her that wanted to feel his thick hair between her fingers.

She took the mop and bucket to the back and washed her hands in the back basin. When she came back out, he'd taken off his jacket and settled himself in the chair, with his neck resting in the cutout of the basin so he was staring up at the ceiling.

He was wearing a plain black T-shirt that hugged muscular biceps; the outline of two colorful tattoos were visible on both arms, partially hidden by the shirt sleeves. The shirt was tucked into a pair of slim jeans belted around his lean waist. His long, lean legs were ever so slightly spread apart. She couldn't help but wonder what he might look like without all those pesky clothes.

The thought shocked and thrilled her. She wasn't in the habit of imagining men naked. She liked to think she was more attracted to potential partners for their minds, rather than their bodies.

But this guy wasn't a potential partner, was he? What he *was* was incredibly sexy. So sexy that Rose's body was reacting in a way that was energizing, exhilarating, and very out of character for her. Her body was thrumming in places that it hadn't since…She thought back. Maybe since high school. That was kind of sad.

'Mack the Knife' vibrated through the speakers. *How fitting*, she thought. A smooth, jazzy song about a knife-wielding serial killer. You'd never guess how dangerous the titular character was from a listen of the upbeat song. She'd do well to remember that, she cautioned herself.

Again, she thought she could hear Mid laughing at her. Telling her she was being *so dramatic*.

The man lifted his head from the sink. "Everything okay?"

Rose rubbed her hands together, the picture of efficiency. "Yes. Just considering."

He didn't ask what she'd been considering, which was just as well, since she couldn't have told him she'd contemplating him as Macheath in *The Threepenny Opera*, on which the song 'Mack the Knife' was based.

Nor would she have told him she was wondering what his skin would taste like on her tongue.

Pull it together, Rose, she thought. Then she blinked and swallowed.

She leaned over him, twisting the spigots in the

sink. She adjusted the water temperature, and happened to glance at his face to find him watching her. Again with those amused eyes. They were a very light brown. Almost amber colored.

She looked away and focused on the task at hand. Grasping the spray hose, she shot the warm water on her wrist before spraying the gentle jets of water into his hair.

Rose had always found the act of washing hair an intimate activity. Years before, she had developed the ability to create small talk to mask some of the awkwardness she felt in performing the deed, but now that ability seemed to have left her.

His hair was as thick, shiny, and healthy as it looked; she sprayed with one hand while making sure his mane was good and soaked with the other.

Inadvertently, she glanced at his face, and again found him staring at her. She nearly dropped the nozzle, but composed herself enough to avoid beaning him in the forehead. She was probably imagining things, but part of her that wondered if she leaned forward and put her lips on his, would he kiss her back? Her lips parted at the thought.

"What is this music?" he asked, as she leaned over him to reach for the shampoo and conditioner in the cabinet above the sink.

Had she known she'd be styling a male client, she would have worn something other than her form-fitting, thin white shirt.

She was aware that her breasts were right over his eyes. What would she do if he were to reach up and lightly tease one of her nipples through the thin fabric of her shirt?

"Jesus," she muttered under her breath. She needed to get a grip.

Griffin said, "I didn't think Jesus did much singing himself."

"What?" she asked, then realized he'd asked her who was singing. "This is Bobby Darin," she said, picking up a masculine, pine-scented hair product.

"I know who it is." He sounded offended. "Why are you playing it?"

"It's one of Mid's favorites," she said, realizing he had no idea who Mid was. But he didn't ask, and she didn't offer further explanation. "Mine too."

She squeezed a generous amount of shampoo into her palm and began massaging the thick gel into his hair and scalp.

This, she thought, *was the worst, and best, part.*

Mercifully, he had shut his eyes. She thought he may have nodded off, but when her nails scraped his scalp, he let out a soft moan. Rose found herself sucking in a breath.

Oh. My. God. she thought. She felt her blood pounding in her ears. And lower.

She glanced down at his body. Was it her imagination or was the bulge in pants larger than it had been earlier?

It was *not* her imagination.

What would happen, she thought again, if she just…swung her legs over him and pressed herself into his swelling erection. She might immediately orgasm.

A sound escaped Rose's lips; the man's eyes flew open. Their gazes locked. Rose could've sworn he knew what she was thinking. If she didn't know better, she'd swear he was thinking it, too.

She hurriedly finished washing the hair and did a quick rinse before towel-drying the hair and applying a light leave-in conditioner.

She felt his amber gaze on her face as she worked; she cursed the rush of blood to her neck and cheeks.

When the task was complete, she let out a breath. He sat up. She tucked the towel around his neck and wound a hairstyling cape around his shoulders.

"Done. Come on, then," she said briskly, moving to her assigned station on the other side of the room.

"You sound relieved."

And he sounded amused.

She didn't respond. But when he walked toward her, she couldn't help but notice a telltale bulge in the crotch area of his jeans. Her cheeks felt as if they might burst into flames. He had responded to her, just as she had responded to him.

A giddiness bubbled into her chest as she averted

her eyes. She had no idea how to feel.

He sat in the swivel chair in front of the station that was much less cluttered than the others.

Rose borrowed equipment from Hallie's station next to hers, then stood behind him, taking care to look at only his head in the mirror.

She managed to force her mind back to the task in front of her, frowning as she again ran her fingers through his hair.

When she did catch his eye, his lips were twisted in a wry half smile.

"What?" Her tone was peevish, petty. She sounded like a child even to her own ears.

"Nothing. It's just…" He cut himself off and thought about his words. "Are you always this serious?"

"I don't think I'm particularly serious."

"Clearly not always, if your dance routine was any indication."

Even though he was laughing, her frown deepened. She hated that he'd walked in on her in a compromising situation. It wasn't just that she'd been embarrassed; it was not the image she wanted to project for the shop. Not even to this stranger whom she'd probably never see again.

She shifted the conversation back to the business at hand. "What are we doing with your hair?"

He looked at himself in the mirror, and for the first

time, she saw a scowl and a slight look of disgust. As if he didn't particularly like the man staring back at him.

He shrugged. "You're the professional. I'll leave it to you."

Rose sighed. She hated it when people put the onus for their hairstyle on her. Luckily, she was good at assessing face shape and hair type and matching up the style with a person's features. Generally men were easier to please than women—it was because they truly didn't care that much. From the attitude of the guy in her chair, she believed he didn't care at all. And she wondered why.

Without thinking much longer about it, she grasped her scissors between her fingers and went to work. Her fingers flew as she concentrated and snipped away. Thick, dark locks of hair fell to the clean floor as she worked.

Andy Williams's rendition of 'Moon River' flowed from the speaker.

"You look a little like her."

"Hmm?" Rose asked, barely listening. She spun him toward her and looked closely at the sides of his head, deciding the best location above his ears for the fade line.

She was leaning in extremely close when he said, "Audrey Hepburn."

She felt his breath on her lips, and she shifted her gaze to his eyes. His gaze flickered to her lips, and they hovered, suspended in that moment, before she jerked her head away.

She blinked and straightened. She did *not* look like Audrey Hepburn. But she didn't bother to tell him that.

She spun him back toward the mirror and picked up the clippers. She affixed a number-three guard and began working slowly and meticulously around the side and back of his head. More hair floated to the floor.

"I was in the bar last evening. The Sweetwater."

Rose hesitated in her movements. "Sweetwood," she amended. "I remember."

"I'm sure you do."

No response. *Keep clipping.* She switched to a lower guard and continued to work her way around his head.

"I wasn't drunk."

"I didn't say you were."

"Your boyfriend certainly thought so."

Rose paused in her clipping and frowned. "Boy-friend?"

"Or husband. Whatever."

He was staring at her hard in the mirror. Then it dawned on her. He was talking about her brother. "You mean Teddy." She laughed.

He grunted and stiffened, then looked down at his hands.

"Keep your head just like that," she said, and continued working on the fade, the clippers buzzing.

"Did he make you stay in the outbuilding?"

"He didn't tell you?" There was a challenge in his voice.

"He doesn't tell me everything. And I didn't ask." She took his silence as assent. "Teddy tries to do the right thing, even when it comes out…wrong."

She sectioned off the longer top portion of his hair and moved the clippers in an upward motion, creating an arc with each movement. Then she moved the clippers sideways across the fade at the back of his head.

"It's a comfortable room," she said, and again the image of his long lean legs tangled up in the frilly comforter popped into her mind. She placed herself into that setting, and thought about her tangled up in him.

Would it be so bad, she thought, *to have just one night of fun?*

She cleared her throat.

Yes, it would be. She had about a thousand other things she needed to think about. A one-night stand wasn't one of those things. As appealing as this man and his body happened to be.

There was a silence as she switched out the guards, and repeated the process around his neck. Short hairs fell onto the damp towel still at the base of his head, and she moved it down to clip the hair at the nape of his neck.

"How long do you plan on staying in Madison?"

"Tell me about this place," he said.

"Madison?"

"The salon. The Pink Wink."

"*My* Pink Wink."

"That might be worse. What kind of name is that anyway? It sounds obscene."

She smiled because it reminded her of Mid, but when she looked in the mirror, she found he wasn't smiling back anymore. "It's been that name forever. Mid, the former owner, named it. She said a wink was the ultimate form of flirtation, and that's what we were doing with hair. Helping people to feel good about themselves and confident. Pink happened to be her favorite color. I think the obscene part was just a bonus."

"And this Mid person—that was the funeral you talked about to…Teddy?"

More hostility. For someone who drank too much all on his own, he was really holding a grudge.

"Mid's funeral was today. That's why the shop is closed."

There were no more words as Rose cleaned up the fade line. She put the clippers back on their base and again picked up the scissors, trimming the longer top part of his hair. She checked the corners and then used thinning shears to trim it back.

Finally, she did the last clean-up, then found a medium-hold pomade in Jay's cabinet. She rubbed the waxy substance between her palms, heating it up. Then she used her foot to swivel the chair so he was facing her.

As she worked the product into his hair, his amber eyes were just as intense, but they were no longer on hers, either smiling or teasing. In fact, he looked annoyed. She found herself unexpectedly dejected, and she fought the urge to shift the dynamics again.

Frank Sinatra began to croon, "I've got you under my skin…"

She wanted to tell Frank to shut up.

You never can win.

"I'm aware," she mumbled as she finger-styled his hair then molded it until it was sleek but messy, and had a lot of shiny volume.

"Aware of what?" he asked.

She hadn't realized she'd spoken out loud. "You have a lot of hair," she said, recovering quickly.

He arched an eyebrow. He didn't believe her.

But it didn't matter. She used a comb to smooth the final product then spun him back around to look in the mirror. He looked good. *Really* good. But his beard needed a trim.

He studied the hairstyle critically in the mirror. Rose held her breath, waiting.

"It's okay," he finally said. "A little shorter than I

normally wear it." But he didn't look displeased.

"Want the beard cleaned up too?"

He ran his long fingers over the coarse facial hair. "Knock yourself out."

She brushed the beard out first with her comb then started to work on the bulk with the clippers. She meticulously faded the sideburns into the cut of the hair and gradually removed more and more of the facial hair until he had a perfect short-boxed beard.

He looked absolutely amazing. Rose nearly couldn't stop herself from ogling him.

He also looked familiar. She couldn't shake the feeling she'd seen him somewhere before. Perhaps he looked like some movie star or singer she couldn't quite place.

She'd just swept off the cape when the man grabbed Rose's hand. His fingers were warm on her palm, and he was staring at her. He looked as if he were about to say something. Rose gazed into those eyes. She felt herself leaning forward—or was he pulling her toward him?

The door opened quickly, and Julie Newlin stepped in. "Oh…" she said in surprise.

Rose jumped back, nearly falling in the process.

Julie looked from Rose to her customer. "I didn't realize you were taking customers. The sign on the door says 'Closed'." She looked closer at the man in the chair. Her cheeks dimpled with her wide smile. "And who do we have here?"

His face shifted from a grimace to delight.

Julie was beautiful, there was no doubt about it. Her blonde hair was highlighted, her makeup meticulously applied to conceal any signs of aging, and she was plump in all the right places. When it came to Julie, age was a number which didn't matter one bit.

"What can I help you with, Julie?"

"I came to see if I could help *you*. I was just taking a walk, and I noticed the unfamiliar car in the lot. I wanted to make sure you were okay." Rose supposed she was trying to sound caring, but her tone came across as simpering.

The excuse was a load of crap. Julie was only being nosy. She had no interest in helping.

"I'm fine," Rose said. "We're just finishing up."

"Maybe I'm just getting started," she mumbled and walked forward sticking out a manicured hand.

The man took Julie's delicate hand in his large, calloused palm. Rose wondered what he did for a living.

"Julie Newlin," she purred.

"It's nice to meet you, Julie Newlin."

Julie tittered even though nothing was funny. Rose wanted to tell her she was too old to be giggling like a schoolgirl.

"I don't believe I've seen you here before."

"I don't believe you have. I'm just passing

through."

Julie's face lit up. "Are you the man from the Sweetwood everyone's been talking about? The one who stayed in Teddy's little house?" Julie gave Rose a scolding look, as if she controlled what Teddy did. "You really need to talk to him about his manners."

Rose gritted her teeth.

"I guess everyone in town must've heard about that," he said.

"Not much stays secret here. But I wouldn't worry about it. Lots of people have stayed in the house over the years."

That was a lie, Rose thought.

Julie smiled and winked at the man. He winked back.

She hitched her hip, clad in tight designer leggings, against the side of Hallie's station. "Even a man passing through town needs to eat. And you look like a man who likes to eat." Rose grimaced at the innuendo.

"I do like to eat," he responded.

Rose stood awkwardly between them, like a third wheel. She also felt unreasonably jealous of the interaction. How ironic that Rose hadn't been able to bring herself to say more than twenty words to this man, and here Julie was after two minutes flirting shamelessly and inviting him to dinner. Or inviting him for something else entirely.

It wasn't like Rose wanted to date the guy. She just

wanted…*What was it that she wanted?*

She knew what she *didn't* want. For Julie to take this guy home.

He smiled. "You don't even know my name."

"We can fix that easily enough."

A range of emotions played across the man's face. He was thinking about Julie's offer. But in the end, he said, "I'll tell you what. If I'm still around in a couple of days, I'll take you up on the offer."

Julie raised her eyebrows. "Something tells me you'll still be around in a few days."

"You just might be right, ma'am."

Rose stepped in. "Thanks for stopping by, Julie. But I really need to finish up and close the shop." She hoped her words were enough to dismiss Julie, who could be interminable.

To Rose's relief, Julie waived a hand in front of her. "I have to be going anyway. I'm stopping over at the church to finish up some correspondence before Sunday." She gave the man another electric smile. "If you change your mind, I'll be over at the church office. You know how to find the church?"

"I suppose I'll have to look for the steeple."

Julie chuckled. "You do that, sir." She moved to the door, her shapely ass sashaying as she walked.

His eyes were glued to her retreating figure. But she didn't turn back around. She just raised her hand and said "Tootleoo".

After Julie was gone, the air around them remained charged by her aura. But the life had gone out of the man. He would not be flirting with her the way he had with Julie. Instead he stood, grabbed his abandoned jacket from the chair and said, "What do I owe you?"

Rose glanced at the laptop on the desk. She hadn't powered anything on when she'd come in because she'd had no intention of taking customers. Booting up the system and logging into the payment processing app would take longer than she was willing to spend in this awkward interaction. Instead, she said, "Consider it repayment for Teddy's behavior."

"You know, you shouldn't have to make excuses for him. That's not how a relationship is supposed to work."

Rose shrugged. "After all these years, I'm kind of used to it."

"I'm not sure how you're supposed to stay in business if you're giving away your time and talent."

"Believe me—this is a one-time thing."

They looked at each other, and some of the current between them returned.

Then he said, "Well…thanks for the haircut." He reached up and stroked his beard unconsciously. "And the trim."

"You're welcome." Rose wanted to flirt like Julie. She wanted to say something smooth and witty, but her mouth was dry, and her mind was empty.

"Maybe I'll see you around."

"I highly doubt that." Rose just caught the hint of a frown before he walked out the door.

She went to the back of the shop to grab the broom. Cole Porter was singing, "*Here's hoping we meet now and then…*"

Rose switched off the CD. She felt very much alone.

It was just one of those things.

Chapter 9

She was married. Griffin wasn't sure why it mattered. *It didn't matter*, he told himself. This woman, Rose, was not his friend, nor was she the type of woman he'd date. Not in a million years.

He liked women who smiled. Who laughed. Who had fun. He liked women like Julie Newlin.

Now, Julie had been interesting. Beautiful in just the way he liked—blonde, well-built, well-maintained, playful. Julie, he could tell, didn't take herself too seriously. Not like the perpetually frowning Rose. *She would be so much prettier if she just smiled.*

It didn't matter, he thought to himself for the hundredth time since she'd confirmed it. She was married. Hadn't he twice gotten himself into trouble for exactly that?

He folded himself into the Mercedes and sat looking up at the white façade of the hair salon affixed with its bright, frivolous signage—My Pink Wink. He kind of wished he'd never heard of the place.

Pulling down the visor, he looked into the lighted mirror on the back side. Damn, he looked good. He'd still been stinging from the fact Rose had confirmed her relationship with the one arch-nemesis he had in this town, so he hadn't given her the credit she deserved.

He rotated his head from side to side, looking at the haircut. As he'd told her, he normally wore his hair longer. He'd always had good hair. But this was something else entirely. He'd always looked shaggy and rakish with the longer style; this trim made him look downright dangerous. He felt a boost of confidence he hadn't felt in a long while.

Rose had given him that.

He glanced up at the building again. Though his aunt had apparently left him this place, along with whatever other property and assets she'd had, he didn't want it. Did he?

No, he asserted silently. He did not. He didn't want anything to do with this small town.

Through the shop window, he could see the shadow of Rose moving about inside. Mostly likely sweeping his hair off the floor she'd just mopped. His gut gave a little twist.

He did not want to explore the feelings he'd had while she'd been washing his hair. Certainly, he'd his hair cut thousands of times in his life, by many different people, women included. He could not recall feeling like he had when Rose's hands threaded his thick locks.

Married, he reminded himself. Not his type.

Think about Julie Newlin. He conjured her up again—long blonde hair; tight, toned ass; large, perfect breasts. She'd fit right in on the streets of Boston. In the bars he frequented. Waving from the stands at one of his games. Smiling up at him from his bed.

His gut did not twist again.

With a squeal of tires, he backed out of the parking lot into the path of a Jeep, the driver screeching to a halt and laying on the horn.

Griffin lifted his hand in a wave of apology, and then noticed the severe face of Teddy, the bartender and Rose's husband, in the mirror. He smoothly transitioned the wave to a flip of his middle finger, and Teddy lifted both hands in the air.

Griffin shifted the car into drive and sped down the road before Teddy had a chance to react.

He glanced at his phone, which sat on silent. No missed calls from Howard, the lawyer, but three missed calls from Irv, and at least ten missed calls from Boston area codes. All media most likely. Looking for a story. A soundbite. Looking for him to tighten the noose a little more around his neck.

He really needed to change his number. The vultures all had his current number from his failed career in broadcasting.

Then he noticed another number—this one with a name attached. Victoria Bryant. The woman who'd pushed him right over the edge into his current downward spiral. *Hers* as well.

Nope, he thought definitively. He did not want to know what she wanted.

As he drove, he swiped left on the missed call and removed it from the log history.

Instead, he glanced at his email and located the message with the address of his aunt's house. He supposed while he was exiled here, the very least he could do was take a look.

He turned off the main road, such as it was, onto a smaller side street. This one was pleasant and tree-lined, the new growth on the mature trees green and promising in the sunny April afternoon.

What were these trees? he wondered. Maple? Elm? Oak?

He had no idea. He'd never been much of a student outside of physical education. Back in the day, he'd blown them all away. In school, in his brief college career before he turned professional.

He'd shown them all.

Except his mother, who'd continued to be disappointed by his very existence.

He frowned at the memory, then frowned up at the house that matched the address in the email. This house had belonged to his mother's twin sister, who'd failed to plan ahead and leave the property to the right person. Something his mother also would have done.

Then she would have blamed it on Griffin because he was the only one left for her to blame.

But he was also frowning because he knew this was the house where his mother had grown up. Madeline Higgins Stangel—before she'd been just Mad Stangel—had talked about her younger years so rarely, Griffin never thought to question her upbringing or her hometown.

Now that he was here, he found himself with questions. What had happened between the woman named Mid and his mother? Because something clearly *had* happened. Some disagreement or falling out. He supposed he'd never know.

He could ask his father, who lived in Arizona now. But if his father had ever known, the man probably wanted to forget. He'd been married to another woman for the past twenty years, and on the rare occasions Griffin had spoken with him, he never mentioned his former dead wife.

The house was a small, squat ranch-style home constructed of sand-colored brick and surrounded by evergreen trees and shrubbery. A wind chime on the front porch swayed in the breeze. It was utterly ordinary. If he hadn't been looking for the house, he'd have passed it and never known.

It looked empty, but that could've been because he knew the owner was no longer living.

This house would be his, too, if he wanted it. He

didn't.

But there was some pull. Some curiosity. Was there anything of his mother left inside?

On the other side of the street was a large expanse of land with a sad-looking, overgrown ballfield, a pavilion, and a freshly paved track.

On a Friday afternoon, the only occupants were a very young couple hanging out by a swing set that looked like it had seen better days.

Griffin looked away.

In the cupholder beside him, his phone lit up with an unknown number but which looked familiar. It was Howard Lincoln. The phone wasn't connected to the car's Bluetooth, so Griffin answered on the handset and pulled away from the house, talking as he drove.

"Howard," said Griffin into the phone.

"Hello, Griffin?"

"Yes," said Griffin. "It's good to speak with you, Howard."

"This is Howard Lincoln, attorney for your aunt, Mid Higgins."

Griffin frowned. The guy sounded ancient. "Yes, I called you earlier."

"Yes, yes. Apologies. I attended Mid's service today. But that business has all been taken care of. You should know, however, the cost of the funeral will be coming out of the estate assets."

Griffin didn't respond. He turned around in the

driveway and backed out onto the quiet street.

"When can we expect you to arrive?" Howard asked. His voice had become faraway sounding, as if he'd angled the mouthpiece of his phone away from his face. Griffin struggled to hear the next sentence. "Your attorney mentioned some pressing legal matters."

"Actually, I'm here now."

"Here?" Howard's voice was still distant. "Dealing with your legal matters?"

Griffin paused, trying to decipher the conversation. "Here, as in, I'm here in Madison."

There was a long pause. The lawyer's voice was loud again when he said, "Excuse me. I don't think I heard you clearly."

"I arrived yesterday. Thought I would just get the lay of the land before we spoke further."

"That's…Well, I'm not quite sure what to say. That's something I wish I'd known. Where are you staying, may I ask?"

Griffin looked both ways at the end of the street and turned back onto the town's main drag. He wasn't sure how to respond to Howard's question, but he figured the old man would find out soon enough. "Last night, I stayed out behind the Sweetwood Saloon. I'll be looking for a hotel room this evening. Haven't gotten that far yet."

"The Sweetwood Saloon," Howard said slowly. Just the way he said the name of the bar, Griffin knew

Howard had already heard the story. "Surely you're not the person they've been talking about. The stranger who got drunk and became belligerent with Teddy."

Griffin set his jaw at the man's name.

Howard continued, "Rose…" Her name trailed off, and Griffin found himself sucking in a breath. "She even asked if it could have been you. I told her absolutely not…"

At the woman's name, Griffin felt the same little jolt of electricity. Then the same letdown when he remembered she was spoken for. He inadvertently glanced in the mirror at his haircut, thought about her swaying to the bluesy song that had been playing. *It had to be you…*

Why did it have to be her? he thought.

"So you've already met Rose."

Howard had uttered the sentence more to himself than to Griffin, but Griffin answered anyway. "I met her, but I didn't introduce myself. So she doesn't know it's me. I mean, she doesn't know I'm Mid's nephew."

"Well, I don't see how that's any better. We're all going to have to meet together next week, and I assume she'll recognize you. But maybe she won't. If you just ran into her once in the Sweetwood, she may forget with everything else going on."

Griffin didn't mention the haircut.

"May I ask…" His voice went distant again. "…why you didn't introduce yourself?"

Why hadn't he introduced himself? Griffin supposed it hadn't been the right time, though he wasn't sure what the right time might have been. "I wasn't sure what to say to her. I didn't know who she was until I overheard her talking to her boyfriend about me, and at that point, it was clear she didn't have the warmest feelings. Also, I'd had a few drinks, and I don't always make the best decisions after a few drinks."

"So I've heard," Howard quipped, likely referring to the news coverage of Griffin. "But Rose doesn't have a boyfriend."

Husband, whatever. He didn't want to continue this thread with Howard.

"How long are you planning to stay?"

Griffin supposed it was up to Irv. But a few days seemed reasonable to him. He repeated the plan to Howard.

"Then I will set some time up for Monday morning. We may as well get this over with. I thought about meeting in the office, but perhaps it makes more sense to meet at Mid's house. Then you and Rose can decide how you want to handle the assessment of the property."

Griffin felt a niggle of doubt. He'd considered he and Rose might have to meet about the property, but the truth was, he'd been hoping he could avoid it. Just tell Howard he didn't want any of it, and let them do what they would with it.

But since he'd seen the shop and the house…he still couldn't say he *wanted* it, but he was curious at least. And Irv had told him not to come home, so it made sense to keep up with the charade for just a little while longer. Maybe he could find out some information about his mother—the woman who'd made him into who he was now, he thought bitterly.

"Did you know Mid when she was younger?"

Howard chuckled. "Oh, yes. She was a few years younger than me, but she was a firecracker. Most everyone knew her."

"So you knew my mother too."

Howard was quiet. Then he said, "Madeline. Yes, I knew her, too. She was…different than Mildred."

"My mother and I weren't close," Griffin said. "Do you know why they didn't speak?"

There was a pause, long and filled with hesitation. Finally Howard said, "I'm afraid I don't."

Griffin wasn't sure he believed him.

"I do hope you'll be kind to her."

"My mother is dead," Griffin said.

"I meant Rose. When your aunt died, Rose essentially lost a mother, for the second time in her life. You'll know how it feels." Howard's tone turned brusque and businesslike. A change from the stammering old man. "I'll talk with Rose and let her know the plan for Monday. I trust you can lay low over the weekend? She's had a rough go of it."

Griffin knew what Howard was saying. *Stay away from Rose.* Griffin could do that. He didn't want to see her anyway. "I'm sure Teddy will take care of her."

"Teddy has a hard enough time taking care of himself."

So the guy was a known asshole. That didn't make him feel any better. He just wanted to punch the guy's lights out.

"I'll send you the time for Monday as soon as I speak with Rose," Howard said and disconnected the call.

Griffin sighed. He knew he needed to talk with Irv. Just in case Howard decided to tell him about the situation at the Sweetwood.

For this conversation, Griffin looked for a quiet place to park. He found himself in front of the church. The parking lot was empty, except for one car—a sporty silver SUV with a 'Soccer Mom' decal in the back window. Had to be Julie's car.

He cut the engine and dialed Irv's number.

Irv answered on the third ring.

"Griffin," he said. "I've been calling. I'd hoped to hear from you yesterday."

"Yeah, well, I was a little tired after the drive."

A pause. "I'm going to video call you."

Before Griffin could object, his phone started to pulse. He gritted his teeth and pressed the button. Irv's face was too close to the screen, and Griffin could see the hairs sprouting from the man's nose.

"Whoa," Irv said. "What the hell happened to you?"

Griffin assumed Irv was talking about his haircut and beard. "I just got a trim."

"That's more than a trim," Irv said. "You look like a new man." His lawyer peered closely at the screen. "I like it. You look—" He cut himself off. "I was going to say 'respectable', but that's not it." Irv narrowed his eyes. "Where are you?"

"I'm in Madison, just like you ordered."

"Show me."

Griffin looked up at the church. "There's not much to see here." But he turned the phone around so Irv could survey his surroundings.

When he pivoted the screen back to his face, Irv looked satisfied. "So everything else going okay? Did you check in with Howard?"

"We're meeting on Monday morning to look at the house and the property."

"Good, good. Everything is quiet here. Just stay there and lay low. I put some calls out, but I won't hear anything until next week."

"I did want to let you know, though—I've met some of the people in town already."

Irv's tone slowed. "Okay. Like what people?"

"Like the niece."

"Is that a problem?"

"Well, no. It's just…I ran into her last night at a bar—"

"Let me stop you right there. I thought you were going to lay low. What were you doing at a bar?"

"I just stopped in as I was passing through town."

Another pause. "All right. Well, as long as nothing happened that might attract any attention. You know, like from the media. Because that will certainly not help your case *here*, if you get in trouble *there*."

"I don't think anything happened that might attract the media attention." No one in town knew who he was, so they wouldn't know to contact the media.

"You don't *think*?"

Griffin didn't respond.

"We've been over this before, Stangel. I can't help you unless you tell me everything. And I have a feeling you're not telling me everything."

Griffin debated what to say next. In the end, he decided to change the subject altogether. "I stopped by My Pink Wink." Just saying the name gave him the willies. "The *salon*," he amended. "Just to see what it's all about. I thought the place was open, but it turns out Rose was in there alone. I needed an excuse for being there, so I said I needed my hair cut, and she agreed. She still doesn't know who I am."

There was a long slow exhale on the other end of the phone. "Well, she did a bang-up job on you. But you see how this looks, right? You went in there, didn't tell her your name, and now she's going to meet you. How suspicious is that going to look?"

"I don't see how it matters, Irv. Sure, it might be awkward. But I have no intention of accepting any of my aunt's property. I don't need it, and I don't want it." Even if he *had* been interested, too much here reminded Griffin of his mother. "I have no intention of staying here any longer than I absolutely have to."

"You sure about that? You want to know how much the salon brings in on a yearly basis?"

Griffin didn't particularly want to know, but Irv told him anyway. Griffin's eyes nearly bugged out of his head.

"See?" Irv said, staring at Griffin's reaction.

"That can't be right. This town is tiny. There's no way the place is pulling in that kind of profit."

"Apparently, a few years ago, one of the stylists created some sort of new hairstyle which was all the rage. The trend even got picked up nationally. Since then, the shop has had a very steady clientele, and yet they haven't capitalized on the popularity beyond the small town. Now, I don't know much about hair salons, but I do know something about business. And I'm telling you—there's an opportunity to do much, much more with the place."

"I'm not a businessman," said Griffin.

"You can hire a business manager. And as annoyed

as I get with your antics and having to clean up your messes, can you imagine the publicity you might get from opening up a hair salon? With that head of hair of yours? Hell, with the new style you're sporting now? You've got the bones right there. It's just waiting to be brought to life."

"Who was the stylist?" Griffin asked.

"Huh?"

"The stylist who created the popular hairstyle."

"Who cares? What matters is the reputation. People remember."

Griffin thought the name mattered very much. Especially if the name was Rose. "How do you know all of this?"

"Who are you talking to? I do my due diligence."

Griffin certainly knew that. For better or for worse, Irv did his due diligence. "Still, Irv—I have absolutely no interest in living in this town."

"But that's the thing. You don't need to. All you need to do is attach your name to it. You could cater to older women. I know how popular you are with that demographic."

He ignored the crack. "But what about Rose?"

"What about her?"

"She's running the salon now."

Irv shrugged on the video. "Apparently, she's not running it all that well if she's leaving opportunity on the table. Besides, she doesn't own the salon, and even if you don't want it, there's a good chance she won't be able to afford it. It'll go into probate."

He remembered those mournful brown eyes. That lovely full mouth with the downturned corners. "It just doesn't seem fair."

"Life isn't fair. Besides, if your aunt wanted this woman to inherit her property, she would have willed it to her. That didn't happen."

Griffin knew Irv was right, but it didn't sit well with him.

Irv's voice turned serious. "Can we go back to something you said earlier?"

"What's that?" Griffin said, glancing out the window. The light of day was starting to fade, and he still hadn't booked a hotel room for the evening. He wanted to get off this call.

"You said you stopped at the bar. Anything else happened at this bar?"

Shit. Irv knew him too well. "What do you mean?"

"It's just that the last time you stopped at a bar, all hell broke loose. In fact, the last couple of times you've gotten in trouble has been directly related to bars and women."

Griffin hesitated. He contemplated feigning cell coverage issues and just ending the call. But in the end, he knew he had to tell Irv what happened. It wasn't a big deal, anyway. And if he didn't tell Irv, Howard probably would.

"I may have had a little too much to drink after the long drive."

Irv puffed out his cheeks. "And?" he asked, resigned.

"And I got into a bit of an argument with Rose's husband who happens to own the bar. He took my keys and insisted I stay on an outbuilding on the property."

"Jesus Christ," Irv said. Griffin glanced up at the church in front of him. The lawyer sighed, his full face still too close to his screen. "Did anything else happen?"

"No. There may be some talk in the town about me."

"You know, for someone who claims to hate the spotlight, you sure do like to seek it out." Irv pursed his lips. "Do me a favor, Griffin. Go to your hotel room, order some room service, watch some TV, and stay the fuck in. Do you think you can do that?"

Griffin hated it when people spoke to him like he was a child, but he didn't say anything.

"Try not to screw up any more than you already have, huh?"

Griffin's face burned. Irv sounded just like his mother. He ended the call abruptly.

Sitting in the parking lot, his hands gripped the steering wheel of the white Mercedes as the sun sank below the horizon, coloring the sky various shades of orange, purple, and pink.

He took a few deep breaths, calming himself down from the conversation, and the day. Trying to calm himself from life.

Griffin wasn't sure how long he sat like that before he heard a light tapping sound on the window next to him. He glanced over to see the woman from the salon—Julie—peering inside.

He blinked up at her smiling, artificially pretty face—artificial blonde hair, artificial long eyelashes, artificial perfect nails, and artificial full lips. But those lips smiled a real smile, and her blue eyes looked delighted to see him. And that was a welcome feeling.

He powered down the window.

"Hey, stranger," she said in her seductive purr. "You came looking for me after all."

Griffin was about to tell her he'd just needed a quiet place to take a phone call. But he didn't say that. Instead, he said, "I may not have been looking, but I sure found you."

She beamed at him. "What are you doing tonight?"

"Not a damn thing."

Chapter 10

The invitation from Howard to meet in his office on Monday morning had come in typical Howard fashion—through a voicemail filled with extraneous information, shuffling papers, and stuttering. But even for Howard, the lawyer had seemed flustered and apologetic. Rose didn't think much about it, thought it had struck her as faintly odd. Perhaps he was dreading the meeting as much as she was. Perhaps it was because they were meeting at Mid's house instead of Howard's office, and he knew it would be painful for Rose. The last time she'd been inside the house was when she'd found Mid on the kitchen floor.

On Sunday morning, her day off, she was drinking coffee and still contemplating the call. She found her mind wandering to the mysterious Griffin Stangel. She was surprised the man was coming into town this soon. And if he could make it by Monday, why hadn't he attended his aunt's funeral? She vacillated between relief that he had *not* attended and resentment that he *should* have. But in the end, she decided she was glad he had not been there. He would have been an unwelcome distraction, to say the very least.

She'd spent her entire Saturday at the shop with the staff, trying to adjust to their new normal. Luckily, it had been so busy there hadn't been a lot of time to think about Mid *or* Griffin Stangel, and she'd barely had time to think about the handsome stranger who'd wandered in the day before. Though every time she used the sink in the back, she had vivid memories of her fingers threaded through his hair…

She was shocked none of her staff had known about the haircut. She'd expected Julie Newlin to blabber the news all over town. But none of them had said a word, and Rose wasn't sharing.

She glanced out the window at the rising sun, shining through the oak trees on the rise behind her house. For the first Sunday in years, she felt dread. Rose wanted to be at the salon, but Hallie had told Rose that if Rose insisted on coming in, Hallie would, in no uncertain terms, zip-tie Rose's wrists together and march her right back out. She said she'd even call Teddy if she had to.

Rose, Hallie and the rest of the staff had decided, needed a break; some time to herself, despite Rose's insistence to the contrary. Because, in truth, Rose had nowhere to go, nothing to do, and no one to see.

How sad was that?

In the end, she decided to attend church. Though she was angry with God at the moment, something told her Mid would not want her to stew in those feelings forever. Rose had even managed to convince herself that some hymns and one of Pastor Ballentine's inspiring sermons might drive her out of her doldrums.

She dressed in a long-sleeved pink silk blouse, plain brown slacks, sensible shoes, and a spring jacket. The temperature was in the upper fifties, and it was a good day for a brisk walk.

Rose strode the short distance up Main Street to the quaint white chapel, listening to the birdsong of early spring as she went. The leaves on the trees were not quite in full canopy, yet new growth was all around her. It was ironic, really. So many things seemed to be ending while the world was undergoing its annual renaissance.

Rose knew every ending brought a new beginning, but she didn't feel fresh and new. She felt rather old and weary. Where was she going with her life? She had no husband, no children, and soon she might have no job. She couldn't even find a boyfriend.

She sighed as she walked into the church, and felt depressed by the chatting of the members and the soft tittering of laughter as people filed into their familiar pews.

In that period between Lent and summertime, the time of rebirth and spring, the church was crowded. Just like the unfolding of the flowers and the trees, humans were also hungering for growth of the spiritual kind. At the end of May, when the weather turned hot, and summer activities were abundant, the congregation would shrink again until fall, when people felt the need to rest and return inward.

Rose took her usual seat, two rows from the back along the righthand side of the church facing the pulpit. She was aware of how alone she was in the midst of the families and the couples who passed by on the way to their seats. A number of congregants gave her small, sympathetic smiles as they passed, in remembrance of Mid. And maybe in sympathy for Rose's entire sad life.

Poor Rose, she imagined them thinking. *Lost her parents at sixteen, barely graduated from high school only to be saved by Mid, then left with nothing.*

Rose shut her eyes and bowed her head, as if in prayer. But she wasn't meditating. She was avoiding the gazes and glances of the people chatting quietly around her. She was sorry she'd come.

After a few minutes, the choir, dressed in their long burgundy robes, moved in single file to the loft at the right of the pulpit.

The sanctuary was a simple one. The stained glass in the tall windows was lovely but not elaborate. There were no statues, sculptures, or paintings. The treasure here was the people—both the congregation and the townsfolk.

But people were people. They meant well, but they were insecure and curious. They meddled; they judged. They also loved and supported. And as frustrated as Rose sometimes was with small-town life, this was her home. And mostly she loved it here.

As Mark Highberger, the music director, began to play the organ, and the tall, thin figure of Pastor Phillip Ballentine made his way down the aisle, Rose relaxed into the service.

Rose always enjoyed Pastor Ballentine's sermons and the sweet sounds of the choir. She enjoyed the quiet reverie of prayer, and the peace she felt while singing the familiar hymns. But despite all this, Rose couldn't say she was a religious person.

Rose preferred to believe there was a divine source—an unseen force connecting all things, all animals, and all people. The belief gave her much more peace than the idea of a judgmental human-like old-man figure watching over every thought, action, and intent.

She stared up at the calm presence of the pastor whose service today was about forgiveness. She didn't flatter herself to think the sermon or the prayer readings or the hymns had anything to do with her circumstances, but she considered the subject on her own terms anyway.

She carried some resentment, and it wasn't just because of recent events. There had also been her parents' accident, which had never been explained to Rose's satisfaction. She felt some misplaced bitterness toward Teddy, even though that wasn't fair. Teddy had only been a few years older than Rose when their parents had died. He'd put his life on hold to come back here, and he'd never quite restarted his own existence. She knew he blamed himself for so much. What could she possibly have expected of him? He'd been a kid.

Rose noticed Julie Newlin in her place front and center. Her two teenage boys on one side of her and a woman named Stella on the other. Every so often, Rose would catch a glimpse of Julie's striking face turned toward Stella, and she'd whisper something to which the other woman would raise her shoulders or tilt her head. Rose couldn't see Stella's profile—only the back of her head.

The frequent exchanges distracted Rose, and she found herself starting to resent Julie.

The woman seemed to thrive on human interaction. And a lot of that interaction, in Rose's experience, had been chatter about other people. Rose didn't think Julie meant any harm, but she found it concerning that in her position as church secretary Julie possessed access to sensitive information, and she sometimes shared things she ought to keep to herself. Or opinions better left unsaid.

Before Rose knew it, Pastor Ballentine was asking

the congregation to rise for the final hymn, the sermon over. Rose had missed much of it thinking about Julie.

She set her jaw, but she sang 'There Is Sunshine In My Soul Today', despite feeling rather gloomy.

Then the pastor left his place in the sanctuary. He smiled his way down the aisle, pausing every so often to share a word or two with a member of the congregation. He smiled warmly at Rose, then took his place at the door of the church to shake hands with the parishioners as they filed out. People would be on their way to after-church lunches, family dinners, or other Sunday afternoon activities.

Rose got up, taking her place next to an elderly woman named Gladys Curry.

"How are you holding up, dear?"

The woman's tone was kindly, and Rose was appreciative of the concern. "I'm fine. Tough week."

"Of course," said the woman. "You know, I'm eighty-three. I've experienced a lot of loss in my life. It doesn't get any easier, but you do get through it. I know you know that too, dear."

Rose smiled. "It doesn't hurt to hear it again."

When Rose reached Pastor Ballentine, he took both her hands in his. He was about forty, if Rose had to guess, and had been assigned to the church two years earlier. As far as Rose knew, he'd never been married. He had kind, soft eyes, and wore black horn-rimmed glasses that overwhelmed his face.

He didn't become involved in petty politics, and he didn't engage in gossip. He was a gentle steadying force for not only the church, but the entire town.

"Ms. Glasser…I am so glad you made it today."

The use of her last name was a bit jarring. Certainly, he knew her as Rose. But she managed a light laugh. "Where else would I be?"

"You could have chosen to be anywhere, but you've chosen to be here with your church family."

Rose didn't think of church as family. They were a sympathetic group of people who she felt marginally comfortable with. And she was confident they would help her if she needed it.

"Thank you, Pastor, for everything. I know we didn't get to talk after Mid's service on Friday, but it was lovely. She would have been very pleased."

He leaned forward. "You can call me Phillip."

Rose knew others called him by his first name, but she just didn't feel comfortable with that level of familiarity. So she just smiled.

"I do hope you know how much Mid loved you."

"Of course."

"I don't think Mid would mind me sharing that the last conversation I had with her was about you. About how much you touched her life." Pastor Ballentine dipped his head to look at her over those heavy glasses. "You've touched a lot of lives here."

Rose's smile faltered. She knew she was part of this

community, but she always felt a little bit on the outside even though she'd lived here her entire life. Despite this being home.

"I'm only a phone call away if you need me," he said.

"Thank you, Pastor."

"Phillip," he corrected.

Aware of the line behind them, Rose pulled her hands from his, murmured a thank you, and moved out the front door. She was about to start her walk back to the house when she heard her name from the parking lot. She turned.

Julie Newlin was coming toward her. Rose sighed, but pasted a smile on her face.

"Rose," she said, her name ending on a small squeal. "I feel like I should thank you."

"Thank me for what?"

"For introducing me to your friend."

At Rose's blank look, she said, "You know, your friend in the salon." She winked.

Rose realized she was talking about the handsome stranger. She had hoped he was gone, out of her life forever. She didn't want to spare another second of energy thinking about him, and yet here she was, remembering the feel of his hair in her fingers.

Rose's defenses were up. And by the self-satisfied look on Julie's face, Rose knew she wasn't going to like what the other woman had to say.

Julie wanted Rose to ask questions. But Rose wasn't playing. She just blinked at Julie.

Julie made a small, impatient noise at the back of her throat. "I ran into him," she said. "On Friday evening. Or rather, he ran into *me* right here in the church parking lot." She gestured toward a spot at the end of the parking area.

A slow burn flowed through Rose's limbs—a combination of anger, jealousy, and fear, she realized. *What was that about?*

If Julie noticed Rose's vexation, she didn't show it. "I hate to see a man who's so down on his luck. You know?"

Rose didn't know, and she didn't want to know. "I should really be going. I've got some things to take care of this afternoon."

That was a lie. Rose had absolutely nothing going on that afternoon.

Julie ignored her comment. "You have to admit, he is a fascinating guy, with an absolutely captivating background and story. Don't you think?"

Rose clenched her jaw and let out a slow breath through her nose. "I wouldn't know."

Julie's eyes went wide. "You don't *know*?" She drew out the 'o' sound in the last word. "He didn't tell you?" Julie made a tsking sound with her tongue. "I'm not sure I'm the one who should be giving you the news…"

Rose had had enough. She'd had enough meddling,

enough gossip, enough drama. She'd had enough of this strange man whom she didn't want to know anyway.

"I would agree with that assessment," Rose said, her tone more caustic than usual. "I don't need to know anything from you. And I don't need to know anything about him."

Julie looked surprised at first, then she narrowed her eyes. "I don't know what you're implying."

"I'm not *implying* anything. I'm flat-out telling you—I don't want to be party to your gossip. Please, for once, just keep it to yourself."

The other woman put a hand to her chest. "I was just trying to help."

"Sharing information that isn't yours to share is never helpful. In fact, all it does is stir up trouble."

Julie's mouth dropped open. "Are you calling me a troublemaker?" Her tone was one of incredulity.

"I didn't call you anything, but if the shoe fits…"

Rose was relatively certain Julie had been called worse things in her life. So Rose was not prepared for the tears that welled up in the other woman's eyes.

"Is that what you think of me?"

Rose let out a breath. She certainly hadn't meant to make the other woman cry. And she said as much. "I'm sorry," she said, softening her voice. "I'm not making excuses, but I've had a really tough week. And next week isn't going to be much better. I'm happy you made a new friend, but I don't need to know about it."

"I just thought you would have wanted to know his intention." Her voice was wobbly.

The conversation was painful. Rose just wanted to go home.

Julie dashed away a tear quivering on the end of her long eyelashes. "I'm just so sorry I offended you."

"You didn't offend me," Rose said.

Julie nodded once, but her normally cheerful face had lost all its joy.

"I appreciate you were trying to be nice. And I'm sorry if I hurt your feelings."

Julie gave a small nod of her head.

Rose didn't know what else to say, so she let out a sigh and simply walked away. The whole walk home, she replayed the conversation in her head, wondering if she should have reacted differently. But honestly, she couldn't come up with a better response. She didn't want to know Julie had interacted with the handsome man. She didn't want to know what they had done, or even what they'd said. It really didn't matter.

When she got to her house, she changed out of her church clothes into a pair of yoga pants and a long-sleeved, soft gray T-shirt, bearing the name of a college she hadn't attended.

She texted Della, who was working the front desk of My Pink Wink.

—How is everything going there?

—All good. Back-to-school rush.

Rose was about to type a response when an ellipsis appeared, indicating that Della was typing. The message came through a few seconds later.

—Don't even think about coming in today. It's your day off. Go have fun.

Rose didn't respond. She didn't even know what fun was.

As if to drive the point home to herself, she shoved her feet into a pair of sneakers, donned a light windbreaker, and walked toward the cemetery, which extended down an isolated lane next to the Sweetwood. *How fun was that?* she thought wryly.

But the temperatures were warm, the breeze was light, and the sky blue. There were much worse ways to spend a Sunday afternoon.

The memorial lawn was quiet and empty, except for one small car parked on the lane. Lena Newbury was clearing stray leaves and debris from the tomb of her mother.

Lena didn't look up, and Rose kept her eyes averted.

She reached the end of the lane and hiked up the small rise where Mid had been laid to rest just two days earlier. The dirt was a fat brown mound marked by a small bronze placard supplied by the funeral home. Rose would meet with the monument company in the next few weeks to have the headstone designed and placed after the ground had settled, most likely in late autumn.

Atop the mound of dirt was scattered a blanket of pink petals from the plethora of flowers that had celebrated Mid's life. It was a cheerful pop of color on a melancholic scene.

She couldn't quite picture Mid's body—so full of life just a week earlier—lying underneath the heavy soil. The thought of it made her claustrophobic.

Rose stared at the dirt for a long while, trying to summon some words or a prayer. But she didn't have anything to say to Mid here. Mid's essence wasn't in this cold, lonely cemetery. It was in the bustle of the shop, in the song of the church. This place, Rose felt, was nothing more than a repository.

Rose's parents were buried in the cemetery, too, but she didn't visit them. When she'd been younger, the place seemed to hold a dark energy—likely coming from a place inside of her, rather than the cemetery itself. When she thought about their resting place, a weight settled in her sternum and prevented her from breathing deeply.

As she shoved her hands into her pockets and turned to walk away, another small bronze marker, identical to Mid's, caught her eye. Rose leaned forward, peering at the name, wondering whose family had forgotten their loved one by not erecting a more permanent memorial.

To her surprise, the name on the marker was Madeline Higgins Stangel. Mid's sister. And mother of the man Rose was to meet at Mid's house the next day.

Rose peered at the date, marked five years earlier. Then she frowned. She could not recall Mid mentioning a service for her sister. Was it possible Mid's sister had died and been buried right here in this town without anyone having realized it?

The thought made Rose incredibly sad. It also made her angry. This Griffin Stangel person could not even be bothered to order a headstone for his mother, and yet he was inheriting all of Mid's property? She hadn't met the man, yet she despised him desperately and with a passion she rarely felt about anything in life.

She was scowling when she turned to walk away, and still scowling when she reached the crest of the small knoll on the road leading out of the cemetery. The sound of an engine coming toward her caused her to move to the side just before a white Mercedes traveling well over the ten-mile-per-hour speed limit barreled toward her.

It was that man again, looking even more dashing than he had two days before. His eyes widened in surprise at her presence.

"Slow down!" Rose yelled, and threw her hands up in the air for emphasis.

He stopped abruptly, but she kept walking. What the hell was he doing here? And why did she keep running into him?

Rose knew some people tended to exist on the same threads of energy. They were the ones she encountered over and over again at the grocery store or at the dentist's office. Normally she thought it was benign, and rarely gave it more than a moment's thought. But this guy—she had to wonder what the universe was trying to tell her.

Her conversation with Julie Newlin came back to her and she quickened her pace.

"Hey," he said, as he leaned out the window.

She wanted to keep going, but her blasted manners made her stop.

She turned around. "What?" she asked in a belligerent voice.

He reversed so he was right beside her. She glared at him.

They stared at each other for a few long seconds without speaking. It was Rose who finally broke. "What are you even doing here? I thought you were just passing through town. You've said that multiple times, if I recall correctly." And she did recall correctly. "If that's the case, why in the world are you in the cemetery?"

He looked at her with his mouth slightly open as if he was contemplating saying something. When he didn't, a prickly perception crawled up her spine. Rose couldn't quite interpret it, but she knew she had to get away. She turned again.

She told herself she was overreacting. There was no reason in the world she should be getting this worked up about this particular person. She was letting her emotions run away with her, which was something she didn't normally allow.

"Rose…"

Her name on his lips was soft and easy. It sounded like a whisper. A breath. How did he know her name? He may have overheard Teddy in the Sweetwood. Or more likely, he'd learned it from Julie. She bristled. "There's something I need to tell you," he continued. The words were just as low, just as soft.

They were dangerous. Portentous.

Rose's senses, already heightened, tingled. Her extremities cooled, and a shiver of apprehension ran through her. Whatever it was he had to say, she didn't want to hear it. Because, deep down, she knew what it was. She wondered if she'd known the first time she saw him.

"I'm in town…" He stopped and wetted his lips. "I came here because last week, I received a phone call."

"From who?" she asked softly. But she knew the answer.

"Howard Lincoln." He paused. Rose looked off into the distance at the neat rows of monuments lining the hillside, at the tops of the trees surrounding the cemetery swaying in the breeze.

He continued. "I came to the cemetery today to see where my aunt was buried. And also to visit my mother's resting place for the first time."

Rose wrapped her arms around her middle. She couldn't look at him. She was silent.

"I should have told you this the first time I met you, but I didn't know how. My name is Griffin Stangel."

Chapter 11

The blood drained from Rose's face.

She was a fool. She should have known from the beginning who he was. She'd even voiced her suspicions aloud. But Howard had assured her Griffin Stangel wasn't yet in town. And she'd wanted to believe it.

She had painted a much different picture of the man in her imagination. In her mind, Griffin Stangel was a miserly and unpleasant man with a wispy combover and crooked teeth. He was small and he was greedy. He was someone who had abandoned his own mother and never bothered to meet his aunt.

This last part was true of the man in the car idling beside her, but Rose couldn't quite reconcile the striking face and perfect hair as that of Mid's absentee nephew.

Why hadn't she thought to do an internet search of the name?

But Rose knew the answer to the question. The woman who had been like a second mother to her had just died. Rose had other things on her mind. She didn't spend a lot of time online as it was. She had no social media, and she got her news the old-fashioned way through newspapers and the nightly news on television, which she'd watched every evening with Mid.

It was unusual for a woman of her age to avoid an online presence, but honestly, the constant connection and instant access to the World Wide Web and social media made her itchy. She didn't want everyone to know her business.

My Pink Wink had social media accounts, and Halle and Alyssa often posted pictures of clients' hairstyles online. This was all perfectly fine with Rose. She understood the need for branding. But it wasn't something she had ever felt the need in which to personally participate.

So, no. She would not have immediately thought to run a search on Griffin Stangel.

She stood there silently for so long that this man—Griffin—said to her, "Are you all right?"

His low, smooth voice brought her out of her reverie. "What are you doing here?" she finally managed to ask.

"I told you—Howard called me."

She shook her head. "What are you doing *here*, in this cemetery? And don't tell me you're paying your respects to Mid. You couldn't even be bothered to come to her funeral."

Griffin looked straight ahead for a moment. "It didn't seem right to show up at her funeral just because she died without making a will, and I happened to be her beneficiary. It seemed hypocritical."

He was right. "I'll repeat my question then. Why are you here?"

Again, the sulky, petulant look, making the man look like a little boy.

He lifted a shoulder. "My mother…she's here. Somewhere."

The realization hit Rose. Of course. Madeline Higgins Stangel. The lonely plot beside Mid. The one without the marker.

"You didn't even go to your mother's funeral."

He had the grace to look guilty. But then, with a note of defensiveness in his voice, he said, "My mother had no funeral. She was cremated and buried here a couple of years ago. It was months before I even found out she died."

That shocked Rose into silence for a moment. But then she realized what it meant. He'd been so estranged from his mother that he hadn't known she no longer held space on this earth. No phone calls, no impromptu visits. Not even a quick check with another family member to question her well-being.

As someone who would have given nearly anything to have one more conversation with her own mother, she couldn't imagine willingly giving up the relationship.

Rose rocked back on her heels, trying to decide how she felt. Anger was infinitely more comfortable than the other emotions sitting deep in her chest.

She felt mostly humiliated. This man had come into her brother's place of business and concealed his identity, laughing at her the whole time. Then he had come into *her* place of business, and…done what? Gotten a haircut she'd offered? Made her feel attracted to him?

And there it was. What irked her most of all. She'd been weak and predictable. He was probably used to that quality in women—using his looks to get them right where he wanted. Just like he'd done with Julie…

"I know the circumstances aren't ideal, but I was hoping—"

"Ideal?" The words burst forth. "This is an utter disaster."

Two figures approached from over the small hill where Rose was standing—Pastor Ballentine and his dog Samson, a German shepherd and husky mix with blue eyes and a playful personality.

When Samson saw Rose, he began whining and pulling at his leash so she could pet him, which she did every time she encountered the pair on their daily walk.

The dog excitedly panted and nuzzled Rose's hand and thigh. He was too well-behaved to jump. Rose reached down and scratched him behind his ears.

A frown creased Pastor Ballentine's forehead as he glanced at the white car and Griffin Stangel sitting inside. "Is everything okay here?"

She wondered if he'd heard her last words.

"Everything's fine, Pastor," she said. "I was just heading home."

Behind his thick black glasses, Pastor Ballentine squinted at the man behind the wheel of the car. Rose could see the concern in his pale blue eyes.

He may have been waiting for Rose to introduce him, but Rose was not going to do that. So Pastor Ballentine leaned forward, his left hand still holding to Samson's leash. "I'm Phillip Ballentine. And you are?"

"Griffin Stangel. Mid Higgins' nephew."

Pastor Ballentine straightened. "Griffin Stangel?" He looked at Rose, who kept her face purposely blank. He turned back to the man. "*The* Griffin Stangel? The baseball player?"

"What?" Rose said. She knew very little about sports in general and nothing about baseball. But the question had still set her on edge.

The man in the car was silent, but Pastor Ballentine became suddenly animated, talking to both Rose and Griffin simultaneously. "He had an MVP season a few years ago. He hit more home runs and stole more bases in the past few years than any other player in the League." He turned to face Griffin. "Wasn't your OBP and slugging average the highest that season, too, with an insane contract with the Red Sox? $200 million?"

Rose's mouth dropped open. Griffin looked embarrassed.

She turned to Pastor Ballentine. "This is not the same man," just as Griffin said, "That's all over now."

"It sure is," Pastor Ballentine remarked. "And after what happened with the Bryants and the trouble you had a few weeks ago…You've been all over sports news."

Rose's head was spinning. She looked from one man to the other. Then she said to Griffin, "You're famous?"

It was Pastor Ballentine who answered. "He's *infamous*. But I don't know if I would've recognized you without your name. Your hair and beard are much shorter than your signature disheveled look."

Rose glanced at Griffin, and he looked at her. She quickly broke eye contact.

"I had no idea you were Mid's nephew," Pastor Ballentine continued, unaware of Rose's shock and discomfort. "She'd never said anything. Unfortunately, you missed her funeral."

"He's Mid's beneficiary," Rose answered.

Understanding finally dawned, and Pastor Ballentine gave Rose an apologetic look.

He turned back to Griffin. "I don't believe Mid has much in the way of assets. It's Rose who's handled all of her affairs."

Rose said quietly, "The salon."

"Oh, but surely there's no interest there for you," he said to Griffin.

Samson gave a small whine at Rose's drifting attention. Rose crouched and took the dog's big head between her hands, burying her face in its soft fur and allowing it to lick her neck.

Griffin's voice was controlled when he said, "Mid's lawyer called me last week. Rose and I are meeting with him tomorrow."

Pastor Ballentine looked between the two of them. He seemed to finally understand Rose might lose the salon. *Madison* might lose the salon. Though he'd been right to question one thing—of what interest could My Pink Wink be to a retired Major League baseball player, who seemingly had plenty of his own money?

Some of the starstruck admiration finally eased from the pastor's face, and his expression reverted back to suspicion. "And you decided to take a drive in our cemetery?"

"My mother is buried here. I just thought I might…" He paused. "I thought I might stop by her resting place. I didn't realize that was a crime here." His tone was annoyed and defensive.

All of the questions had finally gotten to him, Rose thought. Good.

Rose straightened from her crouching position,

though she kept her hand outstretched for the dog to nuzzle.

"Did you know Madeline Higgins was buried here, Pastor Ballentine?"

"I don't believe so, but I wouldn't necessarily know every occupant in the cemetery. Especially if I didn't officiate the service."

She turned to Griffin. "Who did you say it was performed your mother's service?" It was a low blow. Given the man hadn't even known his mother had died, she doubted he'd any idea what arrangements had been made for her memorial.

A muscle ticked on the side of Griffin's face.

Pastor Ballentine, who finally sensed the animosity between them, in addition to the tension, glanced from one to the other. "Rose, can I walk you back home?"

"It's fine, Pastor. You just got here for your walk with Samson. I'm capable of walking back on my own."

"Both Samson and I will enjoy your company more than a prolonged stroll." He smiled at her, those kind eyes seeing more than she was comfortable with.

To Griffin, he said, "It was nice meeting you, Mr. Stangel." Rose caught the slight dip of his voice on the word 'nice'. "I'm sure you won't be in town long, so we probably won't cross paths again."

The pastor turned his back on the car, dismissing the man. And at that, Rose gave a slight smile. She knew Pastor Ballentine hadn't meant it as a threat, but there was definitely an emphasis on the words. No one wanted to see Griffin Stangel in this town. Not even the people who apparently had followed his career.

In that moment, Samson jumped up on the car and sniffed into the open window.

"Samson, down." Pastor Ballentine gently tugged the leash.

But Griffin was nuzzling the dog's neck while Samson licked his face.

Rose didn't want this guy to be a dog lover. He was the villain in her story. It was hard to hold that position when he was making kissing faces at the big, friendly creature.

Pastor Ballentine's manners kicked in, and he said "Down" more forcefully.

Samson obeyed and gave his owner a guilty look. He sat on the ground panting and looking mournful.

"I'm so sorry," he said to Griffin. "He doesn't know how big he is."

"It's fine," Griffin responded. "I've always wanted a dog, but my lifestyle just wasn't conducive to having a pet. And my apartment in Boston doesn't allow furry friends."

"Sounds like you need a new apartment," said Pastor Ballentine, some of the veneration returning. The man was a sucker for an animal lover.

Rose had to admit—Griffin looked like a dog person. She could almost picture him playing fetch with a big dog in the park across from Mid's house…

She quickly dashed the unexpected vision.

Pastor Ballentine looked to Rose, and she turned and walked by his side away from the white car. She did not say goodbye.

She was grateful for the pastor's solid presence as they moved in the opposite direction. But she was acutely aware of Griffin, still parked where they had left him.

After a minute, she glanced over her shoulder, and saw him driving slowly toward the end of the cemetery drive, where both Mid and her sister Mad were resting. She hoped his presence did not interrupt their peace.

Chapter 12

Griffin couldn't remember feeling more like a heel. Not even when he'd been confronted by Charlie Bryant as he toasted a glass of 1982 Chateau Lafite Rothschild in Row 34 with the man's wife.

He wasn't sure what it was about Rose Glasser that made him feel so unsteady on his feet. Hell, the first time he'd seen her, he'd nearly stumbled and fallen, and taken her with him.

He considered Rose's effect on him as he showered under a weak stream of tepid water in the cramped bathroom of the roadside hotel just off the interstate. The space was decorated in unflattering browns and beiges, and the taupe shower curtain reeked of mildew.

He twisted the faucet counterclockwise and stood in the steamy room as he dragged a rough, threadbare towel over his skin. Stepping out of the bathtub onto a floormat embossed with the hotel's logo, he wiped the steamy mirror with the towel.

His image was distorted in the steam, yet it still gave him a shock. The short hair and trim beard caught him off guard every time, and just for an instant, he didn't recognize himself.

He'd picked up a cheap electric razor at a chain department store the prior afternoon, and he did his best to replicate the look Rose had given him on Friday.

As he shaved, he thought about Pastor Ballentine and snorted. A man of God, he thought cynically, would not have looked at a woman the way that guy was looking at Rose. Griffin realized the man wasn't a priest, but still. He should have had some decorum, surely. He'd know she was married to Teddy. Even Griffin knew that, and *he* didn't live there.

Maybe Rose and Teddy had an open relationship. The possibility caused a surge of optimism to rush through him. But it was quickly dashed. Rose wasn't the type of woman he'd want to share.

He nicked the teeth of the razor against his skin, causing him to flinch and swear. A small cut under his jaw blossomed red, and he tore off a small corner of toilet paper from the roll on the wall and pressed it against his neck.

His complicated feelings for Rose didn't matter. He'd be gone soon enough. He only needed to stay long enough for Irv to make a deal with the district attorney to keep his ass out of the legal system, and out of the media.

The fog on the mirror had disappeared. He considered his reflection. Maybe it was the sallow lighting in the room, but his eyes looked sharper and his skin clearer than he remembered. The pouches under his eyes also seemed less pronounced.

He looked down at his stomach, which was still relatively flat, but now held the threat of puffiness that came from too little exercise and too much alcohol. Even that part of his body seemed less distended than it had before he'd left Boston. He hadn't had a drink since he'd sat on that stool in the Sweetwood Saloon. Over the past few months, four days was a record for him.

Julie Newlin, his new friend from the church, had offered him wine and beer when he'd taken up her offer of dinner on Friday night. She hadn't had any hard liquor in the house—not with her teenage boys around, she'd said. But Griffin had turned down the drink, though he wasn't sure why.

Julie was a knockout, and exactly his type: pleasant, talkative, lively, and uncomplicated. When he'd shared his career with her—not a baseball fan herself, she'd never heard his name before—she'd been charmingly impressed, asking him all the right questions without being overcome.

They'd been alone; her boys were spending the weekend with their father who lived closer to the city. And after a satisfying dinner of roast chicken and vegetables and apple pie for dessert, he'd sat with Julie in her cozy little living room, decorated in pastel colors and with framed Bible verses on the walls.

Griffin had settled on the sofa, and she'd folded herself next to him, tucking her long legs beneath her and leaning into his space. As they talked, she'd touched him, first playfully then meaningfully, when he said something she thought was amusing or profound.

As the time ticked on, the touch became more suggestive.

Griffin took the suggestion. He'd leaned in and borne down. He kissed her and slid his hands up her soft belly to her softer breasts.

She nipped at his ear with her teeth then slid her tongue down his throat.

She responded when he teased his thumbs over her nipples, working furiously at the zipper of his jeans until she almost—but not quite—worked her hands inside his fly.

And he'd almost let her. It would have been so easy to let her. But all he could envision was Rose's face. Rose's hands. Rose's body.

So he'd gently disentangled himself, thanked Julie for her hospitality, and explained that he wasn't looking for a meaningless fling.

This pleased her more than he'd meant it to, but he didn't bother to correct any misconceptions his words may have caused.

A casual encounter in this small town was a bad

idea. He told himself he didn't want to hurt a woman as nice as Julie. And he would hurt her, there was no doubt.

But none of that had stopped him before.

What stopped him this time was the look in Rose's eyes as she'd looked down at him over that sink. It hadn't been flirtatious, and it hadn't been playful. He'd felt a real connection. And he couldn't remember the last time he'd felt that with anyone.

Not even Victoria, and he'd been willing to throw away his entire life for her.

He kept reminding himself Rose was spoken for, but it didn't seem to matter.

That concerned him too. Was he so addicted to complication and trouble, and maybe commitment, that he rejected the perfectly available and beautiful woman who'd thrown herself at him all evening for the attractive unavailable woman who also hated him?

He tried to avoid thinking about both Rose and Julie as he dressed in a pair of clean indigo jeans, a brown three-button T-shirt, and a blue and beige checked flannel shirt with a warm sherpa lining. He shoved his feet into a pair of good Riomar loafers he'd bought on a whim when he'd been dating Victoria.

Dating, he thought with a scoff. He supposed you couldn't technically date someone who was already married.

He looked in the mirror again and ran his fingers

through the longer hair on the top of his head. It fell perfectly in place away from his brow.

Griffin wasn't a man with a false sense of humility. He'd always known the effect he had on women. In high school, girls had practically fallen at his feet. In one incredibly precarious situation, a female teacher had also seemed more than a little interested in him outside of the classroom. She'd not been much older than him, and if fate had not intervened and the woman hadn't been transferred to another school…He still thrilled at the trouble it may have caused.

All of this had made his mother absolutely livid. She'd done everything in her power to tear him down, and make him believe that, despite his looks, he wasn't worth much of anything.

He wasn't sure why. Part of him wondered if it was because he resembled his father, who his mother had divorced years earlier.

Griffin had no idea what had happened between them, and he never asked. His father had moved to Arizona; Griffin spent time in the summers with him. Until his junior year of high school, when Griffin had moved in with his father and stepmother full-time.

Once Griffin left his mother's house, he'd spoken to her only on rare occasions—the occasional phone call on her birthday and Christmas. Each time they communicated, she managed to make him feel even more like a loser. It hadn't mattered that he'd excelled at baseball or did well in college. Hell, it hadn't even mattered when he'd been recruited to play for the Major League.

To his mother, he'd always been a failure.

Griffin walked through the small, dank hotel lobby, where a few people milling around glanced in his direction but left him alone. This was not the kind of hotel that invited unsolicited conversation—it was the only thing he appreciated about the place.

He climbed into the Mercedes and began his route back to Madison.

As he drove, he took in the scenery. It really was a lovely place, he realized. After the concrete jungle of Boston, he appreciated the trees, the greenery, and the slower pace of this rural area. On his left, farmland bucolic with grazing cows, and on his right, a quaint and inviting country store. He felt like he could breathe here.

He also found himself strangely attracted to the camaraderie that seemed to exist in Madison. After his transitory childhood and career, he'd rarely been in one place long enough for it to feel like home or to create meaningful relationships. And he'd failed miserably the past year he'd been in Boston.

The closest thing he'd had to a real family was the time he'd spent with his father and stepmother during the brief period in high school. But even then, he'd felt like a stranger in their home.

Griffin blinked through the windshield and let out a breath. There was no sense in dwelling on the lovely scenery or the friendly people of this town—he wasn't thinking about staying. Far from it.

When he pulled off the street in front of his aunt's house, there were already two cars occupying the drive. One was an older light-blue hatchback. While it was clean and looked well-maintained, it had seen some miles. The other vehicle was a Town Car. Though he hadn't yet met Howard in person, there was no doubt in Griffin's mind this vehicle belonged to the lawyer.

He picked up his phone from the center console and noticed he had three missed calls from Howard. It was ten past nine; he was a few minutes late. Not, he thought, late enough to necessitate three missed calls. Since he was right outside, he didn't bother to call Howard back. Instead, he jogged to the front door with its frosted decorative panes of glass and knocked once before pushing it open.

"Hello?"

Howard hollered a greeting from the back of the house.

Griffin followed the direction of the man's voice through the outdated living room into a cramped kitchen. Rose sat at a small round oak table, her hands folded demurely in front of her. She didn't look at him.

Howard half stood when he entered the room, looking flustered.

The man was as old as Griffin had predicted, but managed to hold an air of both competence and discomfiture.

In his half-standing position, he offered Griffin a surprisingly firm handshake. Then he gestured toward the empty seat next to Rose. He peered at Griffin. "You're younger than I expected."

Griffin wasn't sure if the words were a compliment or an insult, so he didn't respond.

Rose's eyes were still averted.

Griffin said, "Hello."

She gave a half-hearted twist of her lips in return.

"Shall we get started?" Howard asked.

Griffin had an overwhelming urge to interrupt and simply tell them the truth about all of it—from the fistfight with Charlie Bryant to laying out the reporter in the middle of the street just a few weeks earlier. But who was he kidding? Everyone knew his name now; he didn't need to air his dirty laundry. The internet could do that for him just fine.

He wondered how appalled Rose had been when she'd inevitably searched his name and found all of his not-so-secret scandals.

He glanced over to see her chewing on her bottom lip; she looked about as innocent as they came.

"We are in Mid's house." Howard gestured around him at the kitchen with its dusty floral curtains and yellowish-green appliances that must have been installed in the 1980s. Or earlier. "Obviously, this would be an asset you would inherit, along with the contents. As the administrator of the will, Rose is available to help you arrange for assessment of the contents, should you require that." Howard looked at Griffin expectantly.

Griffin realized Howard was waiting for an answer.

"Is there anything of any value in here?" he asked. He hadn't meant to sound cynical, but his short walk through the house told him there was probably not a lot he'd consider to be in his style.

Rose spoke for the first time. "Not of any monetary value. But all of this stuff is pretty important to me."

It hadn't occurred to him Rose might want this property for herself. The business, yes. But Mid's possessions, and this dated house? Obviously Rose had been close with his aunt, but maybe he underestimated their relationship.

Because it wasn't the right time to ask the question, he said, "Would I have a couple of hours just to take a look?" He directed the question to Howard who bobbed his head up and down.

"Of course, of course. You're welcome to take all the time you need."

"There's probably not a lot here which would interest a man of your wealth." Rose's voice was flat.

"I'd actually be interested in getting to know who my aunt was."

"Like your mother?"

The question came fast, and it cut deeper than he might have expected. As warm as his feelings toward Rose were, this woman, whom he'd just met, had no right to judge him based on circumstances she didn't understand. Especially when he didn't understand them himself.

Before he could respond, Rose said, "I'm sorry. That was uncalled for."

Howard broke into the conversation. "I was hoping the two of you might tackle this project together. Estate administration is inherently challenging for many reasons. Is that going to be a problem?"

It was the most forceful Griffin had heard the man, and Rose gave a small shake of her head. He looked at Griffin.

"I don't have a problem."

Howard paused for good measure before continuing. He slid a slim stack of papers across the table toward Griffin.

Griffin thumbed through the report. Mid had a healthy financial portfolio, and though it was a sizable sum, it wasn't going to make anyone rich. He nodded and slid the papers to the side as both Rose and Howard watched him carefully.

"Of course, the cost of the funeral and burial will need to come out of this amount. Or the life insurance payout, when that comes." The lawyer slid another printout across the table with Mid's insurance policy information.

Rose added, "I have all the receipts from my personal expenses, and Jack Cummings can be paid directly when we're ready."

Howard opened his mouth to speak again, but Rose interrupted. "Just one more thing—the headstone. I'm meeting with the designer this week to talk about the monument, and that cost has not yet been incurred."

Griffin took a breath before asking his next question, then braced for the answer. "Do you think we might be able to…add a headstone for my mother?"

A shadow passed over Rose's face, just as he suspected it would, but this time, she just said, "I'm sure it can be arranged."

"Do you know how Mid felt about my mother?" The question had escaped from his lips as the thought was formed.

Rose gave a small shake of her head. "Mid only rarely spoke of her." She opened her mouth to say something else, then appeared as though she'd thought better of it and clamped her lips shut again.

"I suspect there was a reason for that."

Howard cleared his throat. "Let's get back to the subject at hand," he said. "My Pink Wink."

This time, it was Rose who supplied the report. She handed a manila envelope, stuffed thick with papers, to Griffin. "Financials for the past five years."

Griffin riffled through the paperwork—first the summary, followed by the detailed numbers. The summary document outlined the businesses, profit, and loss over the past half decade. It was a substantial increase, and Griffin noted Irv had been right about the growth potential.

He flipped through the other papers which were mostly detailed tax documents and general bookkeeping, then he turned back to the profit and loss report, noting the employees' salaries. Rose made a pittance compared to the other stylists.

Her eyes went to the page. When he glanced at her, she was ready with a response. "I don't need as much as some of the others. My house and car are paid for, and I have no family to raise."

He wondered why that was. He frowned, blaming it all on Teddy, the bastard.

"Seems to me maybe you should be paid more based on your management of the business."

She lifted a shoulder. "Others need it more than I do."

"You should be paid for your worth," he murmured. His eyes stayed on the paperwork, but he was thinking about his own situation. He'd been paid as much as he had for both legitimate and questionable reasons. He'd started out as a standout talent for the League. But after a while, his worth was based on his bad-boy antics which had brought fans into the stands and views to their televisions. The on-field fights—all justified, in his opinion—and off-field romances made him both admired and hated. In any case, the publicity had been good for his teams and for the League.

That assessment of his worth hadn't sat as well with him, but it had benefited him too, so he'd kept his mouth shut.

Griffin shut the folder with a snap. "May I ask why you've never expanded?"

Rose seemed surprised by the question. "We've added new stylists over the years as the business has grown."

"I imagine there have been offers from bigger, more well-known brands for partnership or acquisition." He knew from Irv this was indeed the case.

"I...I suppose there may have been a few inquiries."

Griffin waited, and then Rose said, "Mid wasn't much for progress. She liked the salon the way it was."

Something in Rose's voice made him doubt that excuse. She didn't meet his eye, and her voice sounded unsure. He had to wonder if Mid had even known about the offers if Rose had been the one managing the salon.

"I'd like to talk more about the potential."

Rose opened her mouth, but Howard interrupted. "Well, it will be your property. You're free to discuss whatever you wish with whomever you wish." He cleared his throat. "Next steps are to get your signature on a few things, and my office will take care of filing all the paperwork to make the necessary transfers." He pushed a separate stack of papers toward Griffin. "My Pink Wink will require restructuring, and probably a few separate meetings once you decide how you'd like to proceed. You may want to engage your own legal services. I'd recommend it, in fact. But for now, we can have the ownership transferred into your name rather easily, and the salon can keep operating under the same model as it is today."

Griffin looked down at the paperwork, tabbed with small, pointed sticky notes indicating where he should initial and sign. Howard held out a black pen.

Was this what he wanted and how he wanted it?

He glanced at Rose whose eyes were shiny.

He didn't take the pen. "I'd like to think about all of this, if I could." It wasn't meant to have gotten this far.

Rose's gaze snapped toward him and then away quickly.

For a long moment, Howard didn't say anything, the pen hovering between them. "This is a standard agreement to transfer the property. I only have your best interest at heart."

"I'd just feel better if I had Irv take a look at the paperwork."

"I'm not sure what Mr. Abbott would need to add. The assets are the assets."

Griffin looked at the man, and Howard withdrew

his hand with its offer of the pen. "Keep in mind the business has employees. They deserve to feel secure."

Although Griffin nodded, the last thing he wanted was to be responsible for the livelihoods of a bunch of people with families and futures. He could barely be trusted to be responsible for his own life. "Rose can just keep running things, as is?"

Howard glanced at Rose. "For now, yes. But we'll need to figure this out in short order." He began gathering up his papers and neatly sliding them into his worn brown briefcase. "Shall I have my assistant Emily set up another appointment?"

Griffin wasn't sure what to say to that. He had no idea how long he was expected to stay here. "Can we take care of this online?"

"That's certainly an option. Although, I prefer face-to-face interactions, if you're going to be in town…"

Suddenly, the weight of this responsibility sat heavy in his chest. If he signed on the dotted line, everything his aunt owned would now belong to him. After all those years of having no anchor, the offer of one made him feel as if he were about to drown. "I'll let you know."

Rose shifted in her seat, as if she didn't know if she should remain seated or stand.

"As you wish."

Rose kept glancing at Howard, who wasn't return-ing the attention. She finally turned to Griffin and looked at him directly. "I can show you around the house. As I said, there isn't much in the way of valuables, but this was Mid's childhood home, so there might be something you'd be interested in."

Griffin turned to Howard. "You said you knew Mid?"

"I knew Mid for a long time, but I certainly didn't know her as well as Rose did."

"But you knew her when she was young."

"That was a long time ago."

"I'd like to know more about my mother."

Howard hesitated, just for a second, but Griffin clocked it. "I think I mentioned I didn't know her as well as I'd known Mid."

"What can you tell me about their relationship back then?"

Howard shrugged. "They were twins. When they were young, you could barely tell them apart. When they got older—Well, let's just say they were very different people. I can't tell you much more than that." He glanced at his watch. "I'm afraid I have an appointment." He held out a hand. "Please have Mr. Abbott call me if he has any questions. Let's try to get this all settled soon."

Howard shot an apologetic look at Rose then hurried out the door.

Griffin's gaze followed the man's exit. "Well, that was strange."

"What?" Rose asked.

"Did you see the way he rushed out of here when I asked about my mother?"

"I think he just had another meeting." Rose stood from the table and slid her hands into the back pockets of her jeans. She seemed to be waiting for him to say something, and he wondered if this was her awkward version of a peace offering. Maybe because he hadn't immediately signed the paperwork she no longer considered him quite such an opportunist.

"What does Teddy think of all this?" he asked.

Rose frowned. "What do you mean?"

"You know, me being here—inheriting all this." He gestured around him. "I assume you told him who I am."

She lifted her shoulders, and her long hair fell forward with the movement. "I haven't spoken to him. And he's not a baseball fan, so I doubt he knows who you are."

Griffin gave a little laugh. "Of course not."

Her pleasant expression was fast disappearing, and Griffin realized that had been his intent. He preferred it when she hated him. It was safer that way.

"Do you want me to stay to go through any of the contents with you, or not?"

Griffin looked at her; the same electric look passed between them. He wanted her to stay, all right.

She must have felt the connection too, because she

looked away and caught her bottom lip between her teeth.

"I think I'll just stay here alone for a while," he said, though his imagination was filled with images of what he'd like to do with her if she *did* decide to stay.

"It's your house." Rose placed two keys on the table. "One is for the front door, and one is for the back door. I have a set, too; I can return them to you when you're ready."

In the cramped space, she passed very close to him on her way to the front door. He could smell the floral scent of her hair and feel the warmth of her body. He turned his head away.

When she reached the doorway, she turned back around. "Hey, can I ask you something?"

Her voice was soft, and Griffin didn't like the sharp twist in his belly or the stab of protectiveness he felt when he looked at her uncertain expression.

"What?" he asked, rougher than he'd meant to.

She opened her mouth, then seemed to think better of the question. "Never mind," she said. Before he could encourage her further, she was gone.

He shut his eyes and swore under his breath.

But it was better this way. No strings, he thought. At least no strings he didn't mind cutting.

He wanted Rose to stay intact.

Chapter 13

After Rose had left, Griffin looked around. His aunt had been gone for only a week, and already the place smelled close, like dust and the past.

It certainly wasn't a house he would have chosen—the small, squat residence was not much larger than his apartment in Boston. His apartment was spacious, with high ceilings, abundant windows, and an open-concept design. Mid's house was closed in by walls, furniture, and haphazardly placed decorative tables. Every wall was covered in framed art, though the term 'art' would be a stretch. He imagined most of the nature images or inspirational phrases had been purchased at a local department store.

One bold black frame held a print in thick cursive font: 'This Must Be The Place.'

The place for what? Griffin wondered.

On every surface was some sort of tchotchke. He surprised himself with recall of the word—one which had lodged itself in his mind as a distant memory of his mother. Madeline Stangel had hated clutter. As he looked around this home, he imagined the busy style of his mother's twin couldn't have been more different than Madeline's minimalist décor.

From a side table in the living room, he picked up a photograph of a woman and a younger girl standing in front of a rhododendron bush in full bloom. The woman looked hauntingly similar to his mother—of course this was Mildred. Mid. She was wearing a long bright pink dress splattered with yellow flowers, and one of her arms was thrown casually around the girl.

The girl…she had long, fine brown hair with soft waves. Though she was smiling, those eyes were sober and serious.

Griffin knew those eyes. He knew this girl.

Rose.

He replaced the photo and continued his inspection of the room, picking up a replica Washington monument—a giftshop purchase. He took in multiple dusty pink conch shells. A miniature building that read, 'Branson, Missouri'. And three crocheted items embroidered with Bible verses.

I can do everything through him who gives me strength; For I know the plans I have for you; My power is made perfect in weakness.

Griffin shook his head. He wasn't much of a believer in a higher power, so he didn't subscribe to the meaning behind those random quotations. But he got the appeal. Wouldn't it be nice and simple if those sayings were true?

Above the sofa was a large framed print that upon first glance appeared to be a rolling field split by a wooden fence. Dark mountains loomed in the distance. But upon further inspection, Griffin realized it was a battle scene. Men engaged in hand-to-hand combat on the field. Embedded in the frame beneath the print was a small gold plate reading, 'Gettysburg 1863'.

Griffin raised his eyebrows and blew out a breath. He couldn't say he knew his aunt any better after having toured the living room.

He inspected the other rooms of the house—the kitchen, small back bedrooms, and the bathroom—with the same sense of mystification and amusement. He imagined his mother's contempt, and it caused Griffin to approve of the homey chaos of the place.

But what was obvious was there was no trace of Madeline Higgins Stangel's presence in this home.

When he reached the master bedroom, his senses began to tingle. If there'd been any trace of his mother left, he suspected his aunt would have kept it hidden away in here. In private. His mother had been someone to be tucked away in the dark corner of the mind, where she couldn't reach others you might care about.

Griffin found his palms were sweating. A looming sense of foreboding flowed through him. He pushed through it and looked around.

The king-sized bed was neatly made with a floral comforter and half a dozen matching and coordinated pillows. As in the other rooms, little decorative boxes and photographs covered every surface.

Griffin approached the nightstand next to the bed. Staring up at him was a photograph from what appeared to be a few decades earlier, in which a group of people stood outside My Pink Wink. He recognized his aunt, beaming from the center of the group. Rose was not in this photo.

He moved to the dresser and looked at another photograph, searching with dread and anticipation for some evidence of his mother. But this photo was of a group of children in front of a church sanctuary. Griffin peered at the group; one of the taller boys in the back of the clump of children caught his eye. It was a miniature of the scowling bartender from the Sweetwood Saloon. Rose's husband, Teddy.

Had everyone in this town been here forever?

He found himself scouring the photograph for Rose. There was one child—much younger—with those same eyes.

Staring at the group of children made him anxious. He'd never been particularly good with children.

But that wasn't quite true, he thought. He'd not been around many children at all, save for the organized activities his teams' PR departments had planned with groups of disadvantaged children.

There'd been one activity which had solidified Griffin's decision never to have children of his own. He didn't like to think about the experience, but he found himself remembering it now in vivid detail, as if this bedroom was a commemoration of the past.

The Last Wish program for terminally ill children was one Griffin had wanted to refuse but found he couldn't. Other teammates were deeply touched and honored by those requests. Griffin accepted only one in his career, and he'd been mortified. He wasn't worthy of that sort of honor. But he'd gone to the children's hospital alone with a pit in his stomach and a weight on his chest.

On his walk to the room—Room 323, he remembered—he was thoroughly unnerved by the bright colors on the walls, the cheerful scrubs worn by the nurses and doctors, and the smiling faces of the staff, juxtaposed with the rail-thin and pale children who stared up at him with humongous, haunted eyes from hospital beds and wheelchairs.

Many of the kids had no hair, or wispy strands clinging to their smooth scalps, and most were attached to tubes and wires, while parents leaned forward with falsely optimistic expressions on weary faces.

In room 323, eight-year-old Chase Gordon lay in his bed wearing a red shirt with Griffin's number and name which swallowed the boy's ravaged body. His eyes were impossibly blue behind red plastic glasses. Griffin had never seen a smile so wide and welcoming.

No one in his life had ever been as happy to see him as Chase had been that day.

Chase was missing his two front teeth.

Chase's mother was a blonde slip of a woman who looked a lot like Chase. She pumped Griffin's calloused hand with her two small ones and explained that Chase's dad was at work and wished he could've been there. Baseball was something they watched together, and Griffin was their all-time favorite player because he played and lived with reckless abandon. Chase and his father agreed that's how it should be done.

That wasn't true, but Griffin let them believe it was. In reality, Griffin simply didn't think about consequences until it was too late. Then he regretted every moment.

Griffin was awkward during the visit, but neither Chase nor his mother seemed to notice. Chase smiled and giggled the entire time, looking like he'd be awarded the ultimate prize.

Kid, you have no idea what a loser I am, Griffin had wanted to say. He'd never felt like a bigger fraud in his life.

He gave the boy a signed ball and his favorite glove, and then leaned in close while the mother snapped a photograph of the two of them. Chase beamed, but Griffin wore a pained expression. He leaned forward, his body tilted toward Chase and his right hand hovering somewhere in the vicinity of Chase's narrow frail shoulders. Chase held up his ball and glove like an offering to the heavens as his entire being brimmed with joy and life.

Griffin had itched to get out of that room, and he hadn't stayed as long as he should have, looking back. The next day, the team's publicist texted him a copy of the photo; Griffin closed the text quickly. Two weeks later, he received a copy of Chase's death notice, featuring the same photo as the boy's memorial.

Griffin had never cried so hard in his life.

Both the photograph and the write-up of Chase's short life had been printed out and were tucked in with Griffin's most important belongings, kept among the scant items Griffin moved from place to place.

He rarely looked at them. He just knew they existed as a reminder of…of what? Of the fragility of life, he supposed.

He wished he could've lived up to Chase's belief in him.

But one thing the encounter taught him—the potential pain of losing a child was not worth the risk of feeling that way again. When he looked at the photograph of the children on Mid's dresser, all he saw was potential pain.

He sighed and continued walking around the room, scowling now.

He halfheartedly began opening and shutting drawers, feeling like an intruder.

There were items of clothing—sweaters, polyester pants, silky robes, and nightclothes. He barely peeked into the drawer holding his aunt's underthings.

He looked around. Searching this house was a big task, and he didn't think he was up to it.

The nightstand next to the bed caught his eye, and he moved toward it. Underneath the table's surface was a nearly hidden compartment. Griffin ran his fingers across the varnished wood and felt an indentation and a smooth latch.

He tugged and a drawer slid out.

The compartment was deep and held a stack of paperwork. He pulled out the papers—old business documents, canceled checks, random items. Church pamphlets which must have held some significance to Mid, the program for a musical in Toronto, a number of receipts for household purchases—a new dishwasher, garage door replacement, and installation of an air conditioner.

At the bottom of the pile of papers, Griffin discovered a slim leather-bound journal.

It fell open to a page holding a photograph between sheets filled with spiky blue handwriting.

The photo was an old Polaroid turned sepia with age. A young woman who looked like his mother sat on a bench wearing a short skirt and an impressively low-cut flowery top. By the jaunty tilt of her head, Griffin could tell this was not Madeline Stangel. The nose of this woman was elongated, the cheekbones more pronounced, and the chin ended in a heart-shaped point.

The young woman's hand was on a man's knee, and she leaned close to him. His head was thrown back, his mouth gaping, his eyes closed—as if he'd just heard the most hysterical joke in the world.

Griffin had no doubt who the man was. This was his father, Max Stangel.

He stared hard at the photograph, trying to decipher it. A woman—not his mother but his aunt—sitting very close to his father. The diamond on her left ring finger, hand rested on his knee, caught the light and created a slender beam radiating upward, like a beam toward the heavens.

He squinted. Perhaps he was mistaken. Maybe the woman was his mother after all.

But no. Beyond the laughter and the sharp features, the hair was a shade lighter than his mother's honey-blonde hair. He also noted a birthmark on the side of this woman's neck that hadn't existed on his mother's skin.

He sat on the edge of the bed and gently laid the photograph beside him, next to the pile of discarded papers.

He turned his attention to the words in the journal and began deciphering the pointed handwriting. This was a poetic accounting of a long-ago relationship between the author and Max.

A first kiss: *He took my head between his hands and kissed me as the sun dipped below the trees.*

A date in an amusement park: *The rides weren't nearly as thrilling as the emotions he made me feel when he looked into my eyes.*

Holding hands as they walked near a river: *I can't imagine a day more beautiful and simpler than this one. A miracle.*

Griffin quickly turned the page on the consummation of the relationship: more dates, milestones, connections. More love. Then there was a proposal.

Surrounded by the vibrant autumn leaves, on a day where the sun shone brilliant through the trees and the sky colored the world sapphire blue, he sank down to one knee, and in front of God, nature, and the splendid tumble of Cucumber Falls over the edge of the cliff, he asked me to be his wife. There was no other answer but Yes!

A photograph of what must have been the waterfall in question marked the page. On the back of the photo, written with the same blue pen was a date. *October 19.*

More pages followed: musings on wedding plans, wedding dresses, and locations for the honeymoon.

Then an undated entry, the handwriting darker, deeper, more forceful. A heavy hand had scratched through the words, nearly tearing through the page. Griffin tried to make out what had been written beneath the violent scribble, but other than random words, nothing was legible.

That was the last entry. The remainder of the pages in the journal were unwritten.

Griffin picked up the photograph of his father and stared at it, a growing sense of unease spreading through him. His father had grown up closer to the city. He never talked about Pennsylvania, nor did he come back to visit. An only child, Griffin was unaware of any remaining family here. He'd never asked.

It was months since Griffin had spoken to his father. That was not unusual in their relationship. They'd never had a pick-up-the-phone-and-catch-up kind of relationship. Griffin assumed his father had read about his most recent run-in with the law, but Max Stangel wouldn't think to call or check in, just as Griffin wouldn't have called to ask his father for help.

Before Griffin had developed fully formed memories of his mother and father as a parental unit, his parents had divorced. He couldn't say what their relationship had been like, other than the nasty and snide comments his mother regularly made about his father. His father never talked about his mother at all.

Griffin tried to remember if he'd ever seen his father laughing the way he was in the photograph. If Max Stangel felt joy like that, it certainly hadn't been with

Griffin. During the time the Griffin had stayed with his father and stepmother, he'd seen his dad chuckle a few times, but the man had been mostly stoic.

Griffin glanced at the time. Monday morning, it was still early in Arizona, and at sixty-five, his father still taught at the local college part-time. Griffin would reach out later, he thought, with a sense of relief. He wasn't sure he was ready to hear answers to the questions he had.

He kept the book out and slipped the rest of the papers and receipts back into the drawer.

Griffin then opened the bifold closet doors, the roller wheels sliding smoothly in their tracks. The closet gave off a stuffy smell, like a consignment shop or a used bookstore. A moth fluttered out of the dark space behind the rack of colorful clothing: blouses, pantsuits, skirts, dresses. So many items hung on the metal rod that the bar bowed in the center.

Unlike Griffin's mother who purged and replenished her clothing every season, his aunt appeared to have kept every item of clothing she'd ever owned: bright pinks, lurid greens, vivid oranges, vibrant yellows. Griffin smiled. He liked this woman, who seemed unapologetically brilliant.

He was about to close the door on the mess when a small clear plastic box on the top shelf caught his eye. Griffin pulled it down. On the top of the pile was a large yellow envelope with 'For Howard Lincoln' written on it and underlined three times in black.

Griffin unwound the thread wound around the plastic fastener. He pulled out a number of handwritten papers with handwriting similar to that in the journal. The words caught his eye immediately:

I leave all of my possessions, including my house, my car, and my business—My Pink Wink—to my dear friend and surrogate daughter, Rose Glasser.

Holy shit. Griffin blinked and shoved the paperwork back into the envelope.

He stared at it. The paperwork hadn't been notarized so it was in no way legally binding. He'd just pulled out his phone to call Howard when the phone began to buzz with an incoming call.

Griffin hesitated, then answered the call. "Hey, Irv."

No greeting. Just a statement. "Howard called and said you neglected to sign the paperwork." Griffin glanced at the papers in his hand. "Why the hell not?"

"I wanted time to think."

"Think about what? Why are you making this so difficult?"

"It's just—Well, Rose."

"Jesus, Stangel. What about her? Rose is no one. She has no legal claim to the property."

Again, Griffin glanced at the envelope. He was no

lawyer, but even he knew without signed and filed paperwork, his aunt's handwritten letter meant nothing.

Griffin slid the envelope back into the plastic container and shut the closet door.

There was a pause on the other end of the phone. "Don't tell me you've got a thing for her."

"Of course not. She's married."

"Just your type."

Griffin didn't dignify the comment with a response.

"Can you just get through this? I think I can get the district attorney to sign off with a slap on the wrist. Maybe a little community service, maybe a fine, but no jail time. That's our goal here. Can you help me out? Just a little?"

"My aunt wanted someone else to own the property, Irv. And I don't see what my inheritance has to do with whether or not you can cut me a deal so I can come home."

"For all the time I've known you, Griff, you have been one of the least, shall we say, *moral* clients I've had to deal with. Why the attack of conscience now?"

"I just don't see what one thing has to do with the other."

"I've told the DA you're traveling because your aunt passed away and you've inherited some property, and you need to take care of the estate. If they find out you didn't actually inherit the property and decided to give it away, then I look like a liar. And so, by the way, do you."

Griffin wandered out of the bedroom and back into the kitchen, where a manila folder still sat on the kitchen table. He looked away from it and instead pulled open the refrigerator. It was filled with half-empty bottles of condiments, a carton of eggs, and a drawer full of cheese and rotting vegetables. A foul smell wafted toward him and he shut the door again.

"Are you there?"

"I'm here. Look, Irv, when I first got the call last week, you told me to just come here and check it out. I never wanted any of this property. Now you're telling me I have to sign. Why?"

Irv exhaled again in his ear. "I already told you the business is worth something. Why are you looking this gift horse in the mouth?"

Griffin hadn't eaten breakfast, and he was starving. He opened a few cabinets and found everything but food inside. He found one cabinet containing some moldy bread, another with expired puffed rice.

"Of course I know the answer to that," Irv was saying. "There's always a woman at the end of your troubles. Can you just listen to me? For *once*?"

Griffin sighed. "Fine."

"I'll believe it when I see it," Irv quipped. "Sign the paperwork. Got it?"

"Roger that."

"Just do it, Griffin."

Irv hung up, and Griffin made a face at the phone.

A light tapping sound met his ears; he paused and listened. It came again from the front of the house, louder this time. He walked out of the kitchen and into the living room, where he saw a shadow through the pain of glass in the front door. A small thrill ran through him. *Rose*, he thought. A million thoughts raced through his mind, not least of which was the envelope atop the closet in the bedroom.

But when he opened the door, he found Julie Newlin standing on the small porch.

"Hey there," she said brightly, her pretty face flushed with pleasure at seeing him.

He smiled back at her.

"I just happened to be driving past, and I noticed your car. I thought maybe you'd like to get some lunch."

Was the woman a mind reader?

But Griffin hesitated. Maybe it was the overeager way she was looking at him. The rise of her eyebrows, the too-bright gleam in her eyes.

Then again, he could've been assigning emotion to her because of his complicated feelings for Rose. Besides, he was hungry.

"What did you have in mind?"

"Well, there's the Tin Roof Café next to the salon on Main Street that serves sandwiches and pastries."

She held up her hands. Or," she said, drawing out the word, "hear me out. We could head to the city if you're up for an adventure. More of a selection and less people we know."

It was evident which option Julie preferred. And if Griffin was honest, he'd always take the option where less people might recognize him.

But Julie's energy was hopeful and eager. Maybe he was being overly sensitive, but something told him to go with his gut on this one. "The café is fine," he said, and when the corners of her mouth pulled down, he added, "I have some things to take care of here."

She recovered quickly, and the joy returned to her face. "Want me to drive?"

Griffin did not, but he hated to disappoint her again. Besides, it didn't make sense to take two separate vehicles. So he agreed and followed her sashaying backside to the small convertible parked in the driveway. The car was a powder blue and freshly shined.

Julie gracefully folded herself into the front seat.

"This doesn't seem like a practical car for a mom with teenage boys."

Julie laughed lightly as she reversed onto the rural back road. "The car was my divorce present to myself, courtesy of my ex-husband. I also have a practical SUV, if it makes you feel any better." She winked at him.

He didn't wink back.

They pulled into the parking lot in front of My Pink Wink. Griffin noticed the restaurant housed in a white building behind the salon, tucked back from the road. He hadn't noticed the place before, hidden like it was.

He followed Julie in her tight jeans, her blonde hair fastened in a high ponytail at the back of her head. From behind, she could have been a teenager, even though she was at least as old as he was. Probably older.

He hurried ahead of her to open a glass door decorated with brown vine threaded with red berries. When he pulled, the powerful vacuum of the door forced him to put some muscle into it. The smell of coffee and vanilla drifted from the interior, and his stomach rumbled.

Julie scrunched her nose and beamed up at him. "Aren't you a gentleman?" she cooed. "I knew I couldn't believe all those stories I read about you." She playfully bumped his chest with her shoulder. Then her smile faded, and she snapped her fingers. "I nearly forgot my coupon," she said. She dashed back to the car, leaving Griffin holding open the door while she leaned in the passenger side to retrieve the coupon, her backside on full display.

He gazed at her a second longer than was necessary, then looked away, immediately locking eyes with

Rose who was approaching the next-door salon.

Her gaze flitted from him to Julie who triumphantly held up a small card.

"Found it!" she announced gleefully.

Griffin nearly yelled out to Rose, "It's just lunch," before remembering she was married, and it was none of her business anyway. He didn't have to defend himself to her. Or to himself.

Did he?

To overcompensate for his guilt, he smiled widely at Julie as she walked toward him. As she passed, he put a hand on the small of her back. She beamed up at him.

His smile faded when she passed into the building. He didn't turn back around to see if Rose was watching.

He knew she was.

Chapter 14

"So it's true?" Hallie asked as Rose opened the door.

Rose's mind was still on the image of Griffin and Julie, and that's immediately what she assumed Hallie was referring to.

But before Rose could respond, Della interrupted. "We heard he was a baseball player. A hot one."

Rose briefly shut her eyes. So much for Julie keeping her mouth shut.

"Griffin Stangel," Alyssa affirmed. "He's a zaddy." She was concentrating on the hair of a middle-aged woman Rose didn't know.

"What's a 'zaddy'?" the woman asked.

Alyssa held opposite ends of the woman's hair, checking the evenness of the length. "A hot older gentleman." Then she clarified. "Well, older to me."

"Do you think my bangs are short enough?" The woman was more interested in her hair than hot older gentlemen.

Alyssa nodded in affirmation. "Your hair is still damp—your bangs will shrink a bit. We'll see how they look when you're dry and styled."

Jay had just put Kelly Mitchell, a longtime customer, under the hairdryer. He put his hands on his hips and stared at Rose. "Does this mean we won't have jobs? Is he going to shut the place down?"

Jay was the stylist least prone to drama and hyperbole, and Rose held up her hands. "Nothing is changing right now. No paperwork has even been signed."

"Why not?" asked Hallie, narrowing her eyes. She was setting the hair of the elderly woman in her chair in narrow pink rollers.

"He's checking in with his attorney." Rose couldn't tell them what that meant. Like Howard, she had no idea why the action was necessary.

Jay walked to the front desk. Out of earshot of the customers, he said, "My cousin owns a salon in Baltimore and has offered me a job. I wasn't really thinking about moving at this point, but maybe I should take her up on it." It wasn't a threat, but Rose's chest tightened at the thought of her salon family scattering across the country.

Griffin Stangel might turn out to be the storm that blew them away.

Rose was still reeling from the sight of Griffin and Julie walking into the coffee shop together, and she hadn't been prepared for an interrogation.

Della steered the conversation back to Griffin. "I

don't know what he'd want with a salon here of all places. Have you Googled his name? He's dated actresses, models, celebrities. Most of them were married at the time," she said wryly. "He also had a tendency to get into fights on the field *and* in the dugout. The guy has issues."

Alyssa picked up a hairdryer. "I'd still date him."

Hallie shot her a look. "You have a boyfriend."

"Exactly his type then," said Della. Then she added, "Actually, you're a little young for him." She brightened. "Maybe I've got a shot."

"I heard he's been out for dinner with Julie Newlin," said the woman in Alyssa's chair.

"Shocker," Della scoffed. "I bet dinner isn't *all* they had."

"I heard she met him here—at My Pink Wink."

Della's eyebrows shot up. "Here?"

Hallie frowned. "That's impossible."

Jay raised an eyebrow at Rose, and before this line of questioning could continue, she said, "Let's not gossip and speculate, okay? You all know better than anyone you can't trust half of the information zipping around Madison. Besides, the situation is very fluid."

"Well, *that* sounds like a crock."

Rose frowned. She was done talking about this. Not only did she have no good answers for what might happen with the salon—or their jobs—the last thing she wanted to do was spend more time dwelling on

Griffin Stangel.

After Pastor Ballentine had revealed the man's identity the day before, Rose had gone home and done a deep dive worthy of a private investigator. She'd read about the teams he'd played for, his contract agreements, and a bunch of statistics that hadn't meant much to her but seemed to indicate he'd been a talented player. She also read about his temper—the on- and off-field fights—that didn't quite line up with the quiet man who'd sat in her salon chair two days earlier.

The way his eyes had stared up at her with an intensity bubbling just beneath the surface.

Rose quickly tucked the memory away. Because she'd also read about the women—so many beautiful women. Even sheltered Rose knew who model-turned-newscaster Victoria Bryant was. Rose had studied the images of Griffin and Victoria taken by a detective hired by Victoria's husband—their heads bent together, their lips pressed together, their bodies molded together.

And of course Rose had seen the aftermath of those sensual photographs. She'd watched the videos of the confrontation with the imposing Charlie Bryant—the shouted insults, the shoving, and finally the bleeped-out language leading to Griffin's powerful right hook to the man's jaw.

Then the arrests. First, after Griffin had knocked

out Charlie Bryant, then just a few weeks ago when he'd decked a reporter on the street in front of God and everybody.

Why in heaven's name anyone should want to defend the man was beyond Rose. Except Rose had felt herself softening toward him. In every photograph and video, just like in real life, she'd sensed something beneath the surface: a barely contained sorrow which seemed to confuse him. She wondered if that sorrow was the reason he lashed out.

Hallie finished setting the hair of the woman in her chair and plied it with pungent chemical solution. She wiped her hands and set her gaze on Rose. "Do you think he's going to sell the salon?"

"As I said—he doesn't even own it yet."

"But he will. Mid left it to him."

Rose cringed. "She didn't leave it to him. She didn't have a will. She didn't leave it to *anyone*. That's why we're in this situation."

Then there was silence, heavy with judgment.

As painful as it was to think about the loss of the salon, and the challenge of all the other logistics after a sudden passing, Mid herself was still gone. There was a stark and naked grief which was now Rose's ghostly companion, like a shadow attached to her every movement.

And as much as Rose wanted everything to work out with the estate and My Pink Wink, what she wanted more than anything else was for Mid to simply be here.

Della stood from her seat at the front desk and began to walk toward the door.

"Where are you going?" Rose asked.

"I'm picking up the lunch order from the café. Do you want something? I can have Olivia add it on when I get over there."

Rose felt a moment of panic. She did not want Della to see Julie and Griffin together and then come back to report on it. She wasn't sure who she was protecting from this gossip—maybe herself.

"I'll go."

"Nonsense. You just got here."

"I'm going to grab a coffee. Besides, I can charge it to the salon. Care of Griffin Stangel."

There were murmurs of assent, and Rose felt a short rush of relief followed by another stab of panic. She didn't want to see Julie with him, her head bent close just like Victoria Bryant's had been.

But Rose set her jaw, drew herself up, and walked out the door.

Julie's sporty blue sportscar was still parked unevenly, barely within the parking spot guidelines. She knew Julie only drove this car on special occasions. She supposed Griffin Stangel was a special occasion.

Rose braced her feet and tugged open the heavy door of the coffee shop. The blast of warm air and fragrant coffee hit her, and she sucked in a breath. She made a beeline for the counter, not daring to turn her head toward the tables. In her periphery, she could see bodies, but she congratulated herself on her ability to ignore them.

Olivia Thomas, the owner of the Tin Roof Café, smiled at her. "Hey, honey. How are you holding up?"

Rose had seen Olivia at Mid's service last week. She smiled back. "One day at a time," Rose said, and Olivia nodded in understanding. Rose had attended the service for Olivia's mother just before Christmas.

"I'm here to pick up the lunch order for the salon."

"It's nearly ready," said Olivia, heading to the small kitchen. "I'll just be a minute."

Rose stood rigid at the counter. The tinkling of some sort of Celtic music mingled with the hum of low chatter. She heard the murmur of Griffin's deep voice and the answering lilt of Julie's higher pitch followed by her distinct laughter. She had the feeling they were laughing at her.

She counted her breaths as she stood stock still. *One…Two…Three…*

"Oh, Rose, is that you?" Julie's voice broke into her forced mediation. "I didn't even notice you come in."

Rose exhaled and her shoulders slumped forward. She turned, telling herself she wouldn't look at Griffin, but of course he was impossible to overlook. And his dark eyes were fixed on her.

"I'm just here picking up an order," Rose said, even though no one had asked, and that's clearly what she was doing.

"We're just having lunch." Julie smiled, gesturing toward Griffin. If she still had any hard feelings over their interaction in the church parking lot the day before, she gave no indication.

Olivia reappeared at the counter, holding a large bulky paper bag and two carriers each holding three large, steaming cardboard cups. "I added a coffee and chicken sandwich for you, on the house."

Rose stared at the bounty, trying to work out how she was going to carry it all. She handed Olivia the credit card, and after the transaction had been processed, Rose looped the twine handle of the bag over her arm then picked up both carriers, balancing them on her palms. The coffee wobbled precariously in her hands.

Olivia said with a laugh, "No one will judge you for making two trips."

But Rose didn't want to come back. "I've got it." She turned and moved slowly toward the door.

The heavy door, she thought with dismay.

She knew the customers in the restaurant were watching her, perched to see if she'd drop the coffee.

The handle of the heavy bag was digging painfully into her forearm.

"You forgot your receipt," Olivia called to Rose

when she was nearly at the door.

Rose gave a small shake of her head. "Can you hang onto it? I'll pick it up later." She didn't wait for Olivia's assent.

Rose caught sight of Julie watching her, the shadow of a smile playing on the woman's lips.

At the door, she braced her feet, and pushed with her upper arm. The door didn't budge. She shifted, and backed against it. Her feet slid against the slick hardwood, and the cup carrier in her right hand tilted dangerously. Before it could tumble to the floor, Griffin grabbed it, easily balancing it in his large hand.

He plucked the other carrier from her as well, and with a small effort, he pushed open the door.

She opened her mouth to protest, but he interrupted. "I've got you."

The ghost of Julie's smile was gone, and the other woman was frowning nearly as deeply as Rose was.

When she and Griffin emerged in the parking lot, Rose turned to reclaim her items. Griffin dipped his head toward the salon and began walking toward the door. "You really need to learn to accept a helping hand," he said, shooting her a slow smile.

Their eyes met, and Rose felt what was becoming a familiar sense of electricity she didn't want to experience.

He walked into the salon with the coffee, followed closely by Rose. All conversation and movement inside halted, and every gaze in the place turned toward the pair. Even the devices in the salon were muted. The only sound was the voice of Mel Tourmé singing 'Comin' Home Baby' over the speaker system.

"What's with the music in here?" Griffin said to Rose. "Don't you play anything from this century?"

Rose shut her eyes briefly as the stares of the staff shifted from Griffin to Rose. She sighed. Then she said, "Everyone, this is Griffin Stangel. Griffin, this is…" She paused. "…everyone."

He set the coffees on the counter and awkwardly held up a hand. No one spoke for a moment. Then Alyssa said, "Oh…my…god," under her breath, but plenty loud enough for everyone to hear.

Rose thought Griffin actually blushed.

Della followed with an overly loud, "Hello."

Hallie's mouth was set in a hard slash across her face. Jay's eyebrows were raised, and his expression amused. He was looking directly at Rose.

Rose introduced them by name. Griffin nodded at each of them as they all stared at each other. Finally, Griffin turned back to Rose. He held out his hand and brushed her arm with just the tips of his fingers. Then he hitched his thumb toward the door. "I should get back to my…lunch."

She nodded, the recall of the pressure of his fingers hot through her sleeve.

When he was halfway out the door, she called,

"Thanks for the help."

He didn't seem to hear her.

She took a steadying breath and began unpacking the food bag. "Lunch," she said brightly.

"What was that?" asked Alyssa.

"What was what?"

Alyssa turned to Hallie. "Did you see how he was looking at her? Am I crazy?"

Hallie said, "How does he know what music we play in here?"

Rose had hoped no one had picked up on that comment.

"He's way hotter in person than he is in his pictures," Alyssa said. "Like, so much hotter." She drew out every syllable.

Jay said, "Maybe I'll stick around after all. See what he does for this place. And for Rose."

The woman in Alyssa's chair was finished. She examined her hair in the mirror and nodded in approval, smiling at Alyssa. "You know, my husband and I have one celebrity agreement." She emphasized the word 'agreement' with its intended innuendo. "One person we're allowed to be with, no questions asked. Mine was Bradley Cooper. I think I've just made a revision."

"All right," said Rose, aware she hadn't answered Hallie's question and had no intention of doing so. She picked up her coffee and gulped it, ignoring the fact it was still scalding and burned her tongue. "With any luck, the man will be in and out of here, and our lives will go on unchanged."

"How do you think that might happen?"

"Maybe he'll want a similar arrangement to the one we had with Mid—he'll own the place and we manage the business, and him, from afar."

"*You'll* manage it," Della corrected. "And him."

"That's different," said Jay. "Mid was here every day. She knew exactly what was going on."

Rose thought about a potential arrangement with Griffin. She didn't want that much contact with him. What she really wanted was for him to go away.

But that wasn't true, and she knew it. She wanted a whole lot more than that, if she were being honest with herself. And sometimes, she hated being honest with herself.

She checked the time on her phone. It was one in the afternoon. She had a client coming in at half past, so she grabbed her sandwich and went to the back of the store to run payroll before the woman arrived.

She could hear the loud whispers of the staff, but she couldn't make out the conversation. She caught a few phrases: *More than once. Doesn't know anything. He looked like he wanted to devour her.* The last phrase was in Alyssa's voice and loud, Rose knew, so she could hear it. It also made her belly clench tight.

She needed to get a grip. There was no way in hell a

man like Griffin wanted anything to do with a very simple, very plain, very small-town girl like Rose. Those romances didn't happen outside of movies and novels.

Besides, he lived hundreds of miles away. Any romance would be long-distance, and…

Rose cut into her thoughts and chided herself again. She wished Mid were here to give her a good dose of reality. Then she remembered Mid was the reason she was in this mess.

She popped out the Mel Tourmé CD and shuffled through the collection.

Jay called plaintively, "Please don't put on Harry Connick Jr."

Rose located the case. The handsome face of the crooner smiled up at her. She popped the disk into the player, and the upbeat piano notes tinkled through the salon. Then that smooth, even voice.

Jay groaned, but the ghost of Mid, ever attached to Rose's psyche, laughed beside her. And Rose laughed along with her.

Chapter 15

Rose managed to get through the rest of the day without seeing Griffin Stangel. That didn't mean he wasn't on her mind. When she walked into the Sweetwood Saloon that evening to pick up a sandwich for dinner, Teddy had taken one look at her and said, "What's up with you?"

"Nothing's up with me."

"You have a weird look on your face," he said.

She insisted there was no weird look, but she knew what energy Teddy was picking up on. It was concerning. Teddy picked up on very little.

The energy wasn't all positive. There was desire and anticipation, which were kind of thrilling. But there was also envy, resentment, dread, anger, and fear. In other words, she was a mess.

Her sleep that night was filled with strange vivid dreams of her parents dancing with Mel Tourmé, while Mid and a woman who looked suspiciously like Mid whispered furiously at each other in the corner of a room on fire. In a grove of trees across the fiery room, Griffin was showing something in his palm to her father, whose hand was slung across Griffin's back.

Rose floated above them, yelling, but none of them could hear her. The louder she called, the more they ignored her.

She woke exhausted and far too early. Then she ate a bowl of cereal.

She would go into the salon early to get a jump on the day, and avoid entering in the middle of conversations which would most definitely be about her.

But first she'd run up to Mid's house to pick up the packet of financial information she'd left sitting on the table. It wasn't that she was afraid anyone would break into the house. But it *was* unoccupied, and the paperwork contained the social security numbers and financial information of every member of staff at the salon, her included.

She dressed for her run and tucked her keys into the small pouch inside her vest.

The sky threatened rain, but the cool sharpness of the breeze cleansed her lungs and cleared her foggy head. She hadn't been eating as well as she should over the past two weeks, and the stress, grief, and emotion were wreaking havoc on her body.

She needed to resume her normal, boring routine.

When she approached Mid's house, it looked the same as it always had, but for Rose, it would never be the same. The spring rains had caused the grass to grow tall, the place overgrown and unkempt and the porch devoid of its spring decorations and flowers. Rose placed her hands on her hips as she gazed up at it, hoping Mid's nephew would make a decision soon so she could clean out the place and sell it. If Mid wasn't in the house, another family should be.

She walked up the empty driveway and sidewalk, lush with new weeds.

It was before seven, and there was no movement from the surrounding yards or from the abandoned ballfield across the street, but Rose felt as if someone were watching her. She spun around, but no one was there.

She shook off the sensation and inserted her key into the lock. With a twist of her wrist, she heard the tumblers engage, and she pushed open the door.

The air inside felt different—energized. And there was a strange odor in the air. Not bad…just different. She took three steps into the living room, before she became aware of a sound. A steading whooshing coming from the back of the house. Her heart began to pound. Someone was here.

The sound abruptly stopped, followed by a silence, and then a light thump.

More noises. Shuffling. A tapping sound.

Rose stood frozen in the living room.

Her first thought was *squatters*. She'd read about people who'd returned from vacation to find strangers living in their home. She'd reacted with horror at the nightmare of being unable to have these criminals evicted when they suddenly had more rights than the homeowners.

Madison was not a high-crime area, but these people did their research—scoured obituaries and targeted empty homes. She slid her cell phone out of the pocket of her leggings, ready to call the police.

Then she remembered the financial information on the table. She moved quickly and silently toward the kitchen. The folder was in the same place, undisturbed.

But there were other things on the table—three full plastic bags and a case of bottled water. Her eyes scanned the room. A brand-new, expensive-looking coffee pot was on the counter, along with a vacuum-packed container of upscale coffee.

She moved toward the table and snatched up the folder, tucking it under her arm. She held up her phone, ready to dial.

There was a movement in the doorway. She looked up and gave a little yell, nearly dropping the phone.

Her eyes registered the sight in front of her.

Griffin Stangel stood naked in the doorway. Rose's eyes took him in. All of him. Every inch. Her mouth dropped open.

She wasn't sure how long they stared at each other. Griffin made no move to cover himself, and Rose couldn't seem to look away.

"What are you doing here?" they both asked, the

words overlapping and tangling together.

The question seemed to shake them both out of their state of surprise, and Rose covered her eyes while Griffin ducked out of the room, coming back with one of Mid's green bath towels slung low on his hips.

When he returned, she was the first to repeat her question.

"You gave me a key. I figured it made more sense to stay here than in a hotel."

"Where's your car?"

"In the garage," he said.

Rose frowned. It must have been a tight squeeze in the small garage with Mid's car also parked inside.

"I wish you would've told me."

"I wish you would've mentioned you were stopping by," Griffin countered, holding out his hands. "I would have dressed for company at…" He glanced at the clock on the stove. "…six forty-five in the morning." He held out his hands.

Rose blushed. The site of Griffin's body was now permanently etched in her brain. As vividly as she'd imagined his physique, her imagination hadn't done justice to the reality of the man himself.

Her heart pounded hard in her chest. At first, the thrumming was born of surprise. Now it was something else entirely.

She held out the paperwork. "I'd forgotten this yesterday."

They stared at each other for an uncomfortably long moment until Rose looked around the kitchen, desperate to say something, but loathe to leave. "Making yourself right at home, I see."

"Isn't it my house now?"

She swallowed. "I don't recall you signing the paperwork."

He moved forward, into the space where she stood. She stiffened. As he moved around the table, his body brushed hers in the cramped space. Her heartbeat began pulsing in her ears. Mortified, she realized it was also pounding other places in her body.

When he passed by, she took three steadying breaths.

"Coffee?" he asked.

The towel was knotted so loosely, there was no way it was going to stay in place. If he noticed, he gave no indication.

He looked over at her, awaiting a response to his question. *Coffee. Right.* She nodded.

He put the coffee on brew then turned back to her and leaned against the counter, his palms resting on the service behind him, revealing strong, ropey forearms, and the full tattoos on his biceps she'd glimpsed the other day.

His chest was lean and toned. A line of thin, dark hair led down his abdomen to a place she'd already seen, and wouldn't soon forget.

Her eyes locked with his; she watched a shadow move across his face. She wasn't sure how long they stared into each other's eyes, but before she realized what was happening, he crossed the short space between them. He took her face between his large palms, and brought his mouth down hard on hers.

She dropped the folder, the papers fluttering like leaves to the floor.

Rose had been kissed before. She'd had relationships before. There hadn't been many, and they hadn't been long. But nothing any of those men had done even came close to what Griffin was doing to her now.

His tongue was gentle, hesitant at first, then exploring. After a minute, he deepened the kiss and it became insistent and demanding. His rough palms slid from her face to her hair, and he threaded his fingers through her long waves, pulling it from the ponytail on her head.

Rose nearly forgot to breathe.

She reached around him, her hands splayed on his smooth, hard back.

He was pressed hard into her belly, and she felt all of his desire deep within her. She let out a moan.

An animalistic sound responded, and he picked her up against him. The towel lost its losing battle and slid to the floor.

Rose would have gone anywhere with him. Allowed him to do anything to her.

But just as suddenly as the kiss had begun, Griffin tore away from her, leaving Rose stunned. And empty. He snatched up the towel and turned away from her, wrapping the cloth around him, much more securely this time.

He faced the counter and leaned over, head hanging down.

Her face burning, Rose distracted herself by bending to retrieve her scattered papers.

"Jesus," he said, and swore violently. "I am so sorry."

Rose wasn't sure what she was supposed to say to that. She managed a weak, "It-It's okay."

"I'm an idiot."

"I'm not upset," she said. Trying to figure out a delicate way of telling him she'd *wanted* it to happen.

"It's not *you* I'm worried about," said Griffin hotly. He swore again.

Rose blinked, stunned. This was about Julie Newlin. She'd been tested and found wanting to another woman who, like her, he'd met less than a week ago.

She was a fool. Of course this handsome, successful man would choose pretty, perky, pleasant Julie over overanalyzing, overthinking, over-emotional Rose.

She drew herself up and tried to speak calmly. "We can just forget it ever happened."

He shot her a look over his shoulder. "You think you can just forget that?"

Rose wouldn't forget it as long as she lived. But she shrugged. "It was only a kiss."

He scoffed. "Right." He shook his head and without turning around, he banged open and shut cabinets until he found the coffee cups in a cabinet to the right of the sink. She watched his wide, muscled shoulders move, and her gaze traveled down the length of his tapered back.

Had her arms really just been around his waist?

Her fingertips were still tingling with the contact, but the rest of her was now flooded with shame. Tears welled up in her eyes before she could quell them.

"I have to go," she said, mortified her voice betrayed her emotion. She moved quickly through the living room.

"Rose…wait," Griffin called, but she didn't wait. She fled down the overgrown sidewalk, the paperwork haphazardly tucked under her arm.

✝✝✝

Rose wished she'd driven to Mid's house so she could cry in her car in peace. Walking home at seven in the morning, she was exposed to anyone who happened to pass by. And plenty of people tooted their horns and waved as she walked, bedraggled, down the street.

She managed to hold herself together, swallowing down the tearful lump in the back of her throat.

Entering the house, she shut the door behind her and slid to the floor. She'd protected herself and her heart for so long. The minute she'd let her guard down for a second—just one small slip—her heart had nearly broken in two.

Beyond Mid, she hadn't even allowed herself to have friendships. Now, she had no one.

She pulled the phone from the pocket of her Lycra pants and dialed the number of the person she knew wouldn't understand but who was the only one she had.

He answered on the second ring, though by his thick voice she could tell he'd been sleeping.

"Rose?"

"Teddy…" As she said her brother's name, the rush of tears threatened all over again. "I fucked up," she managed to get out before all her emotions flooded forth.

Ten minutes later, she was perched at the bar of the Sweetwood, her eyes puffy and her nose red.

Teddy placed a shot glass filled with amber liquid in front of her. "Drink it."

"It's not even eight in the morning."

"When you need a shot of bourbon, time doesn't tend to matter."

Rose hated bourbon. But she gulped down the strong liquid. Then she coughed and sputtered.

After a few seconds, a warmth spread through her

and she took a deep breath. A sob hiccupped in her throat. Her shoulders slumped.

Teddy poured her another. She shook her head.

"Drink," he ordered. Then he poured himself a shot.

They downed the liquid together; another spread of warmth flowed through her. It dried her tears.

"Now talk."

She stared at the varnished bar and spread her hands in front of her. She remained silent.

Teddy sighed. "You can't call and tell me you fucked up then refuse to tell me what it's all about. You asked for my help, and now you're going to get it. So talk," he said again.

Rose wasn't sure what to say. Her mouth felt fuzzy.

After a minute, she said, "I-I went to his house to pick up some paperwork this morning…"

Teddy looked mystified. "Whose house?"

"Griffin's."

"Who the hell is Griffin?"

Rose looked up at his face. Rage had begun to distort his features. How was it that everyone else in town had heard about Griffin Stangel, but the man who owned the town's only bar—where Griffin's identity had probably been discussed the most—had no idea who she was talking about?

She rolled the empty shot glass embossed with two S's between thumb and fingers.

"Mid's nephew," she said. "He was at her house."

Some of Teddy's rage dissipated. "And?"

"It turns out he's the guy from the other night. The one who stayed in the outbuilding."

Teddy's eyebrows shot up. "*That* guy? The drunk?

"He's not a drunk," she said.

"He knew his way around a good bourbon."

"He's a baseball player."

A look of recognition crossed Teddy's face. "Griffin Stangel…" His voice trailed off. "I've heard of him. He had an affair with the wife of the head of the Sports News Network. Broke up their marriage." Teddy made a sound at the back of his throat. "I should've known just by looking at him he was trouble."

Rose swallowed down the urge to stand up for Griffin. Why would she even want to defend him after what he'd done? She let her head fall forward on the smooth brass bar.

Teddy didn't seem to notice. "He got kicked out of the League, didn't he?"

Rose mumbled into her arms, "It was because of an injury."

"What?"

Rose raised her head a few inches and looked at her brother.

He looked back at her. Then his mouth fell open. "Oh, Rose. Please tell me you didn't sleep with him."

At that, Rose sat up. "Of course I didn't sleep with

him. How could you even think that?" But her indignation was unfounded. If Griffin had carried her to the bedroom, as she was nearly certain he'd planned to, there was no question she would have let him do whatever he wanted to her.

He frowned as if he didn't believe her. "Then what's the trouble?"

"I kissed him."

Teddy narrowed his eyes. "You kissed him." It was a statement.

She let her head fall into her arms and nodded miserably.

"You're sure that's all you did?"

The alcohol was running swiftly through her brain. She couldn't be bothered to feel indignant. "I'm sure."

"Okay. So what?"

Rose raised her head an inch and frowned. "He's dating Julie Newlin."

Teddy laughed. "No, he's not."

Rose nodded.

"Even if both of them came in here and took a blood oath they were dating, I still wouldn't believe it."

Rose raised her head. She wanted to be as sure as Teddy. "Why do you think that?"

"Because Julie is not the dating kind. She's the fun kind. Now, if you told me the guy was sleeping with her, I would have a different reaction. But dating?" He shook his head. "No."

Rose now felt indignant on Julie's behalf. It was some misplaced 'girl's girl' loyalty. But she couldn't be bothered to argue with her brother.

"But you should have seen him, Teddy. He regretted it."

At Teddy's confused face, she continued, "He regretted kissing me. Like it was the worst thing he could've done. It was mortifying."

Teddy sighed. "He doesn't regret kissing you. He regrets how much he *liked* kissing you."

She gave him a skeptical look. "You didn't see how he acted."

"I don't have to see it. I'm a guy."

"I don't get it," she said.

"Unlike Julie, you are the dating kind. Even though you've sworn off men for whatever reason. But a man like Griffin Stangel is also not the dating kind. The fact you made him want to be probably scares the shit out of him."

"How do you know?"

"Let's just say I'm probably a little bit more like Griffin Stangel than I'd like to admit. The difference is I'm not dating models and newscasters."

In her slightly altered state, Rose thought about what he was saying. She had a hard time thinking about Teddy as anything other than her surly brother.

He began to wipe down the bar, avoiding eye contact with her. He probably wished he hadn't said anything at all.

"So what do I do?"

He glanced over at her. "About what?"

"About kissing him."

"What do you want to do?"

"I want to kiss him again," she admitted. It was the damn alcohol talking.

Teddy made a face. "Not the answer I was expecting. But if you want to kiss him again, then kiss him again."

"He doesn't want to kiss *me* again." She sounded whiny even to her own ears.

"I can assure you, he does."

"But he's the enemy." She was getting tired, and her words were starting to slur together. At her brother's questioning look, she continued, "Of me. And Mid. And the salon. He's going to inherit all the property then sell it."

"Did he say that's what he's going to do?" Teddy asked.

"No," she said miserably. "He didn't even sign the paperwork."

Teddy leaned toward her, resting his elbows on the bar. "I can't tell you what you should do. I can tell you that this guy appears to be transient. He probably hasn't spent much time in one place most of his life or put down roots. With his lifestyle, I would imagine, comes a lack of commitment.

"You, on the other hand, have spent your entire life in this small town. If you decide to pursue this thing—whatever this *thing* is—with this man, there's a very good chance you're going to get your heart broken."

Rose didn't want to hear what Teddy was saying, but she knew he was right.

He placed a glass of water in front of her and she drank it down.

"I'm going to take you home, and you're going to wallow for one day, and one day only. You got it?"

"I need to be at My Pink Wink."

"You haven't even properly grieved for Mid. If you're not going listen to me, at least do it for Mid."

Rose lifted one shoulder indecisively. Teddy was right—she'd spent the last two weeks running around and concentrating on everything *but* her emotions. It certainly didn't help that Griffin had complicated all the emotions she already felt. She was tangled up inside, and confused. And all she wanted was for Mid to be there to give her advice.

"Please?"

Teddy's normally sullen expression had shifted to one of concern. Rose felt her rigid resolve weakening. Teddy very rarely asked anything of her. And he almost never said please. Could she really refuse him?

His eyebrows were raised and his palms stretched toward her.

"Fine," she grumbled. "But what do I do about

Griffin?"

Teddy reached forward and covered her hand with his. "Unfortunately, sis, that's a question only you can answer."

Chapter 16

Griffin nearly packed up the few belongings he'd brought with him and drove right back to Boston.

What was the worst that might happen if he did that?

Likely, Irv was close to working something out with the district attorney. Griffin couldn't imagine this trip mattered to anyone in the grand scheme of things. Especially if he signed over the property to someone who needed it more than he did. Surely, Irv's PR team could put a positive spin on that.

Hell, if he had to spend a few nights in jail, what did he care? It wouldn't have been the first time.

But there were two things keeping him in Madison. First, he needed to get to the bottom of his mother's relationship with his aunt. He'd never been much of a believer in fate, but he'd been feeling an invisible pull lately—a tingling sense he was right where he needed to be, and a deep knowing of the reason behind that.

And as much as he didn't want to admit it, his feelings for Rose were keeping him here. He'd spent his entire adult life dating women who were just beyond suitability for an actual relationship. Women he would never consider spending the rest of his life with. Women who were married; women who were too mature for him; women who were just like him.

He had carefully engaged in relationships that he knew, in the end, would never work.

This was something he'd never admitted to himself before, although, on some level, he must have known it.

He wasn't much for examining the childhood trauma of his past, but it didn't take a genius to follow the path of his younger years to the man he'd become today. He'd never been loveable enough to get the full attention of his parents. Why would he risk that kind of rejection again?

But this time, it was Griffin who was different. His feelings for the woman were different. The connection he felt to her ran deep and was attached to an anchor— a protectiveness he didn't remember feeling about anyone else. Ever. What was it all about?

It was because of those emotions he was determined not to hurt her. He needed to apologize, not only to Rose, but to her husband.

After Rose had gone, he dressed and made himself breakfast. Then he waited.

He got two text messages from Juile, thirty minutes apart.

—Hey, stranger. Let me know if you'd like to grab dinner this evening.

—I can cook, if you'd like to stay in. I grill a mean steak and baked potato.

When he hadn't answered those messages, there had been two missed calls.

Griffin knew he needed to get back to her. She was sweet and kind. She didn't deserve to be ghosted by the likes of him. In the afternoon, after the second missed call, he sat in the dusty living room of his aunt's house and dialed her number.

"Hey, you," she said, the delight and relief evident in those two words.

"Hi." His voice was more restrained.

"It's good to hear from you. I was getting worried."

Griffin shut his eyes. He knew what she was worried about, and she was right to be concerned.

Before he could speak, she continued. "So what do you have in mind for later? Dinner in?"

A pause. "Julie, I'm just going to be honest—"

"I know what you're going to say," she interrupted, "and I agree. Dinner out would be best. There's a great place in Greensburg that's a little more upscale. Probably more your speed. I can—"

"Julie," he broke in, trying to ensure he spoke firmly and gently.

"Or we can grab something quick. Fast food, even. I'm not opposed to burger and fries."

"Julie," he said again, more softly this time.

There was silence.

"This isn't going to work out."

He heard her clear her voice on the other end of the connection. "I thought we were just having dinner," she said. "Some company while you were in a strange place."

"I appreciate the offer," he said, "and I thank you for the company you've already provided. You're a nice person."

"A nice person," she repeated. There was ice in her voice. A long silence followed before she said, "Was it something I said or did?"

"No," Griffin said quickly. "You've been lovely. It's just that…" His words trailed off. He didn't want to use distance or lifestyle as an excuse. Because that's what it would've been, and it wasn't fair. So he admitted out loud what he'd only just admitted to himself. "I have feelings for someone else."

"I see," Julie said. "Someone in Boston."

Griffin didn't answer.

"The woman on the news?" she asked. "The one who was with you when you punched that reporter?"

Griffin blinked. He was embarrassed to admit he'd nearly forgotten about her. He still couldn't remember her name. "No," he said. "It doesn't matter who. What matters is that those feelings would prevent me from offering you what you deserve."

"I just thought we could be friends," she said. "I'm not looking for anything serious or complicated."

But Griffin knew by the way she'd looked at him, her words weren't true.

"I'm sorry, Julie."

Another pause, then a curt, "Suit yourself. It was nice meeting you. I hope you find what you're looking for." Then she ended the call.

Griffin looked down at the phone. He felt like an ass even though he knew it was the right thing to do. It was easy to think there was no harm in an innocent dinner, but he knew where those harmless, innocent encounters led, and it was never anywhere good.

After, he had another missed call from his father. Griffin didn't pick up. He needed to ask Max Stangel some questions, but he wasn't quite ready for his father's answers. He let the call go to voicemail.

As he waited for the Sweetwood to open later in the afternoon, he turned on Mid's television and found her subscription included just about every channel and streaming service imaginable. Griffin had never had a lot of time to watch television, but he found himself embarrassingly enthralled by a silly show in which young people attempted to find love on an island.

He also scrolled the latest headlines, and didn't find his name appearing anywhere. The new cycle had moved on. It tended to do that. Give it just a few days, and people forgot who you were. Which meant he could go home just as soon as he'd done what he needed to do.

His mind kept wandering back to the kiss, which had been so much more than a kiss. Then he'd remember Rose was spoken for and what he needed to do. And his chest would clench, along with his fists. The last thing he wanted to have to do was apologize to Rose's husband.

At four in the afternoon, he finally picked up his cell phone and looked up the number for the Sweetwood Saloon. When he dialed it, a voice he recognized answered the call.

"Just checking the hours today."

"We open at five."

Griffin glanced at the time. He had another hour to kill.

"Thanks," he said and was about to end the call.

"Is this Griffin?" Teddy's voice sounded gruff.

Griffin startled. "How could you possibly know that?"

"The incoming call popped up with 'Maybe Griffin Stangel'. The magic of technology."

The invasiveness of technology more like it, Griffin thought.

"You can come in now if you want. I think there are some things we need to discuss."

Griffin tensed. What could Teddy possibly have to discuss with Griffin unless Rose had already said something? Griffin felt like he was on his back foot now.

"I'll get there when I get there."

He hung up and let out a long exhale. So much for easing into the conversation.

Restless, Griffin got up and went outside. A light rain misted from low gray clouds, and the air held the leftover chill of winter. He walked across the street to the small field he'd noticed on his first exploration of his aunt's property. The land was overrun with weeds, including the two overgrown ballfields which, by the looks of them, hadn't been used for their intended purpose in years.

A white concrete building ran along one side of the property, and on the other side of the field were three small pavilions holding rotted picnic tables. At the far end was a playground including a swing set missing a few of the swings, a rusted sliding board, and a precarious-looking jungle gym.

The only new thing on the property was the out-of-place track circling the periphery.

Griffin was assessing the area with his arms folded when a boy appeared from behind the block building. He noticed Griffin and startled. He quietly turned around as if to walk in the opposite direction, but Griffin called to him.

"Hey kid…"

The boy stopped and his shoulders slumped before

he turned around. He skulked closer, but not too close.

"Why aren't you in school?"

"School's done for the day," the boy said. From his gangly limbs and awkwardness, Griffin guessed he was eleven or twelve.

"What're you doing here?" Griffin asked.

The boy pointed up a gentle rise on the north side of the field. "I live over there. There's nothing to do." He kicked his shoe against the wet grass.

"You play baseball?"

He nodded. "At the middle school."

"You any good?"

The kid gave a little laugh. "No, we suck." Then in a smaller voice, he asked, "Are you Griffin Stangel?"

"How do you know that?"

"My mom and dad were talking about it last night, and everybody in school was talking about it today."

Griffin nodded. "My aunt lived right there." He pointed to Mid's house.

The boy seemed to know that already. "We went to church with Ms. Higgins. She never mentioned you." If Griffin didn't know better, he'd have thought the boy was skeptical of the fact that Griffin was actually Mid's nephew.

"Not many people mention me."

"Why not?"

"Not much good to say, I guess."

A pause. The boy looked into the sky and let the

drizzle fall on his face. "Are you moving here?" he asked.

The question caught Griffin off guard. Of course he wasn't moving here. But he didn't answer directly. "I'll go back to Boston in a few days." But he didn't want to talk about that, so he walked over to the squat, white building and tried the door. It was locked.

"Do you know what's in here?" he asked.

The boy shrugged.

"Who would have a key?"

"Probably Pastor Ballentine or Ms. Newlin. The church owns the ballfield."

Griffin chuckled without much humor. He didn't want to ask either the pastor or his assistant for anything. He said, "I wonder why they spent money on the track but didn't clean up the rest of the park."

"My mom says because of Ms. Glasser."

That stopped Griffin in his tracks. "Rose?"

The boy nodded. "Pastor Ballentine didn't like her running on the roads, so he built the track."

"Why would he do that for Rose?" The question was more to himself than for the boy, but the boy shrugged again. "Your mom said that?"

Perhaps sensing he'd shared something he shouldn't have, the boy didn't respond.

Griffin wondered how Rose could be so blind to her own appeal. Every other woman in his life—both those he'd dated and those he hadn't—had been all too aware not only of their beauty, but the power that came along with it. For Griffin, the mutual recognition of their position had created a game—a friendly battle for the upper hand. He'd learned to play the game well. He'd learned to win.

But Rose wasn't playing any sort of game at all, it appeared, which took all of Griffin's control away, and left him mystified and confused.

And why *would* she be playing? She wasn't available. He kept having to remind himself of that.

He thought again about the imminent conversation with Teddy. No matter what happened, he wasn't going to fight the guy. If Teddy came after him, Griffin would take the hit. He deserved it.

"Are you okay, Mr. Stangel?"

He realized he'd been frowning deeply. To the kid, he said, "To be honest, I've been better."

"How come?"

Griffin sighed. "Did you ever really, really want something, like, so bad you didn't know how you were going to live without it?"

The boy thought about this, then he nodded. "A puppy," he said.

Griffin opened his mouth then shut it again. Rose was nothing like a puppy, but for the purpose of the conversation with this child, he guessed it was a comparison that made sense. He'd also wanted a puppy when he'd been young. He hadn't gotten one, which made sense as he looked back on his childhood, but caused a ripple of emotion in his chest, too.

"Kind of like that," he answered. "I just found out the thing I didn't even know I wanted—that I now want more than anything—I can't have it, and I'll never be able to get it. It hit me like a punch in the gut. You know?"

The kid looked very sage when he said, "Yeah, I know."

They both stood lost in thought for a minute.

Griffin looked again around the overgrown baseball fields.

"How would you and your buddies like to help clean up this place? Maybe make some real, playable fields before summer?"

The boy's face lit up. "We'd like that a lot. But I thought you were going back to Boston."

Yeah, that's what I thought too.

"Let me see what I can do." Then he checked the time. He'd put off the conversation with Teddy for long enough. "It was nice meeting you." He held out his hand to the boy, who shook it in a very mature fashion. "You too, Mr. Stangel."

"You can call me Griffin."

The boy nodded.

"I don't think I caught your name."

"Chase," the boy said, and Griffin's eyebrows shot up. The hair rose on the back of his neck.

The abrupt, metallic clanging of the bell of a dog collar echoed through the quiet field. Griffin looked toward the source of the sound. A burly chocolate lab bound toward them, and the boy turned around. "Miles!" he yelled as the dog jumped at the kid, nearly knocking him over.

"Hey," Griffin said, and the dog ran toward him, slobbering on his hands as Griffin bent to pet him. "I thought you said you didn't get the thing you wanted most."

"I said I knew what it felt like to want something that much," Chase said. "But then I got it. Maybe you will too."

"Chase," a woman's voice called, and without a word of goodbye, the boy and the dog began running across the field as fast as their six collective legs could take them.

Griffin watched them go, envious of the child. He'd never gotten the puppy, and he wouldn't get the girl.

But life was a tradeoff, wasn't it? He'd been blessed with fame, fortune and notoriety.

But he'd give it all up in a heartbeat, he realized. For all these years, he'd been chasing the wrong thing.

A short time later, he found himself in the nearly empty parking lot of the Sweetwood Saloon. Griffin cut the engine and gripped the steering wheel for a moment. Then, with a breath, he unfolded himself from the car and slammed the door harder than he needed to.

When he pulled open the door of the saloon, 'Take it Easy' was playing too loud over the sound system. Two older men at the bar glanced up then back at their drinks. They were the only customers in the place at five o'clock on a Tuesday afternoon.

Griffin took a seat at the bar, the same place he'd sat last week. A few seconds later, Teddy walked out of the door in the back. He spotted Griffin immediately, and his face darkened.

"Griffin Stangel, at long last. The homewrecker and the heartbreaker."

Griffin's pulse picked up. Rose had already told him. And for a shameful second, Griffin felt a flash of hope. Maybe Teddy had broken up with his wife.

What an awful thing to think. That would not be the way he'd want a relationship with Rose to begin.

He reminded himself that as amazing, glorious, soul-altering as their kiss had been, it had still been just a kiss.

"I imagine you probably need a drink as much as Rose did earlier." Teddy grabbed a bottle of The Saint bourbon—the variety he'd ordered nearly a week earlier—and poured him a generous tumbler.

One of the other guys seated at the bar twisted

around and looked at Griffin curiously. He clearly had a flash of recognition, but just when he looked as if he would call it out, he turned around again and huddled back over his beer.

Griffin looked from the drink to Teddy. Teddy stared back at him. He was taller than Griffin, and taller still standing behind the bar. Griffin realized it was a mistake meeting him here, on his own turf. Griffin had given up any upper ground he might've had.

Then again, he thought, he was here to apologize to Teddy. The high ground was not his.

He took a drink then a breath. "About Rose…"

Teddy narrowed his eyes and waited.

"I assume she told you what happened."

"A version of it."

Griffin shook his head. He wished the guy would just sucker punch him already, instead of standing over Griffin looking morally superior.

Griffin took another swallow of the smooth bourbon and shut his eyes. "I'm not sure…" he started then abruptly stopped. He tried again, "It just kind of happened. I'm not even sure how."

"Are you talking about the kiss or your feelings for her?"

Griffin looked up sharply.

Teddy leaned forward. "Here's the thing you need to know about Rose. She's had a rough go of it. Both of us have. But it was harder on Rose, I think."

Griffin stared up at him. He had no idea what he was talking about.

Teddy continued. "Mid was the best thing that could've happened to Rose—she swooped in and saved her. I didn't have the emotional capacity for what Rose needed. I don't know what would've happened to her if it hadn't been for Mid."

Griffin opened his mouth and then shut it again. He wasn't even sure what question to ask.

Maybe Teddy sensed Griffin's confusion because he crossed his hand in front of him, like a slash. "What I guess I'm trying to say is Mid's death was harder on Rose than she'll ever admit, probably even to herself. She copes by putting her head down and getting shit done. Even after our parents died. And she tends not to see things around her, and she doesn't give herself enough credit."

Griffin shook his head. "You're not angry?"

"Oh, I'm angry about plenty of things," Teddy said quickly. "Rose isn't one of those things."

"You don't want to punch me?"

Both of the guys next to Griffin looked over at them. Whether or not they recognized Griffin, they were much more interested in witnessing a potential fistfight.

"Yeah, I want to punch you. I'd want to lay you out if you broke her heart. But honestly, I don't think you're going to do that. The more I consider the situation, and especially after seeing you… If anything, I think she's going to break yours."

Griffin frowned, trying to piece together this conversation. Then something Teddy had said clicked. "Our parents…You said 'our parents'."

Teddy waited with an expectant expression.

"Did your parents pass away at the same time as Rose's did?"

Teddy looked angrier than he'd had since Griffin entered the bar. "What the hell are you talking about, man?"

"You said 'our parents'…"

"Yeah, our mom and dad. They passed away in a car accident when Rose was sixteen and I was twenty."

"Rose is your *sister*…" He said it quietly at first, then yelled it over the 38 Special song now playing over the speakers. He stood up so quickly that the barstool wobbled, before banging to the ground.

Teddy swore and rushed around the bar. "Watch what you're doing. These things are irreplaceable."

He examined the furniture for damage.

Griffin didn't care. "You had the same parents?" he confirmed one more time.

"That's what I just said. What is your trip?" He set the stool back in place.

"I thought you were married."

"To Rose?"

The guy closest to Griffin barked out a laugh, laying to rest any pretense Griffin had that the man hadn't been eavesdropping.

"Why on earth would you think that?" Teddy asked, moving back behind the bar.

Griffin took his seat again, and Teddy eyed the stool as if Griffin was going to crush it.

He was nearly positive Rose had confirmed her marriage to Teddy. In the salon while she'd been cutting his hair. And nothing anyone else had said to him indicated otherwise.

Griffin took another long drink of the bourbon and slammed the glass down on the counter, sloshing the liquid over the rim.

Teddy immediately wiped up the liquid with a low growl.

Griffin stood again and thrust out a hand.

Teddy stared at it. "What are you doing?" But he shook Griffin's hand anyway.

"I've got to go. There's something I need to do." He pulled out his wallet and placed two fifty-dollar bills on the bar between them.

Teddy said, "You don't owe me that much." He slid the bills back toward Griffin.

"No, man. Keep it. I owe you everything."

Chapter 17

The knocking was loud and insistent.

It wasn't yet six in the evening, but Rose was watching television in bed, where she'd been for most of the day. She had taken Teddy's advice because she'd promised she would, and she typically kept her promises. She glanced at her phone.

Nothing.

She muted the TV set and listened, hoping the visitor continued on his or her way. There was a long pause, then three sharp raps followed by the muffled sound of a voice.

Rose wasn't dressed for company. She was wearing a long T-shirt and nothing else. Her hair hung in tangled waves around her mottled face, and she was certain her eyes were still puffy with both tears and sleep.

The knocking continued, and Rose assumed the worst. What sort of emergency awaited her?

She grabbed a threadbare robe from the end of her bed and threw it around her shoulders as she hurried down the stairs.

When she reached the landing, she opened the front door a crack.

Griffin Stangel stood on her front porch. Her breath hitched in her throat.

"Rose…" he said, his voice thick with relief.

She wasn't sure what to make of that. "Can I help you?"

"It's Griffin…"

"I am aware. What do you want?" She wasn't sure how she'd react when she saw him again. She wasn't hurt or embarrassed or sad. She was angry.

"I was hoping we might be able to talk."

She stood silently, waiting. Finally, she said, "So talk."

"Can I come in?"

There were so many reasons she didn't want him in her home. Most of all she didn't want his memory ruining the comfort of her own space. "If you're here to apologize again, you can save it. Everything's fine."

"I know. That's why I'm here." His voice was upbeat. Gleeful.

"I'm glad you feel so good about everything. I suppose you worked things out with Julie?" It was a lame shot, but it was the only one she had.

But at least the comment wiped the smile from his face. "What does she have to do with anything?"

"You tell me."

He leaned forward but stopped short of crowding

the door. "Can I just come in? There have been some big misunderstandings on my part. But maybe on yours too. We really need to talk."

Rose clenched her jaw and tightened her shoulders. He didn't look like he planned on going anywhere anytime soon. With a noisy exhale, she opened the door and stepped to the side.

He gazed at her as he stepped in, but if her unkempt, unwashed appearance bothered him, he didn't let on. He came close. Too close. Rose felt what was becoming the familiar pull of attraction, and she backed away, crossing her arms tightly over her chest.

He gave a cursory glance around the dining room to the left and then the living room. He tilted his head. "Can we sit?"

She stalked into the living room, assuming he would follow. He did.

Rose sat on the edge of the sofa, and to her chagrin, he sat beside her rather than in the armchair across from her.

She shifted over in a huff.

"I just left the Sweetwood. I went there to apologize to Teddy."

That got her attention. "For what?"

"Somewhere along the way, I'd gotten the impression Teddy was your husband."

Rose stared at Griffin with wide eyes. He stared back, his expression so earnest, she burst out laughing.

She laughed until her stomach hurt and tears streamed down her face. She laughed until she wasn't sure if she was laughing or crying.

And when the laughter had subsided, a wide grin still split her face.

Griffin didn't laugh, but he gazed at her with his dark, dark eyes, one corner of his mouth turned up. "You're beautiful when you laugh," he said.

That caused both her laughter and her smile to fade. She turned away so she wasn't looking into those eyes. "Why are you telling me this?"

"Because of what happened this morning."

Then she understood. "You thought I was married to Teddy," she said, repeating what he'd just told her, but this time without the laughter.

He nodded.

"And that's why you stopped…"

He nodded again.

"And Julie?"

"There was never anything between Julie and me. I told her so in no uncertain terms this afternoon."

"But the dinner and the lunch…"

"Meals only. Nothing else."

They sat in silence for a long moment. Rose listened to the ticking of the wall clock in the kitchen.

"Rose?" His voice was low, and he filled her name with significance.

Rose looked back at him, self-conscious of her

knotted hair and splotchy face.

He looked like he was trying to decide the best words to use. Finally he said, "I'm going to kiss you now."

Rose was not prepared for the hot jolt of desire that coursed through her. She sucked in a breath.

He closed the distance between them quickly and took her face in his hands. Unlike the earlier kiss this one didn't begin sweetly. This was all desire. A promise of more.

Rose closed her eyes, heart pounding in her chest. His lips were hot and urgent against hers. The world around them seemed to fade away as the kiss deepened. His tongue moved against hers in slow, urgent thrusts.

When he finally pulled away, Rose's cheeks flushed with heat. He looked at her intently, searching her eyes, not speaking.

She reached up and cupped his cheek with her palm, his beard beneath her fingertips rough against her skin.

"That was…" she began, but the words trailed off.

He smiled, a crooked grin that made her heartbeat pound in her chest. "It was," he agreed softly, his gaze never leaving hers. "Do you want me to kiss you again." It wasn't a question.

Rose took a deep breath to steady herself, before leaning in and closing the gap between them.

His lips filled her with a heat and a desire for something so powerful she didn't think the need could ever be filled. It was both exhilarating and terrifying. She pulled back, gazing into his eyes; she saw a reflection of her turmoil and vulnerability mirrored back at her.

"Rose…" His whisper was dark and husky with desire. "…I want to be with you."

The words hung between them, substantial and heavy. Whatever her next words, they would have the power to change her life.

For years, she'd taken the safe road, dated safe men, made the safe decisions. And when her emotions became too unwieldy, she walked away before she could get hurt.

Here, there was no safety net. She could either plunge in or stay back, always wondering what might've been.

She searched his eyes for any doubt or hesitation. All she found was an intensity, and a fear matching her own feelings.

She let out a breath. Then she said, "I want to be with you too."

He let out an audible breath. Then he took her hands in his. It felt like a promise between them. Of what, she wasn't sure.

She stood and gently guided him to his feet.

He followed her lead, up the stairs and into the bedroom. Her body was filled with anticipation, desire, and an unmistakable looming dread. She prayed with all she had that she wasn't making the biggest mistake of her life.

Griffin's eyes were on hers as he disrobed her. He ran his hands up her arms softly then reached under her nightshirt. The rough skin of his palms against her bare back made her shiver.

He kissed her again, pulling her against him. His body was hard and hot. He sat on the edge of the bed and positioned her between his legs, staring up at her as his hands slid again under the nightshirt. His fingertips explored her hips, her stomach, her ribs.

His eyes were laser-focused on hers as the pads of his thumbs swept over her breasts. The sensation made her knees buckle, and he tightened his thighs against her legs, holding her upright in front of him.

He continued the delicious movement—caressing, pinching, rolling her nipples—until Rose didn't think she could stand one more second of the torture. She leaned forward and kissed him, trying to mold herself against him.

But he stopped her and broke the kiss to slide the nightshirt over her head so she was nearly naked in front of him. He looked at her with reverence. No man had ever looked at her that way before.

"Oh, Rose," he whispered, looking up into her eyes. "You don't know how beautiful you are."

To her dismay, a sob bubbled up in her throat. He stood, holding her close, while she cried softly. After a moment, he took her face in his hands. "You okay?"

She nodded, and he lay her on the bed, positioning himself above her. He kissed her once on the cheek before descending, his mouth working over her skin, caressing every inch of her. His lips moved from her neck down to the valley of her breasts. He stayed there, moving his tongue in circles around her nipple before taking it between his teeth and nibbling gently, first one then the other. She arched toward him, panting.

He moved down her body, his beard scraping roughly, sensuously against her belly. She stared at her ceiling, reveling in the sensations he had awoken in her.

Then he was between her legs, within seconds his mouth on her sex. She pushed herself into him, her hands clutching at his hair.

He alternated between licking and sucking, until Rose called out his name and the delicate skin of her belly began to quiver. He increased the speed of his tongue against her, grounding her with his hands firmly on her lean hips.

The soft moans that had begun quietly built in volume and intensity. Her fingers in his hair were twisted around his locks as she ground against his mouth. Higher and higher he took her, and she stayed on that brink for a long, exquisite moment.

When she crashed back to earth, the blood rushed in her ears and she saw stars. Her belly quivered. Her limbs trembled. And for just a moment, she thought she must might have experienced heaven.

Rose lay very still, staring up at the decorative swirls in the plaster of her ceiling. Her hands were still in Griffin's hair.

She looked down and he looked up; thinking she'd be embarrassed or mortified, instead they both laughed at the other's hopeful expression.

The tension broken, Rose scrambled to her knees, Griffin sliding off the bed onto his feet. She unbuttoned his jeans while he shimmied out of his pullover. In a second, he was gloriously naked. She touched his shoulders, his chest, his stomach…down until her hand was around his erection.

When she began to gently move her hand against him, he stopped her, a pained expression on his face.

"Not like that," he whispered.

He lay down on the bed and guided her on top of him. He slid inside her. Though he was large, and it had been so long since she'd been with a man, the length of him filled her.

She stayed still for a moment, reveling in the sensation of him inside her. She began to move, slow at first.

His hands were on her breasts, touching, teasing, rolling, and releasing. She looked to the ceiling as she slid up and down on him, then her unfocused gaze locked with his.

He smiled. It was dazzling and brilliant. It was

everything.

She rode higher and higher. He grasped her hips, moving her urgently against him. She said his name and he said hers. They rose together, their voices loud, their breathing in time.

Rose felt him crest first and her muscles clenched against him, powerful in the intense pleasure of the moment.

She fell forward against his chest and he held her tight, their bodies fused together.

She wasn't sure how long they lay there, hot and slick, before she stirred, trying to shake the feeling back into her legs as she rolled down next to him.

He reached over and brushed the tangled hair out of her eyes.

He was so incredibly handsome; Rose felt like an imposter.

Her eyes must have reflected her doubt because he dipped his head and touched her cheek. "You okay?"

She caught his wrist in her hand and nodded. "This is just…not my normal Tuesday night."

"Despite what you may have read about me, it's not mine either."

Rose shot him a skeptical look. "It's been…" She thought back to her last relationship. A nice, mild-mannered man named Chris. "…four years," she finished. For the three years they'd dated, she couldn't remember ever once seeing him fully naked. She'd done more with Griffin during their first encounter.

He gave a low whistle. "You have some catching up to do," he said at her ear. "Shall we go again?"

She looked over at him. "You're ready for that?"

"Rose, honey. With you, I can go all night."

And then he did.

Chapter 18

Rose couldn't stop smiling as she walked down Main Street the next morning. She'd lost count of the number of times she'd made love the night before. Griffin had woken early and ravished her again before going out to Alsops' convenience store at the edge of town and picking up eggs, bacon, potatoes, and orange juice, and making her the first decent breakfast she'd had in months. Then he'd despoiled her again before allowing her to dress and go to work.

Jay had the day off, and other than Della who was picking up a coffee order, the rest of the staff were already at the salon getting ready for the day.

Alyssa was the first to look at Rose closely when she walked through the door. "Uh…" the younger woman said, narrowing her eyes. "What's going on with you?"

Rose kept her eyes averted. "What do you mean?"

"Why are you smiling like that?"

"I'm not smiling."

Rose powered up the laptop so everyone could clock in.

Hallie looked over at her. "You're definitely smiling," she said. "Why?"

Rose did her best to assume a serious expression, but trying to look normal only made her want to laugh. She logged into the scheduling system to check the day's appointments. Rose had three appointments back to back.

When she looked up, both women were still staring at her.

Rose shrugged. "I just needed the day off yesterday."

Neither of them seemed to believe her, but they didn't argue as they readied their stations.

Rose stood up from the desk as Della walked in with the coffee.

Della took one look at her and said, "Oh my god, you had sex." Hallie and Alyssa whirled around.

"Don't be ridiculous," Rose said. But her voice was breathless.

"With who?" Hallie cried.

"It's the baseball player," Alyssa exclaimed. "Griffin what's-his-name. The one who couldn't keep his eyes off of her."

Hallie's brow creased. "I heard he was sleeping with Julie."

"He's not sleeping with Julie," Rose said, frowning for the first time that day.

"See," Alyssa said triumphantly. "I told you."

"It doesn't mean he's sleeping with me." Rose

grabbed one of the coffees and took a tentative sip.

Della leaned in close. "How was he?"

Rose couldn't help it. Her lips twisted into a smile.

Hallie placed her hands on her hips. "Well, shit," she said. "You *are* sleeping with him."

"I bet there wasn't much sleeping going on," Della quipped, and Rose smiled wider.

Alyssa rushed to the front desk where Rose and Della were standing. "Tell me everything," she said, grabbing Rose's hand. "Was it as good as I daydreamed it would be?"

Rose pulled her hand away. "Stop. I'm not going to give you details."

She walked to the back of the store to put some music on. It was a Tony Bennett kind of day. Hallie followed her to the back of the store and leaned in the doorframe while Rose went through the CDs.

Rose looked up.

Hallie was not smiling. "What about the salon?" she asked.

Rose pressed her lips together. She and Griffin had not gotten around to talking about My Pink Wink.

"Is he going to sell it?"

Rose looked over at her. "I don't know."

Hallie sucked her tongue against her teeth and nodded once. "Got it. While the rest of us are worried about our livelihoods, you're fu—" She stopped herself. "You're *cavorting* with the enemy."

"I'm not going to let anything happen to the salon," Rose said.

"Really? Just like you didn't let anything bad happen to Mid?"

Rose's mouth dropped open and she put the CDs down on the table in front of her. "That's not fair."

Hallie at least had the grace to look apologetic. "I just meant…" She stopped, threaded her hands through her hair. "Look, if the salon gets sold, you'll be okay. You own your house outright and you don't have any kids. Plus you've got Teddy. I've got three kids, Rose, and it's all on me. Every month, I wonder if this is the month I can't pay rent, or something happens and I can't afford my bills. Is this the month someone finds out I sometimes leave my younger kids home alone with my oldest because I have to work, and the state takes them all away?"

Rose stared at Hallie in horror. "If you need to leave early or take more time—"

"I need the *money* more, Rose. Besides, that's not the point. The point is, while you're sleeping with this guy because he's hot, I'm wondering what I'll do without a job."

"You're a good stylist. You'd get another job."

"Yeah, but how much further away would it be? I'd have to build up my client base again. My base pay would be less. I've looked into it. If My Pink Wink closes, my life changes, and not for the better."

Rose nodded. She felt like a jerk. Hallie was right. She'd been so concerned with Griffin and her feelings for him, she'd lost sight of what was important. "I'll talk to him," she said quietly.

Hallie looked at her a beat too long.

"I promise."

The other woman nodded once. "Okay." Then she walked back into the salon.

Rose glanced down at Tony Bennett smiling at her. It turned out she wasn't feeling any music after all.

After she'd closed the salon, Rose returned to an empty house. For a second, she thought Griffin had had his fill and abandoned her, but when she walked into the kitchen, she saw the handwritten note on the kitchen table.

> *Left to take care of a few things and then heading to Mid's house. I realized we've exchanged words and kisses, but we've not exchanged numbers. Call/text if you need me, or come and see me. ;)*

Rose smiled and immediately input the number into her phone then sent a text message.

—*This is Rose. Headed your way.*

Her phone buzzed a few seconds later.

—*Can hardly wait.*

A delicious shiver of anticipation ran through her followed immediately by the weight of the conversation she'd need to have. She'd made a promise to Hallie.

She drove the short distance to the house. Griffin's car was in the driveway. The lawn had been mowed and the weeds cut back.

Over the past few years, Mid had hired a landscaping service for lawn maintenance, but when Rose glanced into the open garage, next to Mid's hatchback she saw a new lawnmower and weedwhacker along with a number of bags from a home improvement chain.

Rose wondered what type of outfit Griffin had worn for the lawn work. From what she'd seen, he'd only brought designer clothes and shoes with him—understated, but expensive.

She knocked and then walked into the house, her heart pounding. She wasn't sure why she was nervous. Shouldn't the anxiety be out of her system?

The low pulse of music was coming from the back of the house, and Rose followed it to Mid's bedroom.

Griffin caught sight of her immediately as she appeared in the doorway, and his face broke into a grin. Some of her anxiety eased as he crossed the distance and swept her into a deep kiss.

She allowed it for a long, delicious minute, then she

pulled away. They had other things to discuss, and she didn't want this relationship to be only about sex. Although the fact it was a worry at all thrilled her more than it should have. That was something she'd never had to consider before.

"You've been busy," she said, noting he was freshly showered and dressed in his normal designer clothes. She ran her hands over his shoulders. "The yard looks great."

"Do you know how long it's been since I used a lawnmower?" he asked. "I must have been thirteen."

"What did you wear?"

He told her of his adventures shopping at a department store near Greensburg where he'd bought jeans and T-shirts. Then he excitedly showed her his new purchases.

When she looked at the bed, papers were strewn across the comforter and the closet was open.

"What's all this?" she asked.

Griffin quickly moved the paperwork into a hasty pile and sat on the edge of the bed. He patted a spot beside him, and she sat. He picked up a leather-bound book. "Have you ever seen this?"

Rose shook her head and took the book, opening it. Mid's spiked handwriting filled the pages.

"Is this a diary?"

Griffin nodded. "I found it on Monday morning, and I wanted to ask you about it."

Rose skimmed some of the words, but didn't want to invade Mid's privacy. Instead, she ran her fingertips over the pages.

Griffin held up a photo of a man and a woman. "Do you know who this is?"

Rose frowned, studying the worn picture. "That looks like a very young Mid, and…" Her words trailed off as she squinted at the man on whose thigh Mid's manicured hand rested. "Oh, my gosh. Is that Max?"

"You know who he is?"

Rose shook her head. "I never met him, obviously, but Mid mentioned him. He was her first love. Only love, I think. They'd been engaged."

"What happened between them?"

Rose shook her head again. "She would only say it didn't work out, and it was her greatest regret." Rose ran her fingertips over the beautiful photo of young Mid, who was laughing, full of life and hope for the future. She wondered what would have happened if Mid had ended up marrying Max. Rose wondered what might have happened to her.

"She said she'd had a second chance with him, but she couldn't bring herself to take it," she murmured. She peered at the picture. She couldn't see his face clearly because his head was thrown back in laughter. But there was something familiar about the dark hair, chiseled features, and lean muscular frame.

"I was looking for more evidence of their relationship," said Griffin, nodding at the paperwork on the bed. "Maybe more photographs."

Rose handed the photograph back to Griffin. "If any exist, I've never seen them."

"She's got a lot of photos of you."

Rose smiled sadly. "She pretty much adopted me as a teenager, after my parents died. I didn't make it easy on her."

"It seems like you grew into your role."

She didn't respond. She didn't feel like she'd done a particularly great job as a daughter the second time around either.

"Teddy told me there was a car accident. I'm so sorry, Rose."

He was looking at her with his dark eyes. Rose exhaled. "Yeah, well. It was a long time ago. Life goes on whether we want it to or not."

"Did you not want it to?"

Rose thought about her rash and foolish reaction to her parents' deaths at age sixteen when she hadn't seen any clear path forward. She wasn't yet ready to share the story with Griffin.

She plucked the photograph of Mid from his fingers and stared at this new evidence of Max, a name she'd heard on occasion, usually when Mid was feeling sentimental. She wished she'd asked more questions about the man, but she didn't think Mid would have offered more information anyway.

The way his head was thrown back…She'd seen the pose before. Just last night, in fact. She looked from the photo in her hand to Griffin.

"Oh my god," she said looking from one to the other. "You look so much like him."

"I do," said Griffin.

"Do you…?" She halted the question, then plunged forward. "Do you know who this is?" She wasn't sure she wanted to hear the answer.

"This," he said quietly, "is Max Stangel, my father."

Rose's mouth fell open as she stared at Griffin. Then she looked down at the photo. The woman in the picture was Mid, without question.

"But your mother…" Her words trailed off.

"Was unquestionably Madeline Stangel. Mid's sister."

Chapter 19

Griffin could see Rose doing the math in her head, just as he had done—attempting to untangle the years. Griffin's own age was well-documented online, and he assumed Rose also knew this. His mother had been born in the early 1960s, putting the sisters in their early twenties at the time the journal had been written and dated.

She picked up the other photo of the waterfall and let out a breath.

"Do you know this place?" asked Griffin.

"I've been here many times with Mid. We went at least once a summer. The past two years, her knees were giving her trouble, but we still hiked down the precarious steps built into the hillside so she could gaze up at the falls from this very spot."

"She didn't tell you why?"

Rose shook her head. "I knew it had something to do with him, but I didn't pry." She opened her mouth and then shut it again. "Now they're both gone. We'll never know."

But Rose didn't ask about Max, maybe assuming he

was gone too. Griffin didn't offer. She looked so sad that Griffin reached out and touched her cheek. Rose caught his hand in hers and looked up at him.

Her eyes searched his. He waited for whatever question she had to reach her lips, but after a moment, she broke eye contact and stood awkwardly at the edge of the bed. "I guess I should think about dinner."

Griffin reached out and tucked his finger in the belt loop of her jeans. "Would you like some company?"

"Sure. I mean, if you'd like to join me. I didn't want to assume."

He tugged at the loop until she was standing right in front of him. He moved his hands to her hips and she caught her lower lip between her teeth.

"You can always assume I want to join you. Okay?"

She nodded, but he could sense her hesitation. He thought he knew why. Rose had lived her entire life in this small town. She hadn't had many serious relationships, or relationships that would have led to serious long-term commitments. To be thrust into a romantic situation with a man like Griffin...she was bound to question both his level of interest and his level of commitment. She was bound to wonder when he was going to break her heart.

While he had no intention of doing any such thing, he didn't think his empty words would convince her. He'd have to tread carefully and sincerely.

And to be honest, these feelings were as new to him

as they were to her. He wasn't sure what would or *should* happen next. He had a life in Boston. It wasn't much of a life, but it was where he was comfortable. He couldn't see himself giving up his urban lifestyle for an existence in a small town.

But he didn't want to think about any of those things. All he wanted was to enjoy this new connection with this beautiful serious woman who was looking down at him with huge, terrified eyes.

He pulled her down onto his lap and nuzzled her neck. She smelled sweet, like vanilla. It was a warm and comforting scent, and he breathed her in. Then he said at her ear, "It's going to be okay, Rose."

She turned into him, and his desire stirred.

"How do you know?"

"Because we're in this together."

He felt her breath catch in her chest as he hardened beneath her. He'd convinced himself he was going to take things slow and allow Rose to take the lead. After what had happened between them the night before— the *entire* night—he thought she might be feeling vulnerable. He wanted her to feel as if she were controlling the situation.

But with her on his lap, his fingers seemed to move of their own volition. His hands were under her blouse, exploring the smooth, bare skin of her stomach and ribs. She rocked lightly against him and he let out a soft moan.

She stood up quickly, and while Griffin was disappointed, he understood her hesitation.

Then she fell to her knees in front of him, working at the button on his jeans with frantic movements of her hands. His breath hitched in his throat, but he managed to catch her wrists and stop her.

She looked up at him, her eyes hazy and unfocused, her full lips parted.

"You don't have to," he said. His voice was a husky rumble.

"I know," she whispered. "But I really want to."

They stared at each other until Rose pulled free of his hands and continued her exploration of him, first with her fingers and then with her mouth.

She took him in her hands and ran the tip of her tongue up his shaft.

He shivered and placed his hands gently on the back of her head, tangling his fingers in her hair.

She reached her hand lower and cupped him in one palm, licking slowly, lightly.

His body jerked, and he growled, "Rose, you're killing me…"

She smiled up at him. "Just a little bit longer. Then I'll put you out of your misery."

He moaned as she took the length of him in her hot mouth, sliding up and down slowly, while her other hand gently massaged him.

He pressed gently into her, holding back.

When he let out a tortured "*Fuck*", she showed him mercy. Placing both hands on his buttocks, she pressed him deep into her throat with a slow thrust, then increased her speed, guiding with her tongue.

The pleasure was intense and fast. His entire body was taut and strained. Griffin lost all sense of himself. In that moment, there was everything and there was nothing. And then a deep swell from the core of his being rising, rising, until it crested and broke, crashing down around them both.

He rode it for a long delicious moment, though time had lost its meaning. And when he came back to himself, he was bent over Rose's head, his fingers tangled into her long waves.

He breathed again, and she gently disconnected from him.

He inhaled then exhaled. She looked up at him.

"That was…" Words failed him.

She smiled, and his heart squeezed in his chest. He placed a hand on her cheek. "Oh, Rose," he said. He wasn't sure why he was feeling so melancholy.

She didn't seem to notice. She stood and offered him her hands. "Let's get something to eat."

He nodded, but before she could walk out of the room, he pulled her close to him and held her. He didn't want to let her go.

✝✝✝

The next morning, they headed to the monument company for Mid's tombstone. Griffin wasn't sure if Rose wanted him to tag along, but she'd been insistent. "Especially if you want to have a stone placed for your mother."

Neither of them had spoken again of the implications of the journal, and Griffin wondered if it was best just to let the mystery lie with the sisters.

The dusty shop was located on a lonely rural road next to a mechanic who advertised transmission repair on a faded, rusty sign. Across the street was an old house that hadn't been maintained for years.

Blank tombstones leaned against the side of the brick building. Griffin shivered.

They pushed open the door, and a cowbell affixed to the inside announced them with an obnoxious clang.

Inside was a crowded, miniature interior graveyard with blank monuments of varying colors, shapes, and sizes. Griffin averted his eyes from the section that held the children's markers: angels, toy tractors, race cars, and teddy bears. They made him think about Chase—the boy from the hospital. And also the boy from the park across the street. He hated that these fleeting, fragile lives were marked with heavy stone, forever anchoring memories into the lonely ground.

Rose glanced over at him. "You okay?"

He swallowed and nodded as an ancient man

emerged from the back of the shop. His gray hair was thin and Griffin could see his bumpy scalp through the strands. "Help you?" he asked in a wheezing voice.

Rose said, "Hi. Jack Cummings sent us. I'm here to order a monument for my…" She hesitated for just a second. "…my mother," she finished.

The man shuffled to a desk cluttered with paperwork and binders. "Name?"

"Mid Higgins."

"Mid," he said, his face lighting with recognition. "She used to cut my wife's hair. I didn't realize she'd died. I'm sorry for your loss." He gave her a sympathetic look. "What did you say your name was?"

"Rose Glasser," she responded.

He opened a folder and slowly read through some entries, his lips moving with the review. "Here it is," he said. "Jack called last week."

He gave them a painfully slow overview of the ghostly inventory, reviewing all the available styles and pointing them out: upright, slant, flat, bench, and wing styles. Each of those styles could then vary in size and design. It was also possible to order a custom shape: a heart, a vehicle, an angel, a cross, praying hands, or a design to symbolize a hobby or occupation.

The old man walked over to the children's section. "These give you an idea of the variety we've created."

Griffin walked away so he could breathe. He imagined each of those monuments symbolized a cold, lonely grave for a child who'd departed much too soon.

"We can do pretty much anything," said the man.

He then ticked through the options for stone before finally recommending granite as the most durable rock and slowly listing the nearly twenty variations of color.

Rose listened carefully, nodding politely.

Griffin paced around the store.

He heard the man say, "Is your husband okay?"

Griffin's eyes met Rose's, and he waited for her response. She faltered for a second before seeming to decide the explanation wasn't worth it. "He's fine," she said, and gave him a look that made him smile. Some of his anxiety eased.

The man went back to his sales pitch. "You also need to think about the inscription, the placement, and the font." He went to a massive binder on the desk and handed it to Rose who opened it.

"Wow," she said. "I didn't realize the options would be so…involved."

"We can also inscribe a custom artwork sketching within the stone."

He opened another binder. Curious, Griffin came closer. Detailed inscriptions of horizons, sunsets, mountains, and oceanscapes had been artfully incorporated into different sizes and shapes of monuments.

Rose lit up. "Can you design a waterfall?" She described to the man the photograph of the waterfall

Griffin had shown her earlier.

He nodded. "Of course. We work with an artist who can create that for you. If you have a photograph in mind, send it over, and we'll have her do some mockups before you make a final decision."

Rose nodded, looking infinitely more satisfied than Griffin felt.

"If you're going with a design, I'd suggest the imperial black stone." He flipped through one of the binders and pointed to a similar stone with an etching of a mountain scene. "It shows up nicely on that color."

Rose looked at Griffin who felt claustrophobic. "What do you think?"

He tried to give her a supportive look, but he felt the grimace on his face.

As if Griffin wasn't in front of him, the man said to Rose, "Some men don't do well with death. Women either, but they hold it together better."

Griffin wanted to argue with the blatantly sexist comment, but he was in no position to offer a retort, so he just sulked silently.

Rose turned back to the man. "I like that option."

He made a notation on an old-fashioned order pad then moved a mouse around as he peered at a desktop computer. For nearly ten minutes, he hunted and pecked until he looked satisfied with his progress. Griffin had started to sweat.

"Have you thought of her epitaph?"

"Yes," Rose said, and from her purse she pulled out a piece of paper. Griffin glanced over at the writing.

Mildred 'Mid' Higgins
Beloved Daughter, Sister, Friend, and Mother
She Lived 'With a Wink and a Smile'

A final line indicated the years bookending her life.

Rose then pointed in the first binder to a font called 'Emerald' that was robust but had whimsy. As little as Griffin had known his aunt, from what he was learning, it seemed to suit her perfectly.

The man looked from the paper to the computer, and again began to type. After another minute, he looked at them and smiled with his rheumy eyes. He handed them a card and pointed to the email address at the bottom. "Send me a scan of the photograph you want etched, and we'll get it over to the designer. Should take about a week before she has a design ready for you."

Rose nodded, and Griffin stood. He was halfway to the door before he realized she was still at the desk. He turned and gave her a questioning look.

"Your mother?" she prompted.

Griffin's breath constricted even more. He didn't want to do this. He felt like he knew his mother less than he knew his aunt.

"We can do it another time," he said. He motioned

toward the door.

Rose frowned. "We're here. We may as well ask."

She turned back to the man at the desk. "Mid's sister was buried in the Madison cemetery a few years ago but a headstone wasn't ordered. We're looking for a simple option."

The man licked a finger and turned to a fresh page on his notepad. "What's the name?"

"Madeline Stangel," Rose said to the man.

He looked up. "Like the baseball player."

Rose glanced at Griffin then said, "Just like that. Yes."

He moved back to the computer. "I think I have an order. I remember the name."

Griffin walked back to the desk. "You have an order?"

He concentrated on the screen for a minute and moved the mouse slowly around the mousepad. "I remember," he said, "because it was at the same time Griffin Stangel punched out the guy from the other team…" His words trailed off. "Can't remember who it was. They cleared the benches and the kid got a five-game suspension. Helluva player, but an unpredictable kid." The guy chuckled. "The order came in around the same time, and it's not a common name around here."

Rose glanced over at Griffin who dipped his head. He remembered it well. He'd hit a home run against the Phillys, and on his way back to the plate, the opposing players immediately started talking shit. He'd ignored it until his next time up to bat when Jeff Bell had intentionally drilled him. He'd run out onto the field to argue Bell should be ejected; Bell had gotten in his face and said something Griffin couldn't even remember now. Griffin threw the first punch which had led to a brawl. Griffin had taken the brunt of the punishment. Rightly so. It hadn't been his first fight on the field. Or off.

"Anyway," the man continued, and went back to searching on the screen. "Here it is. Jack Cummings placed the order for Mid Higgins." The coincidence occurred to him. "Oh," he exclaimed, and looked at Rose. "Your Mid."

Griffin shook his head. "There was no marker on her grave."

He squinted. "It looks like it was ordered and paid for but never delivered. I have a notation here—'No response'."

Griffin looked at Rose who shrugged. "Mid never said a word." She turned to the man. "What was the date it was completed?"

He blinked at the screen. "September 14. Five years ago."

Rose turned to Griffin. "Mid was diagnosed with late-onset lupus right around that time. Maybe she just didn't deal with it."

Griffin looked at the man. "Where is the stone

now?"

"Probably somewhere in the warehouse." He hitched his chin toward the back of the shop. "I'll have my son take a look when he gets in. We can have it delivered and placed if you sign off on it."

"What does it say?" Griffin asked.

"It's a light gray slant with base. It says, *Madeline 'Mad' Higgins Stangel. Daughter, Sister, Mother.* Followed by the years."

Rose said softly, "Do you want to change anything?"

Griffin had no idea what he could add. He shook his head. "I think that pretty much covers it." He knew it was awful to think, but he felt unfairly resentful that his aunt, who'd never had children of her own, had someone like Rose who had loved her and was grieving her now. He realized the irony of that—he was Madeline's son. He was the one who should've been feeling the same grief for his mother.

Likely sensing the change in his mood, Rose finished up the transaction and they walked out of the shop and got into her car. She drove quietly for a few miles and let him stew in his thoughts. Finally, she said, "I know it's none of my business—"

"No, it's not," he interrupted. He hadn't meant it to come out as abruptly as it had, and he saw the color rise in her face. He exhaled, and after a few minutes said, "I'm sorry. It's just—it wasn't an easy childhood."

She stared straight ahead through the windshield. "A lot of us didn't have easy childhoods."

He remembered the car accident. *Shit.* "I'm not trying to compare," he continued. "I..." He stopped and thought about what he wanted to share. "She wasn't a nice person."

At that, Rose glanced over. "She was your mother."

"And I think she would have preferred I'd never been born."

Griffin had shared the belief with a small number of people in his past, but rarely and not for years. Every single one of those people had told him he must be mistaken; he'd likely misunderstood his mother's words and actions. Every single one of them had made him feel like he'd been the problem.

He clamped his mouth shut and stared out the window.

He felt the pressure of Rose's hand on his knee and glanced over at her with a tight smile.

"If it's true, then she sounds like a truly awful person. I'm glad I never met her. But thank god she existed, otherwise, the world wouldn't have known Griffin Stangel."

He gave a humorless laugh. "There are plenty of people who feel differently."

She lifted a shoulder. "They're not in this car."

Those words hit Griffin. It was true—not one of those people mattered. The only thing that mattered now was the present moment—the time and space shared between Rose and him. He was thinking about his relationship with his mother, which had been over for years, and interactions with other people, the names of whom he hadn't bothered to remember.

"You know," he said, "I'm really glad I met you."

One corner of her mouth lifted. "Yes, I've been able to tell."

He laughed. "And that's been great. But this is deeper. I want you to know that." It was much too early to be throwing out the 'L' word, but it was hovering in his mind.

Rose glanced over at him. She wet her lips and cleared her throat. "Can I ask you a question?"

"Of course," he responded, but before she could continue, his phone buzzed in his pocket. He pulled it out to check the caller, and she turned her attention back to the road in front of her.

Irv Abbott's name was lit up on the screen.

Griffin didn't want to talk to Irv while he was with Rose, but he also didn't want Rose to think he was declining calls in her presence. He may have imagined her glance at the buzzing device, but he pressed the accept button anyway.

He shifted his position toward the passenger side window. "Hey Irv."

"Good news, Griff, my boy. I've gotten written confirmation from the DA you're getting off with a slap on the wrist."

Griffin brightened. "That's fantastic," he said. Then he paused. "What does 'a slap on the wrist' mean in this situation?" Griffin fully expected Irv to tell him the amount of the fine he'd been ordered to pay.

He'd only told Rose in vague terms about the situation, but he assumed she'd read the news coverage. *Everyone* seemed to have read about it, either in the news or on social media, where everyone also had an opinion on his actions.

"No jail time," Irv said. "Not even a fine."

An uneasiness entered his consciousness. "Mike didn't push for a fine?"

"No." The lawyer's answer was quick, but the word itself held a hesitation.

"Give me the details, Irv."

A breath. "First, there's a six-month community service requirement. And they're open to letting you define the details and the organization, as long as it, in some way, promotes leadership and good decision-making." Irv didn't add the unspoken, but those were certainly qualities Griffin had been lacking. "Of course, they'll need to approve whatever you come up with," Irv continued. "I'll need your proposal in writing by early next week."

Six months. Griffin thought about that. He actually had something in mind, but he wasn't sure he could pull it off. He'd need to have some conversations. He'd already *planned* to have conversations.

"I have to say, I'm impressed. I thought for sure the order would be much more involved. I thought Mike would've insisted on more."

"There's something else."

Griffin shut his eyes briefly. Here's where the other shoe would drop. "What is it?"

"Speaking of Mike…" The words trailed off followed by a long pause.

Griffin's thoughts went to the oily man with the slicked-back hair and the superior smile. A queasy feeling bubbled up in his stomach.

Irv continued. "In exchange for not pursuing the charges, he wants an exclusive with you on his new talk show."

"New talk show?" The question exploded from Griffin's lips. "Since when would any network give that guy a talk show?"

"Since you knocked him out cold on the street and made him a household name."

"That was only a few weeks ago."

"Entertainment moves fast. What can I say. You've been part of it. It pays to take opportunities when they come. And you handed Mike McCaffrey the opportunity of a lifetime."

Griffin exhaled long and slow. "I don't know if I can agree to those terms, Irv." He wondered if those terms had been Irv's.

"You want me to go back to the DA to renegotiate jail time?"

"I'd be okay with a fine."

"I'm going to guess Mike McCaffrey will not be."

Griffin said nothing, and Irv clearly took that as concession. Was Griffin conceding? He hadn't decided yet. But he assumed a jail term might last at least a few months after the lenient sentence he'd received after punching Charlie Bryant in the restaurant late last year. He glanced over at Rose. There were a lot of reasons he didn't want to go to jail.

"You'll need to be back next week for production, which will air live. And you'll need to sign your life away that you'll be on your best behavior during filming." It was a warning, and again Griffin kept his mouth firmly shut. "Look on the bright side. You can leave that backwater little town and come home. The news cycle will move on, and you'll become not much more than a quick snicker and a distant memory."

Griffin didn't know if that was supposed to make him feel better.

He glanced over at Rose, who was doing her best to pretend not to listen to his conversation. He was starting to feel like so much more than a quick snicker in this small town. Especially in the eyes of the woman beside him.

When he talked to her, he mattered. He couldn't remember the last time anyone had made him feel like he mattered. In his relationships as in his career, there had always been someone to step right in and fill the gap he'd left. He didn't feel the same way with Rose.

Perhaps sensing his gaze on her, she looked over at him and offered an encouraging smile.

"I need to go, Irv." He moved the phone away from his face to end the call, but he heard Irv's faraway voice.

"One more thing…"

Griffin sighed. "What?"

"Howard Lincoln called to tell me you'd finally signed all the paperwork. Good boy. When you get back, we can discuss next steps with regard to all of that. I'm not an estate attorney, but I've got somebody on staff who can help."

Instinctively, Griffin huddled closer to the window. He and Rose hadn't spoken about the inheritance since they'd slept together, and he wasn't sure how to bring it up. In fact, he *did* have plans for those assets—plans he hadn't communicated to Rose or anyone else. At least, not yet.

"Call me when you get into town. We'll meet and discuss all of this, along with my fees for these super-human feats I've been able to negotiate on your behalf." Irv chuckled. "And I'm going to invite Justin to sit down with us." Justin Dutton's name was a blast from the past. Griffin hadn't talked to his most recent agent and publicist since the Bryant debacle when the man had immediately dropped Griffin as a client.

The fact Irv had mentioned the name meant Justin had wanted to be mentioned. He probably had some sort of opportunity for Griffin to slowly claw his way back into the spotlight using Mike's talk show as a springboard. Griffin imagined a celebrity boxing match or something equally as absurd.

He wanted nothing to do with Justin. But to end the call, he said to Irv, "Sure, Irv. Sounds great." He hung up.

"All good?" Rose asked when he didn't immediately speak.

Griffin managed a forced smile. "All good."

Rose looked over with a tight smile, as if she didn't quite believe him.

She was right to be skeptical. It was not good. Not by a long shot.

Chapter 20

In the silence following Griffin's call, Rose turned on the radio. The last station she'd listened to in the car was an alternative rock station. A tenor voice was lamenting in a haunting minor key what happened when you messed with love.

Rose let the song play through, but she much preferred Mid's generally upbeat pop jazz leanings: Bublé, Connick Jr., Martin, Darin, Sinatra. Those guys knew how to vocalize love and heartbreak properly.

She'd gathered enough information to realize the man called 'Irv' was Griffin's lawyer and they'd likely been discussing his legal troubles. But she couldn't shake the feeling something else had been communicated. Something that had made Griffin deeply unhappy. And that caused her senses to sharpen.

All of Rose's past romances had been carefully cultivated so she'd been in control: she'd been the one to initiate the relationship, she'd set the tone and progression, and she'd ultimately left those relationships when she felt they'd run their course. With Griffin Stangel, she felt as if she had no control at all. It left her breathless, but also terrified.

Rose left Griffin at Mid's house. He said he had some phone calls to make, but she didn't ask.

She then headed to the salon. She dreaded facing the staff because she still hadn't worked up the courage to ask Griffin his plans. Along with the thrill of intimacy with Griffin, she felt off-balance.

The dinners, talking, laughing, and lovemaking were exquisite. Perfect even. But this wasn't a relationship, and whatever it was, it was far from perfect.

It was Hallie's day off, and Rose breathed a sigh of relief. But it was Jay who eyed her instead.

"I've missed some developments on my one day off this week," he said after he'd glanced up at Rose. He looked back to the head of Walter Bixby, who was seated in his chair.

Walter winked. "The whole town is talking about our little Rose's new little romance."

Rose wished she was disciplined enough to ignore Walter. "It's not a romance." And it didn't feel 'little'.

"What is it then?" asked Jay.

Rose didn't answer. She wished she knew.

The mood in the salon was decidedly subdued, and it made Rose feel guilty. Even Della, seated at the front desk, had little to say. She felt as though they'd given up on her, and she couldn't say she blamed them.

They were all waiting for everything to end.

As Rose stood at her own station, she became

aware Della had asked her a question. She looked up. "Sorry?"

"I was reminding you of your bookings this afternoon. I have my own appointment I need to take."

When she said it, she didn't meet Rose's eye, and Rose wondered if the woman had a job interview lined up. She supposed she didn't blame her.

Rose nodded. "Do what you need to do. I can handle the desk for you between clients. I'm going to spend this morning placing orders."

The front door opened, and Rose glanced over. Julie Newlin stepped in wearing a blue pinstriped blouse and a pair of wide-legged navy cropped pants with stylish nude-colored ballet flats. As usual, her makeup was flawless, and she looked more Milan than Madison.

Julie smiled widely and directly at Rose.

Rose felt the tingling of anxiety in her extremities. If Walter knew about Rose and Griffin, Julie had definitely heard the news.

Della didn't seem to notice the sudden tension in the room. She turned to Julie. "Didn't you just have your hair colored and trimmed a few weeks ago?"

Julie stared a beat longer at Rose with a wide smile. Then she transferred her attention smoothly to Della. "My bangs just need the teensiest bit of a trim. I thought maybe someone had time to even them out."

Alyssa, who'd just swept the salon floor, said, "I

have 20 minutes before my next appointment. I can take you."

The corners of Julie's mouth turned down. "What about Rose?" she asked, drawing out the 'o'.

Her face was perfectly pleasant, so Rose couldn't tell what her true motivations might be, and while she could have refused, she didn't. "Sure," she said. "Take a seat." She nodded to her chair. Her palms had started to sweat, and she excused herself to wash her hands.

After taking her time in the back of the shop, Rose took three deep breaths and walked out. Julie was staring critically at her striking face in the mirror. Rose glanced at her own plain reflection next to Julie's and wondered about Griffin's eyesight.

She looked back to Julie. "Do you need a wash first?"

"Not unless it's better for you."

Rose shook her head and swept a clean black cape embroidered with little pink winking eyes over Julie's designer clothes. Then she concentrated on Julie's hair, careful to avoid the woman's direct gaze. Her long, layered bangs looked perfect to Rose.

"Tell me what you're specifically asking for today."

Rose could feel Julie's eyes on her, and heat crept up her neck. She kept reminding herself she had nothing to feel guilty about. According to Griffin, he and Julie had never done anything but share a few meals.

Still, Rose couldn't help but feel she'd betrayed Julie somehow.

After a moment, Julie turned her attention back to her hair. "It's just a little long on the ends." She pulled a long layer from the right side of her face. "I'd like it to blend in better with the rest of my hair so it's not constantly falling into my eye." She let the strand go. "Do you see what I mean?"

Rose lifted the long fringe of Julie's bangs and considered the woman's concerns. "I'll do my best," she said.

"That's all any of us can do, isn't it?" There was an edge to her voice; Rose caught Jay's raised eyebrows in the double reflection of the mirrors.

Rose deliberately sectioned off Julie's bangs in the shape of a 'V', then held the hair between her fingers, using her scissors to trim vertically upwards.

She leaned in close; she could smell Julie's perfume. It was subtly sweet—flowers and vanilla with just a hint of peppery spice.

"I heard you're sleeping with Griffin Stangel." This was said loud enough for the entire salon to hear. Rose nearly dropped the scissors. She caught the sudden movements of Alyssa, Jay, and Walter in her periphery. Then she took two steadying breaths and continued trimming, the scissors open. Slow and light.

"Lois Rhodes, who lives across the street from you. I probably don't need to remind you that she's the secretary of the church's board of trustees. She said his car was parked right out front all night long."

It hadn't even occurred to Rose someone might have been monitoring the cars parked in front of her house. Then again, she hadn't been thinking much beyond Griffin.

"There aren't too many white Mercedes around town."

For a panicked second, Rose's mind raced for an excuse for Griffin's presence. Then she realized she didn't need one. She was silent for the next few minutes as she moved horizontally across Julie's face with the vertical scissors, cutting gradually less hair and moving toward her ear.

"How does that look?"

Julie shook out her blonde hair and frowned critically into the mirror. "I'm not sure," she said. She combed her bangs with her fingers. "It might be okay."

Rose nodded once. "Anything else before I remove the cape?"

Julie sighed and fluffed her long honey-colored locks with her fingers. "I'm thinking I might need something new. Something completely different. What do you think?"

Rose thought it was a trick question. But she considered Julie's inquiry. Julie was a bit mature for the Barbie-blonde color and waves. She might have looked sleeker and more sophisticated with a toned-down color and updated style. Something a bit shorter which would complement the woman's small, heart-shaped face. The long layers overpowered her delicate beauty.

But to Julie, she said, "I can send you some looks I think might suit your face."

"Let's just do it now," Julie said. There was a challenge in her eye.

But Rose knew this game. She removed the cape and shook her head. "Take some time and consider what you want before we do something drastic. You don't want to undertake a change that big on a whim." As the words left her mouth, Rose thought she should be taking her own advice. She wondered if Julie was thinking the same thing.

Instead, Julie fluffed her bangs and said, "I've heard getting an ill-advised haircut is one of the first things women tend to do after a breakup."

Rose managed not to react as Julie gracefully unfolded herself from Rose's chair.

"You know he was at my house last Friday night, right?" Her voice was breezy, but the implication was unmistakable.

Jealousy twisted, sharp and hot, in her chest. She knew everyone was listening intently in practiced silence.

Rose had no choice but to believe what Griffin had told her. Why would he bother lying?

"Griffin mentioned you'd had dinner."

"Did he mention what else we had?"

She bit down hard on the inside of her cheek. "That is none of my business," she finally managed.

"Well, if we're sharing the man's body, I'd think you'd want to make it your business." Julie's voice was late and airy, and Rose's jealousy transformed into rage. She suspected Julie was just trying to get under her skin, but she couldn't be sure. And she'd have to wait until evening to ask Griffin the question.

There was no chance she was going to act the stereotypical jealous girlfriend, calling to hysterically demand explanations for his behavior when he didn't owe her any.

"I think we're done here, Julie."

She gave Rose another bright friendly smile. "How much do I owe you?"

"You don't owe me a thing," she said, and just barely managed to stop herself from saying, *And I don't owe you anything either.*

"Are you sure?" Julie's voice was filled with exaggerated concern. "Because I heard Griffin signed the paperwork to take over the salon. I want to make sure I'm doing my part to take care of you girls." She looked at Jay, and added, "And guys. Just in case Griffin decides he's going to shut you down, or sell the building and the property." She waved her hand in front of her. "Or whatever. I guess anything could be on the table."

If the question about Rose sleeping with Griffin had rattled her, it was nothing compared to the jolt of pure shock she felt when she heard this last accusation.

Now Rose was livid. "I don't know where you think you heard that, but I can assure you—"

"I'll tell you exactly where I heard it," Julie interrupted. "Emily Brown who works in Howard Lincoln's office mentioned it to me."

Rose was stunned. Emily Brown did indeed work in Howard's office. Rose had no idea how Emily would have known Julie, but she supposed it didn't matter. The fact that Julie had cited her name gave credence to the information, beyond that of her other implications.

Julie must have decided her mission was accomplished, because the bright smile reappeared on her face. She wiggled her fingers vaguely at everyone and no one.

"Well, thanks for the haircut. See you all soon."

Then she was gone.

After a short, dazed silence, Jay and Alyssa swooped toward her. Della stood back stoically.

They began peppering her with questions.

"Is what she's saying true?"

"Does he really own the salon now?"

"Why wouldn't he have told you that?"

"Does he plan on firing everyone?"

"When is he leaving?"

Rose held up her hands. "I know as much as you. I

will ask him as soon as I get home."

Alyssa scoffed. "You were supposed to ask him two days ago. It doesn't look like you got around to *talking*."

Jay threw his hands in the air. "That's it. I'm calling my cousin in Baltimore."

Rose reached for him, but he shook her off.

"Let's all just calm down." She was talking to herself as much as the staff. "I'll get to the bottom of this. Please don't do anything rash."

"Like sleep with the guy who holds our livelihood in his hands?" asked Jay.

Rose clamped her mouth shut.

Jay said, "I'll give you until tomorrow, then I'm calling Kerri."

Rose nodded. But she wondered how she was going to make it through the rest of the day.

Chapter 21

Rose's heart pounded as she twisted the doorknob to Mid's front door later that afternoon. It was locked. She hesitated, then pulled out her keys, remembering the last time she'd walked into Mid's house unannounced.

This time, she was nervous for a different reason.

She inserted the key in the grooved slot, turned the knob, and tentatively stepped inside.

"Hello?"

No answer.

"Griffin?"

Silence met her ears, but the space felt inhabited, as if he'd left just a short time before.

She moved through the living room and into the bedroom where the paperwork that had been strewn across the comforter two days earlier was now stacked in a haphazard mass on the edge of Mid's dresser, next to her silver jewelry boxes and other miniature decorations.

The bed itself was rumpled, the comforter carelessly folded back against the pillows and the matching pillows strewn about the mattress and floor.

Griffin had slept here the night before, aware of the possibility of town gossip. Obviously their precautions had been too little, too late.

She left the bedroom and walked into the kitchen, where new items—spices, onions, garlic, and coarse sea salt—were on the counter along with two massive Idaho potatoes.

She let out a long, slow breath and shoved her hands into the pockets of her jeans. A man who was planning on cooking dinner couldn't have the worst of intentions, right?

She felt her resolve wavering.

When she turned to walk back to the living room, her eyes were drawn to the small table in the corner of the kitchen where Mid kept her telephone and a small basket with mail, writing utensils, and an address book. It was where Rose had stood when she'd called 911 on that horrible evening two weeks earlier. Had it really only been two weeks?

An unfamiliar brown folder, fat with papers, had been placed at the edge of the table. Rose reached out to shift its position, away from the brush of a passing hip. She noticed the card attached to the front of the folder. 'Howard Lincoln, Attorney at Law'.

Julie's accusation was still fresh in her mind, and she trailed the tip of her finger over the edge of the thick card stock.

Then she pulled her hand away and instead reached for the mobile phone in her back pocket. She checked for a message from Griffin which might indicate how long he'd be gone. But he'd not been in touch.

With a noisy sigh, she tried to return to the impending conversation with him.

But the fat stack of paperwork was calling to her.

Maybe, she reasoned, there was something in those papers that would answer all her questions and ease her mind. Maybe one quick look would make any conversation with Griffin unnecessary. Maybe she was overreacting and all she needed to do was peek inside the file before all was right in her world.

No, she told herself. Whatever was printed on those pages, Griffin needed to communicate it to her himself.

The loud trill of the landline phone caused her to nearly jump out of her skin. Rose reached for it, half expecting Mid's voice on the other end of the line. But it was just an automated courtesy call from the pharmacy about a refill of one of Mid's medications. Her rheumatologist must have forgotten to cancel her prescriptions. She made a mental note to call them tomorrow.

Rose hung up the phone and stared at the folder again. This time, she picked it up.

The pages were familiar to her. It was the same paperwork Howard had brought for Griffin to sign earlier in the week. Now, instead of the blank signature line, there was a dark heavy scroll, which Rose recognized as 'Griffin Stangel'.

Her breath caught in her chest. She had wanted Julie to be wrong about all of it. But the evidence of at least one of Julie's accusations was staring her in the face.

She flipped through the paperwork. Griffin now owned not only the house and other assets, but right alongside it was all the paperwork for My Pink Wink. Griffin now officially owned the salon too.

She felt woozy. He hadn't told her. If he'd mentioned any of this to her—explained his plans—she may have felt differently. Maybe she'd be able to understand. But now, she felt she'd been duped.

At the very back of the paperwork, two sheets of paper differing in color and thickness. Rose pulled them out. Here was a familiar spiky handwriting.

Rose read the words on the paper.

I, Mildred Annabell Higgins, of Madison, Pennsylvania, being of sound mind and body, leave all of my possessions, including my house, my car, and my business—My Pink Wink—to my dear friend and surrogate daughter Rose Glasser.

I attest to the fact that this will was made of my own volition and was not made under duress.

Upon my death, I appoint Rose Glasser as the executor of this will, as she is the only one who would have any idea what the hell to do when I die. She was the only one who had any idea what the hell to do when I was alive.

Rose is authorized to pay my debts and make any funeral arrangements for me as she sees fit. Make sure Jack Cummings is involved, though, and tell him to make me look at least ten years younger and twenty pounds lighter.

I direct that my remains should be buried in Madison Cemetery, I suppose next to my sister, Madeline Higgins Stangel, and though I have great reservations about lying next to her for eternity, I figure that's as good a place as any to hash out our differences, since we couldn't seem to manage it while we were both alive.

And for god's sake, someone tell Max I forgive him, and also I'm sorry I wasn't able to do that above ground.

Rose stopped reading. There were more words written on those pages, but they didn't matter.

What mattered was that these papers were bundled together with paperwork Griffin had signed. Which meant, even if they were not in themselves legally binding, Griffin knew what Mid's wishes had been. He'd signed the paperwork anyway, giving him possession of his aunt's assets without telling Rose.

If he was lying about this, what else was he lying about?

Rose stared at those pages until the front door opened, and Griffin walked into the room, holding up two paper bags like a trophy.

"I've got steaks and wine and a grill in the car."

She stared at him. His smile faded when he looked first at her face and then at the papers in her hand.

But instead of appearing remorseful or contrite, he looked almost…excited. "I was going to tell you about that tonight."

Did she actually hear a small chuckle?

"Were you?" The words burst forth. "And when were you planning to share? From what I can see, these papers were signed two days ago. The night after we slept together." Her hands shook as she thrust the folder in his direction.

Griffin blinked. "There's no need to yell."

She slapped the folder down onto the table and the loose leaves scattered. The first page of Mid's hand-written wishes fluttered and landed between them. Rose pointed to it. "You knew she wanted me to inherit everything, but you just couldn't help taking it all for yourself, could you? The question I have is *why*?" She waved her hands in his direction. "You clearly don't need it. Though there seems to be a pattern of you making money from cheating, cavorting, lying, and philandering, so maybe this is right in line with your style."

An angry flush had crawled up Griffin's neck and into his cheeks, and his mouth was a hard slash across his face.

Rose couldn't seem to stop the words. "Julie Newlin came into the shop today and told me all of it. I didn't believe a word of what she said about Mid's property, and I also didn't believe her when she said the two of you had been together two days before you slept with me." She pointed to the folder on the table. "Here's the hard evidence of one of her claims. What do you have to say about the other?"

His eyes were angry and intense, and a muscle ticked in his jaw. "I did not sleep with Julie. We had dinner. That's it."

"Why should I believe you?" Her voice was a cry. Then she shook her head. "I don't even know you."

"You're right, Rose. You don't know me. And from what I can tell, you've never been interested in knowing anyone else either." He shook his head slowly. "It was only a matter of time before you found an excuse to end this." He gestured between them. "Because you're too scared to get close."

Griffin was right; she *was* protecting herself. And after all these years of keeping her heart safe, she'd let her guard down with a stranger. Worse than a stranger—a man who had a very public track record of breaking hearts and homes.

She charged toward the front door, rushing past him.

"Rose, wait…"

But there was nothing to wait for. He had nothing to offer her but pain.

Outside, she took deep gulps of cool afternoon air. Then, finding he'd parked his car behind hers in the narrow driveway, she paused.

After the briefest assessment, Rose climbed into the driver's seat, twisting the key in the ignition. She shifted into drive and gunned the engine, praying her old, reliable Honda with its small engine would make it over the sloped embankment next to Mid's house. For less than a second, the tires spun on the damp grass, digging into the soil. Then the tread caught and the car flung forward, bumping over the ground. She managed to maneuver the vehicle back down over the yard, scraping the front bumper onto the curb of the paved road.

The driver of the pickup truck winding up the road slammed on his brakes and laid on the horn, but Rose didn't bother to acknowledge Jacob Wagner, the farmer from up the road, who would surely have something to say to her in church on Sunday.

She returned home, feeling very much alone. She wanted to call Teddy, but she didn't want to hear him say, "I told you so."

What was worse, Rose had warned herself, and she hadn't listened. Rose had escaped Griffin, but she wished she could find a way to escape herself, too.

Chapter 22

Griffin watched Rose walk out the door. He waited for her to return to ask him to move his car.

Maybe if she were forced to talk to him, she might listen to reason.

Then he heard the engine of the small sedan rumble to life, followed by the whining of the transmission and the whir of tires.

He rushed to the window in time to see Rose shoot onto the street in the path of a pickup truck that fortunately had been crawling up the back road at a leisurely pace.

He swore under his breath.

Why had he left the paperwork just lying around?

But the truth was, he didn't think it was a big deal. He'd had no choice but to sign. It was the only way to transfer the property, My Pink Wink included, back to her.

Because Mid's will had not been witnessed, Howard wasn't sure he could push the handwritten will through the courts quickly. The estate may have gone into probate with a chance the property would've made its way right back to Griffin anyway.

The easiest way to get the property to Rose was for Griffin to assume it, then immediately transfer it to Rose.

He'd planned to explain all this to Rose this evening over steaks and wine. They were going to celebrate. He still wasn't sure of his longer-term plans, but once he'd fulfilled his obligations in Boston next week, they could work it all out. He'd been sure of it.

Now, he was sure of nothing.

He waited an hour before calling her, hoping she'd cooled off enough to listen to what he had to say, but his call went straight to voicemail.

He texted her. —*Rose, please let me explain.*

The text was delivered but not read.

An hour later, he tried again. —*We can talk through this.*

No response.

Her questions about Julie haunted him. He may have withheld information about Mid's property in an effort to create some grand gesture, but he hadn't lied to her about the other woman. He had no interest in anyone but Rose.

While that scared him, it did not scare him off.

He called Howard's office to speak to the attorney himself.

Howard's assistant Emily answered the phone. "Howard Lincoln, Attorney at Law. This is Emily. How can I help you?"

"Hi, Emily. This is Griffin Stangel calling for Howard. Is he in?"

"He's just left for the day. Can I take a message?"

He almost left one, then thought better of it. The way incomplete information moved through the town was as frustrating as it was amusing.

"Do you happen to have his mobile number handy?"

The woman hesitated. "I don't usually give that out unless I have express permission from Howard. But I can have him call you back if he checks in."

Griffin remembered Howard had contacted him earlier in the week. From Mid's kitchen table, in fact. He'd scroll back through his calls to find the number. He thanked Emily for her time and ended the call.

He considered his next move. A call to Irv would likely generate a prolonged conversation Griffin was not ready to have. Aside from returning to Boston to fulfill his legal obligations, Griffin had no other immediate plans.

He scowled when he thought about Mike's ridiculous vanity project, hating that the man had found a way to hold him hostage and make him look like even more of a fool than he had previously.

But the thought of returning to Boston caused a surge of relief to flood through him. Boston had become home. He missed the grittiness of the city, the gruff personalities of the people. He was loathe to admit it, but part of him also missed the minor celebrity status he had there.

In Madison, he was somewhat of a novelty, but no one seemed to care who he was. Without Rose, he didn't feel as if he belonged.

Rose, he thought with a sigh. Who was he without her? And what did he want long term? He didn't have answers to those questions, and neither, he realized, did she.

He thought back to his time on the field. All those post-game celebrations with the players and their families. Griffin had usually been alone, though a few times, his romance-of-the-moment had joined him.

He barely remembered them.

More vividly than he could recall the memories, he could fantasize Rose into those real-life scenarios. To his amazement, in those contemplations, she wasn't alone. She had a dark-haired, wide-eyed baby on her hip.

Maybe he knew what he wanted after all.

He thought about the boy in the hospital room and the boy across the street. Chase. He gazed across the lawn to the ballfield. Then he took a breath, steeled himself, and made the call he'd been putting off.

Later that evening, after he'd eaten his steak, alone, he sat in the twilight on Mid's front stoop.

He supposed he should stop thinking of the stoop as Mid's, though he'd become very close to his aunt's spirit over the past week. He wished he'd known her when she was alive.

He sipped the glass of Pinot Noir he'd hoped to share with Rose and pondered his life's choices, most of which had been questionable. But they'd ultimately led him here, and as he leaned his head against the brick column of the small porch, he realized there were worse places to be.

His phone buzzed on the concrete beside him, and his heart stuttered before he caught sight of the name. *Max.*

He picked up the phone. "Max..." He'd long ago stopped calling the man 'Dad'.

"Griffin. Haven't heard from you in quite some time."

From his father, Griffin considered this more an acknowledgment of time passed than a judgment. "I've been busy."

"So I've gathered from the news coverage."

Griffin frowned. "Am I in the news again?" He wondered if Mike had already been promoting him as a part of his silly little talk show. He wouldn't put it past the guy.

"I'm referring to the stunt from a few weeks ago—

the one where you dated the married woman and punched out the reporter. Déjà vu all over again, huh?"

"That's old news," he said.

"What's it going to cost you?"

"An agreement has been negotiated."

Max made a noncommittal noise at the back of his throat. "I'll bet. So, are you just laying low until this thing blows over?"

He thought of his father likely sitting in the study of his Spanish Mission-style home in the foothills of Arizona's red rocks. He'd nearly forgiven his father for leaving and allowing Griffin to languish with his detached mother. Max Stangel had done what he'd had to do, and Griffin respected it, even if he hadn't liked it.

"Actually, I'm in Madison."

There was a pause so long, it prompted Griffin to say, "Max? You still there?"

"When you say 'Madison', I don't suppose you mean Madison, Wisconsin."

It hadn't been a question, but Griffin answered it anyway. "Pennsylvania."

"Why on earth would you be there?"

Griffin thought about the best way to answer his father's question. He remembered the photograph and his father's smile in it. Max wasn't a man of big emotion.

"I am, apparently, the closest relative to my mother's sister."

Griffin could hear the intake of air. "Mid," Max finally said. "She reached out to you? After all these years?"

Griffin thought about the journal entries. He remembered the engagement.

He remembered the one sentence in her handwritten will.

"Her attorney reached out to me. I'm her closest next of kin."

There was another long pause while Max translated Griffin's meaning. Finally, he spoke in a low voice.

"Mid is dead?"

"She left her property to me." Then he amended his statement. "Rather, she officially left her property to no one at all. So I came to Madison."

"You went to the funeral?"

"No, I thought that might be insensitive since I'd never met the woman."

"Then what are you doing there? I would've thought any property transfer could've been done over the phone."

"My attorney thought it was best I go in person. It's a long story." Griffin took a breath. "I take it you knew Mid?"

"A long time ago."

"I have some questions about that. Rose and I found Mid's journal and some photographs."

"Rose?"

"Mid's…" Griffin's words trailed off. What was the best way to describe their relationship? "Mid's surrogate daughter," he finished, using Mid's own words.

Another silence.

"Max, were you engaged to Mid before you married my mother?"

"Look, there's a lot…" He ended his sentence abruptly and cleared his throat. "A lot of things happened that year. It's hard to know where to begin."

"Maybe you could begin at the beginning."

"This is a hard conversation to have over the phone. I don't suppose you'd be willing to make a trip out here anytime soon?"

Griffin considered. He thought about Rose's anger and her unwillingness to take his calls or respond to his texts. He thought about his upcoming travel to Boston and the need to make amends in order to move forward cleanly. And he wanted a clean start with Rose.

Maybe to start over again, you had to go back and sift through the messy past; the pieces that didn't quite fit together neatly. The things you'd rather forget, but which made you the person you'd become.

"I can fly out tomorrow."

Chapter 23

Griffin had taken off early from Pittsburgh International, flown into Phoenix and driven a rental car three hours north. He was exhausted, but it was still early afternoon in the West.

His body felt every bit of the eight hours which had passed as he sat in the bright airy sitting room of his father's spacious one-story home in Sedona. This was not the home in which Griffin had spent part of his late teenage years. That residence had been closer to Phoenix. But the entire area held fond memories for him.

His stepmother handed him a glass of iced tea with plenty of mint from her back garden, and he smiled thanks. She touched his shoulder. Ines Stangel was kind. She'd prepared a simple lunch of fresh salad with chicken, berries, and pecans. A trim, lively woman, she wore her blonde hair short and practiced yoga daily. She looked at least ten years younger than she was.

Max, too, had aged well.

Like Griffin, his father was tall with dark hair nearly free of gray. While he'd filled out a bit around the middle, and some of his muscle had softened, Max looked much the same as Griffin remembered.

And Griffin looked like his father. He'd always suspected the resemblance was part of the reason his mother seemed to have such animosity toward him.

Sins of the father, Griffin supposed.

Ines left the room, heading out to the garden to give them privacy. Through the sitting room's sliding glass door, Griffin watched her move around in the afternoon sun.

His father had been restless and fidgety since Griffin had arrived, and now that they were alone, Max ran his weathered hands through his hair. He leaned back in his armchair and regarded Griffin with those amber eyes so much like Griffin's.

"Your news came as a shock yesterday." He shifted his gaze from Griffin to a point outside, somewhere near those red rocks in the distance. "I never thought I'd live in a world that didn't include Mid in it somewhere."

His breath was steady, and his stare was outside this plane of existence.

Griffin gave his father a few moments of reverie, before prompting him. "Tell me how you met."

"It seems like yesterday—Mid standing up on the stage at Froggy's Bar in downtown Pittsburgh. She was wearing this blue overall-type outfit and had her hair up in a huge pink bow...she was singing Sinatra, of all things." Max smiled and shook his head. "I don't think anyone else was paying her any attention, but I couldn't take my eyes off her."

"What was she doing downtown?" Griffin was under the impression Mid had never left the little town of Madison.

"It was during the school year, so she'd have been down there with some of her girlfriends. She went to Carlow or Chatham, I think. One of the small colleges—I can't remember which. Anyway, when she left the stage, I made a beeline for her, and we talked for hours.

"She sounds great," said Griffin.

"Made me laugh like nobody has since."

"So what happened?"

Max sighed. "We dated for over a year. I went home with her, met her family. But the thing about Mid—she was a homebody. As extroverted as she was, she made no bones about the fact she planned to stay in Madison after college. It was where she wanted to be."

"But not where you wanted to be."

"At first, I wanted to be where she was. But I was young, and I knew there was more I wanted to see and experience. Mid didn't have the same wanderlust."

"Why did you propose?"

Max looked up sharply with a pained expression on his face. "You said you found her journal. I wondered how much you knew."

"Not much," Griffin said. "Just the proposal. At the waterfall."

"Cucumber Falls. It was her favorite place."

"But not yours."

"I wanted something else."

"And *someone* else," Griffin said, referring to his mother.

Max set his jaw. "No." He said the word with force. "That was never the plan."

"And yet, you ended up marrying Mid's sister."

Max leaned back against the cushions. He twisted his wedding ring on his left hand unconsciously. "If I could go back and change my actions at that time, I would do it in a heartbeat. I think about it every day."

At that, Griffin looked at his own hands. He knew his father hadn't meant the implication, but Griffin felt it in his gut. If Max had the power to change his past actions, Griffin would never have been born.

He wasn't sure his father was planning to continue, but he finally said, "Madeline looked like Mid, obviously. But she was cooler, more reserved. There was a mystery to her. At least, I thought that's what it was back then. Turns out she just didn't like to share. But then, I found her intriguing. Where Mid shared everything she was thinking, Mad made you work for her attention." He shook his head. "She also wanted something more. She wanted to get out of Madison, travel the world. She wanted what I wanted. Or so I thought."

"So you broke up with Mid for her sister." It was a statement.

"I wish it had been that simple. I wish I'd had that kind of courage. Instead, I proposed to Mid even though I knew I couldn't give her what she wanted. At least not at that point in my life."

"I don't understand. Where did my mother come into the picture?"

"I'd been visiting Mid, but she had to work the next morning, so she wanted to go to bed. I was leaving when Madeline was coming home. We looked at each other, and we…Well, we made a mistake, is what we did."

"Okay, I get that," Griffin said. God knew he'd made plenty of his own mistakes. "But why not just tell Mid, apologize profusely, and leave the family alone?"

"I was a stupid kid. I pretended everything was okay. Until a month later when Madeline announced she was pregnant."

There was a moment of heavy, shocked silence. Griffin blinked as he tried to process this information, but it kept getting scrambled in his mind. It took him longer than it should have to realize what Max was telling him.

Finally, in a quiet voice, he said, "She was pregnant with me?"

Max leaned forward, clasping and unclasping his hands. He didn't look Griffin in the eye.

"I was the mistake," Griffin said.

"Oh, no, Griff. You were the one good thing that came out of any of this. You weren't a mistake."

"Only the act of my creation was a mistake."

Max looked as if he wanted to argue, but he didn't know what to say. He opened his mouth and shut it again, looking miserable.

"Why did you marry her?"

"I didn't want to, but Madeline said she was keeping the baby. Keeping you," he clarified.

Griffin gathered Max had not been in agreement with her decision.

Max took a breath. "I wanted to do the honorable thing. And so, we eloped, and we never looked back."

"How did you tell Mid all of this?"

"Madeline told her."

"But what did *you* say to her?"

Max lifted his shoulders, and Griffin realized his father had been a coward.

"You never spoke to her again," said Griffin, disgusted.

"Once. After your mother and I split up." He rubbed the back of his neck. Then he took a long swallow of the iced tea, the ice long since melted. He looked at the glass as if he wished it held something stronger. "Your mother and I had some heated conversations about custody."

"Let me guess—neither of you wanted me."

"Not true. We both wanted you. But in an acrimonious divorce, sometimes the child is used as a weapon against the other parent."

Given how much his parents had hated each other, Griffin guessed that had gone both ways.

"I had this deluded idea," said Max, "that maybe I could right all the wrongs with Mid. I called her with a crazy plan to take you back to Madison with me and marry her instead of Mad."

This admission shocked Griffin more than all the others. "You wanted her to raise your love child with her sister?" Griffin was appalled.

"That was essentially Mid's reaction, too. Before she hung up on me. I never called her again. I wrote her a few letters, but never sent them."

"What about Madeline? Did she talk to Mid? Apologize?"

"I have no idea what your mother did or didn't say to her."

They sat in silence for a long while, each lost in their thoughts. Finally, Griffin pulled out his phone. "She wanted to let you know, and I quote, 'And for god's sake, someone tell Max I forgive him, and also I'm sorry I wasn't able to do that above ground.'"

Max stared at his son, his mouth open. "Mid said that?"

Griffin nodded.

"How?"

"It was written in her will."

A sob erupted from Max's throat. His father leaned forward, his head in his hands and his shoulders quaked.

As if sensing her husband's distress, Ines looked in the window and frowned. She turned searching eyes to Griffin who nodded as if everything was okay. Griffin didn't know what Max had told Ines, but obviously she was committed to giving them privacy.

Griffin went into the kitchen and found a box of tissues. He carried them into the sitting room and handed them to Max, who pulled himself together and blew his nose noisily.

"I know it wasn't easy on you, Son, and for that I'm sorry. But I've always loved you. And so did your mother. We were always happy you existed, even if we were too immature to know how to properly show it."

"Mom hated me," said Griffin flatly.

Max shook his head. "Your mother had complicated feelings about everyone in her life, herself included. You not only reminded her of her own mistakes, you reminded her of me. And she had a hard time dealing with that. It wasn't a fair burden to put on a child. Neither of us did what we should have done for your sake. I can't ever make it up to you." He looked as if he might cry again. "The fact you managed to make a success of yourself and your life despite our mistakes—it's nothing short of a miracle. No matter where you ended up, you landed on your feet, and you made it look easy. You did what I couldn't do. And I've always been proud of you."

Griffin felt tears spring into his eyes and he quickly swallowed them away. All his life, he just wanted somebody to tell him he was doing the right thing. And to hear it now, when he'd screwed things up so royally, was bittersweet.

"So," Max said on a breath, "Mid left you all her property. I don't imagine she had much. But maybe I'm wrong."

"A small house—the one she'd grown up in. And a hair salon called My Pink Wink."

Max laughed out loud. "That's the most absurd name I've ever heard."

Griffin smiled. "It's successful. Rose runs it."

"Tell me about Rose."

There were so many things Griffin wanted to say, but he didn't know where to start. So he didn't say anything at all.

"Your voice changes when you say her name."

"She's…" Griffin tried to muster the best way to describe Rose. *Intense and kind. Thoughtful and sober. Beautiful and unaware.* Finally, he just said, "She's amazing."

Max's face broke into a grin. "You're in love with

her."

Griffin had barely admitted that to himself. In front of his father, he shrugged. "I don't know about that."

"I know I'm not the best person to give you advice, but I'm going to offer it anyway as your father. Don't let her go."

It was Griffin's turn to gaze at those red rocks. "I think I may have already lost her." He glanced at his father, who looked at him patiently. Then he let his gaze drop to his feet. "I-I wasn't completely honest with her about something important, and she's not taking my calls at the moment."

"Did you cheat on her with her sister?"

Griffin gave him an incredulous look. "God, no. She doesn't even have a sister. She has a miserable bastard of a brother."

"I know I had nothing to do with the way you turned out, but you're a good person. No matter how this woman feels about you in this moment, don't make the same mistakes I did. Whatever you do, don't let her go without a fight."

Griffin felt helpless. But his father was right. No matter what he did, he had to try to get her back. Even if he had to ruin what was left of his shattered reputation trying.

And just like that, he knew exactly what he had to do.

Chapter 24

Rose ignored Griffin's calls for days. The first day had been easy. She didn't think she'd ever been so furious in her life.

Not only had she felt like a fool falling for his act, she'd had to go into the salon and tell the staff what had happened. She had to encourage them to find other jobs. She had to admit she'd let her stupid emotions get the best of her.

After all those years of so carefully insulating herself, she'd managed to ruin everything in less than a month.

They blamed her, and rightly so.

Jay made arrangements to move to Baltimore at the end of May.

She asked Hallie to hold on for as long as she could until Rose could use her contacts to find something that paid better than My Pink Wink.

Della told Rose not to worry; she'd land on her feet.

Rose knew they all would. She just wished it had been their own decision to make the leap.

Alyssa was the one who suggested they were being

hasty. "Why would Griffin get involved with Rose if he didn't have good intentions? He certainly didn't need to sleep with her to get his hands on the salon. He already had it."

"He's a guy," retorted Jay. "He slept with her because he could. Sex has nothing to do with what he planned from the beginning. I mean, why not sleep with her and still take the property? One thing has nothing to do with the other."

"If he wanted to have a bit of fun, there are better options than Rose," Alyssa argued.

"Okay," Rose broke in. "I'm right here."

Alyssa wasn't deterred. "You know what I mean. You're not what he'd pick if he just wanted to sleep with someone."

Rose felt both proud and insulted at the same time.

In the end, they all knew change was imminent. And aside from being coworkers, they were friends. Maybe they weren't the type of friends Rose would call up and confess her deepest, darkest secrets to. But maybe they could be. Whatever happened, she would miss them all greatly.

The worst of it was Rose felt as if she'd let Mid down. She hadn't been able to hang on to what Mid had built. She hadn't lived up to her half of the bargain.

If only Mid had filed the handwritten will when she'd first gotten sick.

Why hadn't she? Rose wondered. She resigned

herself to the fact she'd never know.

Teddy had been surprisingly supportive. They'd spent more time together than they had in years. He hadn't said, "I told you so." On the contrary, he'd said over a plate of greasy French fries covered in cheese and bacon at a steakhouse in Greensburg, "I'm glad you fell for him. The last guy you dated—what was his name? Carl?"

"Chris," Rose corrected.

He pointed at her with a fry. "You didn't even like that guy, and it was years ago."

"I'm so glad everyone has an opinion about my love life."

Teddy shrugged. "You can't sleep with the mysterious, famous stranger in a town like Madison and expect people not to talk."

Rose frowned and dipped a glob of cheese-covered fries in a healthy coating of ranch dressing. "Do you know how many miles I'm going to have to run to burn off just this appetizer?"

Teddy ignored her. "Now maybe you can date someone more suitable."

But Rose didn't want someone more suitable. She wanted Griffin. "You know, it was more than just sex."

He gave her a look. "It was less than a week."

Rose shrugged. After a day, Griffin had stopped calling, and the texts had ended too. She found herself running past Mid's house. But his car wasn't there, and she couldn't work up the courage to knock on the door.

By the third day, she feared he'd left for good. She was going to have to call Howard to find out if she had any obligations to the house in Griffin's absence.

She'd tuned out of Teddy's rather verbose lecture on how there were plenty of available men for her to date, that all she had to do was open her eyes to suitable possibilities. As if he was one to talk.

Maybe the two of them were just meant to be alone. Some people were like that.

She interrupted his speech. "I fell in love with him, Teddy. I know it was only a few days, but it happened. You said he was going to break my heart, and he did."

Teddy frowned. "Actually, I'd changed my mind. I told Griffin you were going to break *his* heart, not the other way around." He became lost in thought for a moment. "I'm not convinced it isn't true."

"He lied to me."

"Did you give him a chance to explain?"

"The paperwork was dated the day after we slept together. He had three whole days to tell me. And he didn't. Why do you think that is?"

"I have no idea," said Teddy. "But you knew the property was his anyway, even if he hadn't yet signed. Did you expect you were going to sleep with him and he was going to sign the property over to you?"

Rose opened her mouth to argue and found she

had no response. What *had* she expected?

Had she subconsciously thought dating him would mean nothing in her life needed to change? Because if that were the case, she'd done something way worse than he'd done. She'd tried to manipulate his emotions. She shuddered.

But no. *The way her stomach clenched when she thought of him. The way her breath caught in her throat when she saw him. The way her heart softened when he looked at her…*

She felt a deep sense of betrayal.

Those were not superficial emotions. Her feelings for him were real.

The server brought their steaks on sizzling platters and refilled Rose's water. Rose cut into her steak and took a bite. "What about Julie?" she asked Teddy.

"I already told you—Julie didn't mean anything to him."

"What if he slept with her?"

"He said nothing happened," Teddy said around a bite of his steak. He washed it down with a swallow of beer.

"*Julie* said something happened."

"Of course Julie is going to tell you that. She's trying to make you jealous."

Rose rolled her eyes. "We're not in junior high."

"People don't change, Rose. Adult relationships are just adolescent ones with more at stake."

She shoveled a piece of wilted broccoli into her mouth. "He lied about the other thing."

"He omitted information, and you didn't give him the chance to explain. We can go around and around on this all night."

Teddy hesitated. "Rose, there's something else. I know you're holding on for something here. I know you really like him. But a guy like Griffin Stangel—a guy with that kind of track record—he doesn't settle down in a town like Madison. So you have to ask yourself, what were you hoping to get out of this…connection?" he finished after a pause.

Her brother had a point. And Rose had known that. She had no interest in leaving her life and her home. She had no interest in leaving Teddy.

She finished eating her meal in silence with her heart more bruised than when she'd entered the restaurant. Because she had to admit to herself, maybe it was a good thing the liaison had ended when it did.

After four days, Rose stopped glancing at her phone every few minutes, but she was left with a void in her chest. She skipped church that Sunday, but she ran into Julie as she picked up a sandwich at the coffee shop.

Rose avoided contact and conversation, but she caught the smug smile on Julie's face. If Julie couldn't have Griffin, the woman was happy Rose couldn't have him either.

Teddy was right—adult relationships weren't much different than the ones in junior high.

She sighed. Life was exhausting.

She was also left wondering what she was supposed to do about her responsibility as administrator of Mid's estate. Where did Griffin's responsibility end and hers begin?

She nearly used this as an excuse to call Griffin, but she managed to stop herself. Instead, she called Howard's cell phone, mindful of the wagging tongue of his assistant Emily.

She was in the back room of the salon when she finally reached him. 'Call Me Irresponsible' was playing over the speaker system, and Rose thought it was awfully fitting.

"Rose," Howard said. "I was wondering when I'd hear from you. Did everything look in order?"

Rose frowned. She had no clue what he was talking about. "I'm calling about my responsibility as administrator," she said.

"Ah, yes. Well, now it'll be a dual role. Basically, you'll be responsible for everything. But it's not uncommon. And since it's just you, it should actually make things easier."

"When you say 'everything', you mean the role of administrator?"

Howard hesitated. "The new agreements don't change anything there. We don't need to appoint a new administrator."

Rose was quiet while she tried to work out Howard's comment. Finally, she said, "Howard, what are you talking about?"

"Did you read the paperwork?"

"Griffin's paperwork?"

"No. The paperwork I sent in the mail. You should have received it last week."

Rose was mystified. She'd gone to the post office each day, and there had been no mail from Howard.

"I mailed it out as a hardcopy for you to review," Howard continued, "but you'll have to come in to have it witnessed and signed. You can come in now if you like."

"Howard, I don't have any paperwork."

Howard stuttered, then mumbled something before asking her to hold the line.

Bobby Darin was now singing about being impractical, and Rose tapped her fingernail on the counter in time with the music.

The lawyer was back a moment later. "Apparently there was some miscommunication, and Emily didn't get the paperwork out to you. Honest mistake."

Rose doubted that very much.

"But I'm sure Griffin filled you in on his plans."

A shiver of unease passed through Rose. "Griffin's

gone," she said.

"What do you mean?"

"I haven't spoken to him since last week."

Howard paused. "Well, I suppose that's his prerogative. But given the conversation he and I had, I'm rather surprised he left abruptly."

Rose thought it best not to mention her last conversation with Griffin. "Can you just tell me what's going on, Howard?"

She heard Howard's sigh. "Obviously, Mid's handwritten note would've been difficult to get through the courts without some questions, so as I explained to Griffin, the easiest workaround was to put everything into his own name first so he could just sign it all over to you. The paperwork that *should* have been mailed out to you would've explained everything. But as it is, you'll just have to come in and sign it. We can take care of everything else here."

Rose's world tilted. "Excuse me?" she managed to whisper in a raspy voice. "I don't think I heard you correctly…"

Howard repeated everything he'd just said.

Rose swallowed. "Are you telling me I own everything?"

"You will once you sign the paperwork. Griffin was determined to be faithful to Mid's wishes. Also…" He hesitated. "…I gathered from the last conversation I had with him there had been some other developments of a personal nature between the two of you."

Rose leaned against the counter. "My Pink Wink is mine?"

"Yes," said Howard slowly. "Along with Mid's house and assets."

"But…why couldn't they just be signed over?"

"Because that's not how the courts work. This was the cleanest and fastest way to make the transfer."

Rose lost the feeling in her extremities. Her head spun. She sat down heavily in the plastic chair which had been placed in the room.

"And Griffin's involvement is done?"

"In essence, yes. But I got the impression Griffin wasn't necessarily done with you."

Rose stared at the wall and mumbled something to Howard about stopping in the next day and ended the call. She placed her forehead on the cool laminate countertop. As Frank Sinatra sang about doing something stupid, Rose shut her eyes.

"Oh, Mid," she whispered. "I think I fucked up."

Silence met her.

She stood up and paced around the room, her hands threaded in her hair. "Mid, if you're ever going to talk to me, it's got to be now. Can you give me just a little sign? Just something so I know I haven't ruined my entire life?"

For a second, there was nothing but the heaviness of the air filled with ol' blue eyes' melodious declarations of love. Then her phone stuttered with the buzz of an incoming text message. Rose dove for it.

It wasn't Griffin, as she'd hoped. It was Alyssa, who was off that afternoon.

—*Did you know Griffin is being interviewed on a talk show in Boston tonight?*

He'd been talking to his lawyer about it, Rose remembered. But he'd offered no details, and she hadn't asked.

—*Tonight?* she typed back.

—*Yes. It will livestream, according to Eric*, Alyssa responded, referring to her boyfriend. —*Everyone online thinks it'll be a trainwreck. The reporter is a read d-bag. Gotta wonder why G agreed to it.*

Rose thought she might know why he'd agreed. —*What time?*

—*7:00*, Alyssa responded, followed by a hyperlink.

Rose had hours to kill until then.

She came out of the back of the shop and announced to Hallie, Jay, and Della she was leaving. They frowned, but said nothing. Then she went home, before realizing she had nothing to do there either.

When her phone vibrated again, it was a call from Teddy. "Do you know anything about this show Griffin is doing?"

"Not really," she said.

"Well, we're going to be streaming it at the Sweetwood, if you want to watch it here."

As much as she'd have liked company, something

told her she needed to watch this alone. She said as much to Teddy.

"All right," he said skeptically. "But call me if you need me. I don't know what the guy is going to say."

"I don't think he's going to talk about us at all," said Rose, but her heart was thumping.

She spent the next few hours cleaning her already spotless house from top to bottom, and by the time 6:45 rolled around, not a speck of dust was left.

With shaking hands, Rose opened her laptop and typed in the web address. The feed for the show had not yet begun, and Rose stared at the screen, watching the clock.

A comment section for the feed had opened at the bottom of the page, and the general consensus from the commenters was Griffin was going to get destroyed by Mike McCaffrey, the guy he'd knocked out on the street the same day Mid had died.

Rose maximized the screen so she couldn't see the comments. She hated the tendency of a crowd to root for the public humiliation of another person. Just another example of how humans hadn't evolved much past middle-school years.

Finally, the video feed started. An overly dramatic opening, with heavy music signaling hard-hitting news topics.

Then a closeup of a man's face. He was handsome in an oily way, but he was too coiffed, too powdered, too smug to be attractive. He looked like he was trying to be something he wasn't.

He smiled, and his teeth glowed white.

"Welcome to News Fusion Live with Mike McCaffrey, the talk show that blends news with heart. I'm your host, Mike McCaffrey. We're expecting record numbers for viewers for our first episode, most likely linked to our guest and subject matter tonight."

The camera panned out, and there was Griffin, looking polished and pristine in a blue suit with a white button-down shirt. His hair had started to grow out, but his beard was freshly trimmed, and the sight of him made Rose's heart falter in her chest.

She couldn't believe a man who looked like Griffin had ever been interested in her.

His hands were clasped together tightly in his lap, and she swore she saw his throat bob as he swallowed. He looked nervous.

Mike McCaffrey continued. "We're here tonight with a special guest, one that many of you might be surprised to see with me. Former Boston Red Sox player, Griffin Stangel. Many of you remember Griffin was arrested just a few short weeks ago for punching out yours truly on Congress Street in the Waterfront." He smiled in a disingenuous and self-deprecating way. "You might be asking yourselves why I'd choose Griffin as my first guest. But I'm all about second chances. Or in Griffin's case, third or even fourth chances. And I thought you should also have a chance to hear from him while the two of us shoot the breeze and clear the air. It's a win-win-win."

Curious as to what the commenters were saying, Rose opened the window.

—*What an asshole*, someone typed.

—*I can't stand this guy.*

—*Can't believe they gave him his own show.*

—*I think he's sexy.*

—*Gross.*

"Let's get right into it." Mike smoothed his tie as he looked at Griffin. "Mr. Stangel, thank you for being here today, first of all. You didn't have to come."

"Well, it was this or go to jail, so…" Griffin's voice trailed off.

Mike's polished smile faltered. Then he recovered and looked at the camera. "In full disclosure, as part of my generosity, I've elected not to press assault charges against Mr. Stangel in exchange for this interview."

—*Whoa*, one commenter typed. —*Is that even legal?*

—*It's probably legal, but it's sleazy as hell.*

—*This seems kind of like extortion.*

Rose squinted at Griffin's face. In addition to the nerves, there was an angry set to his jaw. What was he going to do? she wondered.

Mike cleared his throat and shifted in his seat. "Griffin, you crafted a career around your reputation as a loose cannon. Can you tell me why, even after all the trouble you've created for yourself, you continue to behave in unpredictable ways?"

Griffin leaned forward slightly. "I don't know, Mike. I think my behavior has always been fairly predictable. If any other normal person were walking down the street with a friend, and a guy with a camera was following him, asking him leading and harassing questions, that person might punch the jerk out too. Don't you agree?"

Mike's smile faded. "That's called assault."

"As you've made me well aware."

Mike glanced down at a notecard in his hand. "You and I had the chance to talk a little bit before sitting down. We discussed a number of topics, all of which you agreed to address." The man stressed the last phrase of his sentence, clearly trying to guide the conversation back onto the approved track. From the look on Griffin's face, Rose didn't think he planned on playing along. Griffin smiled. He looked so dashing and mischievous. Rose's blood pulsed in her ears and she felt woozy.

The commenters weighed in, too.

—*Oh, my god. The man is* hot.

—*Griffin, if you read these comments, come find me. @foxyroxy.*

—*I heard he's dating someone new.*

Rose ignored the last comment.

"Let's go in another direction," Mike said, glancing

down at his card. "You've lived up to your bad-boy reputation both on and off the field. Would you say you have an insatiable need for attention?"

Griffin seemed to consider this question. "It's not so much a need for attention, as it is a need for acceptance," said Griffin. "You see, Mike, despite my success on the field—success you'll never know, by the way—I had a pretty messed-up childhood. My dad was engaged to and in love with my aunt, and my mother, who was far from a saint, stole him away and immediately found herself pregnant with me. So when I was born, I wasn't exactly wanted. My whole childhood I spent trying to gain acceptance from somebody…anybody. I found my niche in baseball, and I was lucky to be able to pursue that. But I never really stopped looking for acceptance from my folks. And I never got it. So I tended to act out. It sucked, but if I had a different childhood, I wouldn't be where I am today. So, here we are."

Rose's mouth dropped open. That's what had happened between Mid and Mad? And Griffin's father? No wonder Mid hadn't spoken to her sister again. She wanted to ponder this new information, but on the laptop screen, she noticed Mike's stare shift to someone offscreen. She figured they were ready to cut the feed at any moment. Mike looked uncomfortable and crossed one leg over the other.

She almost felt bad for the guy.

Mike leaned toward Griffin, ignoring the fact that he was miked-up and the live audience was watching this trainwreck. "This isn't what we talked about."

"It's *not* what we talked about," Griffin agreed. "But I'm changing the narrative."

"You're in violation of our agreement."

"I'd like to tell you what you can do with your agreement."

Rose's eyebrows were raised nearly to her hairline. The comment section rolled fast and furious.

—*You tell him, honey.*

—*Griffin Stangel, the last man to tell it like it is.*

—*I'll give him the approval he's looking for.*

—*They better not cut this feed.*

Rose's phone buzzed, and Rose glanced at it. It was Alyssa. —*Are you watching this?*

—*Yes,* Rose answered.

—*What do you think he's doing?*

—*Telling this guy off.*

—*Cool story, but why bother going on this show in the first place if it's just going to send him to jail?*

Griffin held up his hands and said to the host in a conciliatory voice. "I'm sorry, Mike. I'm just giving you a hard time. Let's get back to the interview. That's what you wanted, right? An interview?"

Mike blinked, and again looked at someone off-camera, who must have told him to keep rolling with it.

"Let's talk about your relationship with women,"

Mike said, but where his voice had been arrogant and cocky before, now he sounded unsure. He was off-balance and not in control of the story. His forehead was shiny with perspiration.

But he continued. "Not even a year ago, you had a relationship with a married woman and destroyed a marriage. More recently, you were caught stepping out with another married woman, and ultimately that's what led to our interview today. Tell us about what led you down that path."

"I was hoping you'd ask me about that."

Mike hooked a finger inside his collar. He'd likely been hoping he'd prompt a reaction from Griffin during this interview, and probably expected anger, outrage, and out-of-control behavior. He hadn't expected self-reflection.

Her phone buzzed again. A message from Teddy.

—*Here it comes.*

Rose frowned. *Here what comes?*

—*You'll see.*

"I just told you about my parents. I don't think it takes a shrink to figure out I have some issues. But my mother died a few years ago, so there's not much hope for me to resolve those directly."

The scrolling comments continued.

—*Aww, poor thing.*

—*I heard somewhere he didn't even know she'd passed away.*

—Do you think he'll have to go to jail?

—I'd rather see Mike McCaffery go to jail.

"I didn't know your mother had passed," said Mike. "My condolences."

Rose thought he sounded sincere, but the online commenters wholeheartedly disagreed. This crowd had definitely skewed for Griffin.

"Thanks," said Griffin. "I didn't feel bad she was gone. I've had a lot of guilt over that."

Mike paused then said, "I've heard you've been in Pennsylvania for the death of an aunt. Can you talk a little bit on that subject?"

"The aunt was my mother's twin sister. I'd never met her."

"Oh," said Mike with mock surprise. "I heard she'd left you her property. I thought maybe you'd been close."

"I wish I could say otherwise. She seemed like a really cool lady."

"So this trip you had to take because of the death of a loved one…" Mike's words trailed off. He was clearly making some implication Rose didn't understand.

"I wouldn't have missed it."

"Why not?"

"Because I met someone there."

Mike's eyebrows shot up. "As in, a woman?"

"Yes, Mike. A woman." Griffin scoffed. "She's probably not watching this, but I'm hoping somehow the word's gotten to her this is being aired. I know you won't find this surprising, Mike, but I may have messed things up with her."

"How so?"

"I've been linked to a lot of women, but there have only been a few I've been interested in dating seriously."

"Victoria Bryant was one of those women."

"Victoria is a great person, and she didn't deserve the damage I caused."

Mike's lips formed an 'O', and he looked as if he were considering his next question, but Griffin kept going.

"But this woman—her name is Rose—is one of a kind."

Rose leaned forward. He was talking about *her*. The whole thing was so surreal.

"So what happened?" Mike asked.

"I wasn't as honest with her as I should have been."

"You lied to her, as you've lied to so many others."

"I never lied to her. But I was trying to be cool and surprise her, and it backfired. One of the reasons was because of her own hesitation." He held up his hands. "Which was totally justified because of my reputation. She told me to get lost. And so I did." Griffin turned to the camera. "Rose, if you're watching this…"

Rose put a hand to her throat. Her heart was pounding. Through the camera, it felt as if he were looking into her soul with those dark eyes.

"Rose, I knew how I felt about you the moment I first saw you in the Sweetwood Saloon. I know I ruined everything, but I hope, in time, you might find it in your heart to forgive me."

—Rose! Where are you? typed someone in the comments.

—How do we find this Rose person?

—Why can't I be Rose?

—She must be smokin' hot.

Rose's phone began to buzz with a barrage of incoming text messages. She ignored them.

"It's all yours," Griffin said. "The house, the money, My Pink Wink."

"My Pink *what*?" Mike asked.

Griffin ignored him, and continued speaking to her. "I want you to know, my days of being a bad boy are over. I may have to report to jail because I highjacked McCaffery's ridiculous, self-serving interview, but it will only be for a short time. I think. But after I get out, I'm coming for you."

Tears sprang into Rose's eyes.

—That's so romantic.

—I wish I could find a guy like that.

—They better not send him to jail. Not after this confession.

Rose held her breath.

"I don't intend to let you go, Rose. Ever. And I'll

follow you anywhere, or stay right by your side. I'm all yours, wherever you are. I love you."

"I love you too," she whispered to the screen.

"If I can get out of here, I'll be on an 8:00 a.m. flight. Meet me at noon…I think you know where. If you don't, just ask Mid." He winked, and then he smiled.

Rose knew exactly where he'd be.

Chapter 25

O f the dozens of texts Rose received, many of which were from people she hadn't spoken to in years, the only communication she bothered to answer was one from her brother.

—You okay?

Rose's reply was simple. *—Wish me luck.*

—You're going through with it, then?

—I have to see where this goes, Ted.

—Go easy on him. Her brother ended his last message with a smiley.

Rose received one phone call which she didn't ignore, and this she answered tentatively.

"Hi, Pastor Ballentine."

"Rose," he said in response, sounding as surprised she'd picked up as she was that the man was calling. "Thanks for taking my call."

"Is something wrong?" Typically, receiving a call from a man of the church in the evening did not bring the best of news.

"Did you, uh…?" He stopped, then started again. "I suppose you caught the broadcast with our friend

Griffin. It's been the talk of the town."

"I saw it, yes." Rose wasn't looking for unsolicited advice on her decisions.

"I thought you might have." He cleared his throat.

Rose waited.

"I think you know me well enough to know I am not one to engage in idle conversation or gossip, but Julie…Well, she casually mentioned a bit about what happened with Griffin and you."

Rose stiffened, but she didn't speak. She knew he was waiting for a response. She would not dignify his comment with an answer.

"I know this man might seem interesting and worldly compared to the men who come from a small town like Madison, but there's a real danger in becoming too close too quickly."

"Thank you, Pastor, but I can look after myself."

"Please. Call me Phillip."

Rose said nothing.

"I'm sorry," he continued. "I know this is none of my business. And I normally try not to give advice that isn't wanted. But I feel especially passionate about this, Rose."

Rose bristled. Frankly, she felt a bit violated. "There's really no need," she said, and her voice was cool. "I can assure you I am, indeed, an adult woman."

"Of course you are," he said. "There's more to it than that." He stopped abruptly.

Rose waited, fully expecting him to bring up his conversation with Julie. But he didn't do that at all.

"I've known you for a few years—since I've been pastor here. And I've come to care about you very deeply." He sounded anguished. Rose blinked in surprise. Was this man saying what she thought he was? She certainly didn't want to jump to any premature conclusions, and her silence seemed to prompt him to continue.

"I'd always thought we might…make a good match."

"A good match," Rose repeated slowly.

"I just never quite worked up the nerve to mention it to you," he said. "I guess I thought there was time. Or maybe you might come to the same conclusion on your own."

Another pause. She thought he was waiting for her to say something. But she had no idea how to respond. "Pastor Ballentine," she said. "I'm not sure—"

"I'm not expecting you to say anything," he interrupted. "Or to give me an indication of your interest. I just want you to know there might be other options out there you hadn't considered. You know, should things not go…as planned."

Rose did not owe this man any explanation. But she knew how he felt. She knew what it was like to be too afraid to share your feelings. Too intent on protecting your own heart to the detriment of your future.

And for that, she would share her perspective. "Thank you for your concern, Pastor."

"Phillip," he said weakly.

"First of all, I'm not sure what Julie told you, but there are multiple points of view about the experience we had. Three perspectives, in fact, and none of them match completely." She took a breath. "Secondly—and I'm sharing this with you because I want to, not because I feel I owe you anything—I've spent my entire adult life running away from feelings and commitment that might cause me emotional pain. There are many reasons for that, some of which you know, and most of which you don't know. I'm not doing that anymore."

"I'm glad for that," he responded politely.

"So am I." She considered her next words carefully. "Griffin Stangel came into my life at an extremely difficult time and under extremely difficult circumstances. Mid was my mother. And I'm still mourning her loss. But Griffin is mourning his own losses, and he has been for a long time. We may have developed a bond too quickly…" Rose stopped herself. She would not minimize her feelings for this man. "The truth is, Pastor, I've fallen in love with him. And maybe that means I will get hurt, but I'm willing to accept the risk. I've already nearly destroyed my chances with him once because I couldn't trust either him or myself. I'm not going to do it a second time."

A heavy silence hung between them before he said, "I appreciate your honesty. I just wish I'd had your courage."

Rose smiled into the phone. "I have full confidence you'll find your person."

"I'm glad one of us does," he responded. She could hear him exhale. "Well, I hope he can do something good with the baseball field."

"What baseball field?" she asked.

"The field across from Mid's house. Griffin offered the church a frankly ridiculous amount of money for those few acres of land. Apparently he wants it for his community service." Judgment hung heavy in his voice. "But with the amount…I couldn't turn down the deal."

Before she could ask for more details, the pastor continued speaking. "I wish you the best of luck and all the happiness in the world." Gone was the tentativeness, replaced by the confident voice he used every Sunday morning. Rose was surprised to realize at least some of what he portrayed from the pulpit was, in fact, an act.

She supposed they were all playing a part to some extent. While it made her sad, it also filled her with compassion for her fellow humans. It wasn't easy, this life.

⸸⸸⸸

The next morning brought the promise of a brilliant spring day—sapphire skies, chartreuse woodlands, and the golden sun lighting it all. Rose tried to borrow from the calm serenity and confidence of nature around her while she drove her way up the mountain roads to her final destination.

The route was familiar to her; it was one she'd taken with Mid many times. But Rose had so many questions about her path forward, she found herself second-guessing everything in her past.

What if Griffin had used the television appearance to gain public support and bolster his image? What if his lawyer had told him what to say to help his legal case?

Rose had tried to call him, but the calls had gone to voicemail, and the texts remained undelivered and unanswered.

So, here she was, driving forward into an unknown situation with an unknown outcome. She kept telling herself that if anything she was safe—even if Griffin walked out of her life forever, nothing would fundamentally change for her. She had her house, she had her business, she had her life. But in just these short few weeks, Griffin had filled a void with his presence. His sudden absence would cause the void to expand and damage her, maybe beyond repair.

Rose pressed down on the gas pedal, and her car's small engine whined with the effort to make it up the long mountain road.

She'd dressed casually in a pair of black athletic pants, white top, and sneakers, but she'd taken extra care in piling her hair atop her head, and she wore more makeup than she otherwise would have for a hike in the forest.

Rose found a spot in the crowded parking area nearest the waterfall. When she climbed out of her car, she found even the parking area brought back fond memories of Mid, who'd always thrown her head back and breathed in deeply when they'd emerged from the long car ride.

She wished Mid would've shared then what this place had meant to her. But maybe that's what she was doing now, after she was gone.

Rose felt Mid's presence as she began her descent down the steep path to the bottom of the gully. But Rose was also painfully aware there had been no white Mercedes in the parking lot, and the handful of people she'd passed on the narrow path hadn't looked her way at all.

At the bottom of the trail, Rose turned and continued the easy hike toward the waterfall. Because of the rain and melting winter snow, the stream feeding the waterfall was running fast and the waterfall gushed hard over the side of the rockface.

A mist of water rose up from the base, and the midday sun shone through the trees, creating a prism of colors around the pool.

Rose gazed at it, reveling in its beauty, but she was the only one on the path.

She sat on a large boulder next to the rushing stream. This was the same rock in the photo Griffin had found in Mid's journal—the location where Griffin's father had presumably proposed to Mid. Rose imagined Mid must have been in love with Max until the very end if she and Mid had made a yearly pilgrimage to this place.

She sat there for a long while. A piece of her was lost in the beauty and the memories. But the larger part of her was waiting for Griffin, vacillating between optimism, anticipation, dread, and anguish. When she finally allowed herself to check the time on her phone, it was hopelessness that prevailed.

Griffin wasn't coming.

Rose took one last look at the waterfall that had haunted Mid. With an exhale, she turned to leave. Her heart felt bruised, but she didn't feel as devastated as she thought she might. In fact, she felt…fine. She was sad of course, but she knew she'd be okay. Even if she never saw Griffin again, she'd be able to smile about the fact she'd met him at all.

Rose, it turned out, was whole all by herself.

The tires on the Mercedes screeched as he steered into his destination, directed by the GPS on his phone. He parked in a grassy spot next to the designated parking area, which was completely full. He tumbled from the car, nearly tripping over himself, and slammed the door behind him.

He was functioning on one hour of sleep. He'd spent the entire night in Irv's office while his lawyer tried to convince the district attorney Griffin had not violated the terms of his agreement with Mike McCaffrey.

Mike had been livid Griffin had not only defied the agreement they'd made, but he'd managed to upstage Mike and make him look like an arrogant and callous ass on his own television show. He'd taken a beating on social media, and he'd been pushing hard for Griffin's jail time.

In the end, social media was what had saved the day. Even the hard-nosed district attorney couldn't ignore the public outcry in support of childhood trauma and the promise of true love. The DA had doubled the community service requirement to a year and added a hefty fine, but Griffin didn't care.

He had all the time in the world for community service.

What he hadn't had was the time to make his flight.

He would've missed the trip altogether if an admiring gate and flight crew hadn't held the plane for him.

And even the inconvenienced passengers had cheered when he'd boarded, many expressing that his vulnerability had moved them to tears.

Who'd have thought the acceptance he'd craved his entire life had come simply by being honest with himself and the entire world?

When he'd landed in Pittsburgh, he'd been quickly recognized and swarmed by new fans. Griffin hadn't wanted to appear ungrateful, but he had somewhere important to be. He said as much, and they cheered him on his way to Rose.

When he finally made it to his car, he gunned the Mercedes through the mountains with the wind in his hair, hell bent on his rendezvous.

He'd tried to call and text, but Rose hadn't answered. Griffin had to hope the issue was down to lack of service in the mountains rather than a blocked number.

Now he was half jogging across the parking lot toward the pathway leading to the waterfall.

"Hey, you can't park there," a woman in a baseball hat said. She was holding the hand of a small child and pointing to his illegally parked car with the other hand. An embarrassed-looking man hunched behind her.

He gave her a half wave and continued on his way.

"That's not a parking spot!" she yelled behind him. "You'll have to find another legal place to park."

He glanced over his shoulder at the woman with

the furious expression, her hand now firmly planted on a hip that jutted out.

"I won't be gone long," he assured her.

"It's not a spot," she reiterated. "If you won't move it, I'll call the park police."

He'd already wasted too much time on this encounter. "Do what you have to do," he said over his shoulder, and he could hear her snort of disbelief.

Griffin ran down the side of the mountain, squeezing past slow-moving hikers on the narrow pathway. They were not as gracious as his fellow travelers on his earlier flight, even when he called words of apology over his shoulder.

He hadn't thought to look for Rose's car in the lot, and he had no idea if she was still here. Or if she'd shown up at all. He had no idea if she'd even watched the interview or heard his plea to her. Though he had to believe *someone* would've passed along the news.

Perhaps he'd gotten too cocky, thinking the entire country was talking about him. Worse, perhaps he'd gotten too cocky thinking Rose would forgive him in the first place.

Then, he turned a corner.

And there she was.

The sight of her nearly knocked the breath out of him, and a deep sense of relief welled up from his very soul.

Behind her was the backdrop of the gushing waterfall. The sunlight filtered through the trees, and the reflection sparkled and danced off the pool while a rainbow showed through the mist.

He raised his hands tentatively in a gesture of submission. "I'm late," he said.

She didn't immediately speak. Her eyes searched his face as if she were looking for a deeper meaning there. He opened his mouth to offer an excuse, but before he could get the words out, she shook her head. "But you're here now."

He couldn't read her expression.

"Rose, I have something to say—", at the same time as Rose said, "Griffin, I need to tell you something—"

They both stopped and laughed awkwardly before Rose said, "Let me go first."

Griffin nodded once, not sure he wanted to hear what she had to say.

"I watched the interview online." She paused as he waited. "I-I'm not good at this." She placed a hand at her throat. "I jumped to conclusions about your intentions," she continued after a moment. "The truth is, I was terrified, and I didn't know what the future would look like. I think I was maybe looking for an excuse to end things."

She stopped speaking, and Griffin waited a beat.

"I should have told you my intentions from the beginning. Or at least my lack of intentions. I never had any plans to accept Mid's property. I didn't need it, and I didn't want it. I let my lawyer talk me into going along with the charade for longer than was necessary."

"So…" She drew the word out. "…it was all a charade?"

"It started out that way, yes." He paused, and saw the doubt creep over her face. "But Rose, my feelings for you couldn't be more real."

She looked up at him, then her gaze flitted away.

"What about the interview last night?" she asked. "Was that real?"

"Do you think I'd be here if it hadn't been?"

She glanced around, and he wondered if she were looking for a camera crew. He nearly laughed. Because he knew as much attention as the interview had gained, it would all be gone tomorrow. Good news faded even faster than bad news. The media cycle would move on, and Griffin would be left in relative obscurity again.

"You spoke with your father." It was a statement; he knew she was referring to Max's relationship with Mid.

"I did. There were a lot of words left unsaid between Mid, my father, and my mother. Among the three of them. They never managed to resolve it."

"I wish they'd gotten their closure."

Griffin glanced behind Rose at the boulder in Mid's photograph. He took her hand and walked with her up the path toward the rock.

When they reached the stone, he said, "Maybe it's

up to us to give them the closure they couldn't manage on their own."

His heart pounding in his chest, he sank to one knee.

Rose's hands flew to her mouth. "Griffin, what are you doing?" she whispered.

"It might be crazy, but Rose…" His words trailed off as he pulled out the small box his father had given to him as he'd left Arizona. "Will you marry me?"

Rose stared at the ring with the small diamond for so long that Griffin blinked up at her.

"Are you serious?" she finally asked.

"I know it's a little small," he said apologetically. "But it was Mid's."

She shook her head. "No, are you serious about this proposal?"

"I've never been more serious about anything in my life."

"God, this is crazy," she whispered. Then she wet her lips. "But yes, Griffin Stangel, I will marry you."

With shaking hands, he managed to slide the ring over the ring finger on Rose's left hand. "We can get it reset if you'd like."

She took his hands in hers and looked down at him. "It's perfect."

As Griffin was still on one knee, a loud voice reached them from the other end of the path. "There he is, Officer. I told you he'd run down this way."

Both Griffin and Rose looked up as the woman from the parking lot marched toward them, a cell phone pointed in their direction, filming. The park official trudged along after her, looking as if he'd rather be anywhere else. Then a look of recognition spread across his face.

"Griffin Stangel," he called. "No shit."

When the woman noticed Griffin on his knee and Rose leaning forward, she gave a small shout of surprise. Then, her phone moving between Griffin, Rose and the officer, she said, "Do you know him?" She sounded torn between regret and outrage that the man who'd parked illegally might get some sort of special treatment.

"The whole world knows him, lady. Are you streaming this? Because you may have just caught the continuation of the story on camera."

The woman's mouth dropped open. She looked unsure, then she doubled down, moving the camera between the two parties again. "Are you going to give him a ticket?"

"Hell no," the officer said. "I'm going to give him a handshake and tell him congratulations." Then the officer did exactly that as the entire world watched.

The woman scoffed as Griffin kissed Rose deeply. Then he looked at the woman's camera. He winked, and smiled.

Epilogue

A crack of thunder sounded from outside the back room of the church. Rose and her wedding party arrived just moments before the dark skies had let loose and rain had begun falling in sheets. The water ran in a river down Main Street, Madison.

A few of the guests were already seated in the sanctuary, but most of them had yet to arrive and would need to brave the downpour.

"This is a disaster," Rose wailed.

Della stood behind Rose and straightened the lace of her train. "It's not a disaster," the woman corrected. "It's going to be fine."

Alyssa appeared in front of Rose and patted her face with a powder puff. Rose sneezed and stepped away.

She looked out the stained-glass window, just as a bolt of lightning lit up the sky. "Do you think this is a bad omen?"

Alyssa came at her again with the powder. "I've heard rain on your wedding day is good luck."

Rose closed her eyes as Alyssa finished blotting off

the shine. "I doubt that very much."

Hallie peeked around the corner and into the sanctuary as the guests hurried through the heavy double doors and into the vestibule with small cries of relief. They shook wet umbrellas and damp coats. Rose heard their complaints about the weather, and frowned.

"Jay is here," said Hallie.

Rose perked up. Jay had been the only stylist to leave My Pink Wink after Rose had assumed ownership. He hadn't been unhappy with the developments; he'd simply decided the universe was giving him the sign he'd been looking for to make some life changes.

"I bet that's his new boyfriend," Hallie said.

Alyssa squealed and rushed away from Rose to look through the partition. "Where?"

Rose was also excited to see Jay and meet his new boyfriend, but right now, she had more pressing concerns.

"Do you think Griffin and the groomsmen are okay in the parsonage?" Rose asked.

Della said, "I'm sure they're fine. The walkway to the sanctuary is covered."

Rose nodded. She'd envisioned brilliant blue skies and colorful leaves on the maple trees which lined Main Street out in front of the church. Instead, they were in the throes of hell. Outside, another crack of thunder and bright bolt of lightning rang out. A few guests screamed, and the lights flickered but mercifully stayed on.

The storm was on top of them.

Hallie handed Rose her bouquet of anemone, chrysanthemum, and roses that offset the navy and golds worn by her wedding party. Rose's white dress was a simple satin design that the designer assured her oozed elegance.

There was nothing to do now but wait, and Rose's mood vacillated between elation and terror.

As if sensing her unease, Hallie placed her arm around Rose.

Alyssa looked over. "Group hug!" she cried and threw her slender arms around both Hallie and Rose. Della smiled and joined them, and Alyssa immediately began to cry.

Rose felt a sob bubble up in her throat, and even Hallie's shoulders began to quake.

Della managed to keep the tears at bay, but her voice wobbled when she asked, "Why are you all crying?"

"I'm just so happy for Rose," Alyssa said, wiping her eyes then grabbing a tissue from a table and dabbing at Rose's face. "I feel like Mid has manufactured this whole scenario for all of us."

Rose blinked as Alyssa made sure her mascara wasn't running. Alyssa had a tendency to be dramatic, but Rose also felt like Mid was with them.

Then the sound of the organ began. Alyssa pulled

back. "Here we go…"

Della squeezed Rose's arm. "You ready for this?"

"As ready as I'll ever be."

"You look stunning." Hallie brushed her lips lightly on Rose's cheek. "You're one of the lucky ones."

Rose smiled as the notes of Bach reached her ears from Mark Highberger's expert rendition of the organ music.

She knew the men would be entering the church right now, and heard Alyssa say, "Oh, my god. They all look so handsome."

Rose's heart was pounding. She shut her eyes and took three calming breaths.

"You okay, kiddo?"

Max Stangel, looking gorgeous himself, appeared at her elbow. In fact, if she wanted to imagine what Griffin would look like in a quarter of a century, Max Stangel was it.

She smiled up at him and nodded. She knew it was unconventional to have the father of the groom walk her down the aisle, but she thought Mid would approve. Besides, Teddy couldn't do it. He was Griffin's best man.

The Bach overture stopped and the sounds of Beethoven filled the sanctuary. Alyssa winked back at Rose and started her procession down the aisle.

"Just breathe," Max said.

The thunder rumbled outside, but this time it was a

gentle sound, and it coalesced perfectly with 'Piano Sonata Number Eight'.

"I may pass out," Rose whispered.

"Then I'll carry you up there. One way or another, you'll get to the alter this afternoon." Max hesitated then said, "Mid would be proud of you."

"She'd be proud of you, too."

"You think?"

Rose smiled. "I know."

They waited. The wedding party reached their positions on the far side of the altar.

Wagner's 'Bridal Chorus' began, and Rose's legs felt weak as she linked her arm through Max's. She heard a collective gasp as the guests stood, but her eyes were glued to Griffin whose smile was wide and eyes filled with tears.

They made their way down the aisle toward her destiny.

Max kissed her cheek. "Knock 'im dead, Rosie," he said at her ear.

She wasn't sure if Max meant the crowd or Griffin. But she smiled and nodded anyway.

Griffin took her hand and gathered her close to his side. "I'm the luckiest man alive," he said.

"Not yet," she said. They both laughed softly through filmy eyes.

Pastor Ballentine smiled, and she smiled back. She wasn't sure he'd completely recovered from her gentle rejection, but he was such a kind and gracious man that he would never have said a word.

He instructed everyone to be seated, and for the first time, Rose glanced at the crowd who'd gathered to help them celebrate their new life together.

"We come together as a family of loved ones to celebrate the joining of the long, happy, and healthy life of Rose Glasser and Griffin Stangel…" Pastor Ballentine said in his confident voice.

Rose's gaze stopped on an unfamiliar woman in the crowd. Though there were a few people from Griffin's past she didn't know, this woman seemed peculiar and out of place. Her long blonde hair was stringy, and her face was drawn and sallow. Her makeup appeared as if it had settled in rings under her eyes. She wasn't old, but she had a rough look about her.

She was glaring furiously at Rose and Griffin.

Pastor Ballentine continued. "We hold marriage up as a sacred union between two people who are committed to loving one another and spending the rest of their lives together, faithful to each other, and to their journey together."

Rose leaned forward and whispered to Griffin, "Who is the woman at the end of the sixth row?"

She watched as his gaze moved to the woman, then to Teddy, who was standing to the left side of the altar. Teddy looked back at Griffin before smiling reassuringly at Rose.

"No one at all," Griffin said. A muscle ticked in his jaw even as he smiled at her.

Rose didn't believe him, but then Pastor Ballentine was saying, "Rose, do you take Griffin to be your lawfully wedded husband from this day forward, to have and to hold, in good times and bad, for richer or for poorer, in sickness and in health? And will you love, honor, and cherish him for as long as you both shall live?"

She forgot about the woman and looked into Griffin's eyes. "I will," she answered.

"And Griffin, do you take Rose to be your lawfully wedded wife from this day forward, to have and to hold, in good times and bad, for richer or for poorer, in sickness and in health? And will you love, honor, and cherish her for as long as you both shall live?"

Griffin opened his mouth to respond, and Rose caught a movement out of the corner of her eye. The woman she'd noticed only moments earlier had stood up, her mouth open, her eyes flashing angrily. Before the woman could call out, Teddy had sprinted down the aisle, causing another collective gasp to rise from the congregation.

Rose barely had time to realize what was happening before Teddy had hoisted the stranger over his shoulder and ran out into the rain.

Griffin looked as if he might be sick. The crowd murmured.

Rose caught sight of Julie Newlin looking exceedingly pleased with this development. Rose wondered if she'd planned it.

Pastor Ballentine said, "Well, we all need a good wedding story, and that's certainly a first for me. Shall we proceed?"

The congregation laughed nervously, and the wedding party exchanged concerned glances.

But proceed they did.

"It's now time to say your vows. Rose?"

Rose took a deep breath and held Griffin's hands. "Griffin Stangel, when I first met you, becoming your life partner was the furthest thing from my mind. But today, I stand before you and vow to support you, cherish you, and love you. I promise to try to be patient and to always be kind. Because you are wanted, more than you could ever imagine."

Pastor Ballentine handed her the plain gold band, and she slid it onto Griffin's finger.

Griffin took a deep breath. "Rose Glasser, when you first invited me into your home, I found this piece of paper held with a magnet to your refrigerator." Rose frowned as Griffin let her hand go to fish into his pocket. He pulled out a small strip of paper. "It says 'Your experiences this week will all make sense within the year.'"

Rose faintly recalled the words and the tiny slip of paper. It was the fortune from the date she'd gone on the night Mid died. She remembered nothing about the man, and had completely forgotten about the words of wisdom in the cookie.

"It hasn't quite been a year, but the moment I met you, my life finally made sense. For that, I thank you, and I vow to do everything in my power to live up to the words in the fortune. I vow to make our lives make sense together."

He took Mid's ring from Pastor Ballentine and slipped it onto her finger.

Pastor Ballentine smiled. "Rose and Griffin, having proclaimed your love for, and commitment to, one another and in the presence of these witnesses, it is my pleasure to pronounce you husband and wife. Griffin, you may now kiss your bride."

Griffin took Rose's face in his hands and looked deep into her eyes before leaning in. Behind them, the cheers of the crowd dissolved as his lips met hers. He seemed tense, but she pulled him to her tightly. She was his anchor now. She would help him sail through.

Their happily-ever-after had just begun.

THE END

Acknowledgments

I must start this section by acknowledging the challenges in writing this particular book. Not only had I just started a demanding new job, that role required an extremely long commute, which necessitated that I dictate much of the first draft of this novel. However, the long hours spent enroute also meant most of my evenings and weekends were consumed with editing and rewriting. So, a huge thank you to everyone in my life who understood when I completely disappeared for a while—either literally or figuratively—into this made-up world of Rose and Griffin.

Many of my friends and family may recognize the small town of Madison, Pennsylvania, the home of my grandparents and extended family—where my sister and I spent much of our childhood; where my mother and father met; where we all were married; where my brother and his family currently lives; where my dad rests. It's a small town like many small towns in Western Pennsylvania. You may pass through it and never know the name of the place. Unless you have a reason for visiting, it's likely not your destination. But it's a special place, and I'm delighted to pay homage to a location that means so much to me.

As always, thanks to my amazing editor, Paul Carson of Seminal Edits, who took on this project, which is outside his normal genre (and mine). He offered comprehensive advice on how to bring the characters to life and tell a compelling story. Additionally, inviting a male editor to offer perspective on the romance side of things really…livened it up. I am eternally grateful for his professionalism and expertise.

There are so many others of you to thank for your support, excitement, enthusiasm: anyone who's commented on my woefully inadequate social media posts; sent me messages of support; offered advice on random writing techniques, points-of-view, plot twists, etc., etc., etc. And sincerest appreciation to anyone who has offered an honest review, purchased a book, or otherwise supported this all-consuming hobby of mine. From the depths of my soul, thank you.

www.ingramcontent.com/pod-product-compliance
Lightning Source LLC
Chambersburg PA
CBHW061107310726
48974CB00002B/423